THE LOVE BET

G.L. TOMAS

Happy Reading!

A + L

Developmental Editing by: Little Pear Editing

Cover Design by: Najla Qamber Designs

Cover Art by Lindee Robinson Photography

Formatting created by: Vellum

ISBN 13: 978-1-943773-50-3 (e-book)

ISBN 13: 978-1-943773-53-4 (paperback)

ASIN: B087RS4Z7R

❀ Created with Vellum

STAY UPDATED!

If you haven't heard anything from us in a while, it means you're no longer on our list.

So if you'd like to get updates on our new releases (And we have a lot of them!) please consider signing up here!

Newsletters not your thing? Consider joining our exclusive Facebook Group!

GET IN CONTACT!

We want to hear from you!
Write us at guinevere.libertad@gltomaswrites.com to discuss your fave stories by us! Comments, Suggestions, even requests what you'd like to see in our next publications!

Also, if you loved this book, please consider leaving a review. It really makes an authors day to read them and they're so, so helpful in determining if this is the sort of read for the next reader who may stumble across it. You can do so by clicking here. And remember no review is too short!

CONTENT WARNING(S)

Below entails a list of may trigger readers. Please take the time to look through them and decide if this is a read you'd rather skip. Thanks for reading! G+L

Mention of death of a parent
A Bisexual Adult with a conservative parent
Toxic family members
Catcalling and toxic male behavior
Mentions of Colorism and Anti-Blackness
A brief mention of miscarriages in a side character's past
Graphic sex scenes

SUMMARY:

Luz De Los Santos thought her job was easy.

Being the Sex and Relationship Director of Modern Magazine, no one knew the art of dating and hookups like she did. When the commitment-phobe beauty gets singled out by her editor to write a challenging column for the coveted, annual Valentine's issue, Luz is forced to confront her issues about relationships with her newly pitched project.

The Love Bet.

Is it possible to fall in love by the third screw? **Maybe***.*

But she's not holding her breath once she recruits her blast from the past, **Evan Cattaneo** *to help test her theory.*

Evan regrets the way things ended between him and Luz.

The girl who charmed him all those years ago was now grown and sexy, making more than ready to aid Luz in her little experiment. Only his plans won't stop at just bedding her. Nope, he plans to make her fall in love again. It's only a matter of time before loving between the sheets turns into stealing kisses in the streets.

When emotions get wild and feelings grow deep, will the insecurities of Luz's past come back to haunt them?

CHAPTER ONE

Before

Luz

If there was one thing I didn't want to waste my time doing today, it was riding the bus to Northland-Lyceum just to tutor some basketball player that the entire student body couldn't stop fanning over. Evan Cattaneo. All-American. Shooting guard. At six feet four, he possessed a six-pack and muscle mass that matched his towering frame. Most students—*regardless of gender*—had a crush on him at my new high school, Irondequoit High, but to me, he was just muscles and a pretty face.

Don't get me wrong. It wasn't that I didn't find him attractive, but what I learned about him after he was an hour and fifteen minutes late to our very first tutorial session was that he didn't take *anything* seriously—unless it was a basketball play or a girl showering him with attention.

To stay on the basketball team, he needed a C+ or higher in Calculus and because my new school provided a paid work-study program for students from low-income families, I was stuck with the assignment, no matter who the student was. It felt like a waste of effort and bus fare to meet him at his preferred place to study, but luckily, tutoring sessions counted in the schools' transportation program. As much as I hated it, though, I had no choice but to spend an entire afternoon with a jock who probably couldn't even spell his own name.

An unfortunate turn of circumstances forced my mom and me to move to El Camino after she lost her salon to gentrification due to the high spike in rent she could no longer afford. She'd gone from owning her own salon and making a comfortable living to us moving into the smallest two-bedroom apartment we'd ever lived in. By day, she continued to do hair in our home, but at night, she cleaned hotels a town over because even with her decent client list, it still didn't match the money she made when she had her own place. Having this tutoring job was the only way I could have my own money and help where I could when Mom needed it. All in all, I couldn't wait to go to college, just so I could have my own space again. Nine more months to go. Trust me, I was counting.

The bus announced the North Goodman street stop as I pulled the string, requesting to let me off at the closest point. Looking at the directions I printed out from school, I hoped I'd gotten the right stop. I didn't venture past La Avenida, but I hoped the side of town he wanted to meet wasn't anywhere I'd deem unsafe. The crime wasn't the only thing to worry about once you left my neck of the woods. Being a black girl in a predominantly white neighborhood, I made sure my phone was charged, just in case I had to call my mom or my Tito Gadiel if something went down and needed to be picked up. The streets were quiet in this sleepy town, and for a mid-January day, I was in awe that I didn't require a jacket. After a few minutes of walking, I found myself in front of the address Evan had written down in the last five minutes of our brief first tutoring session.

In front of me stood a *Pizzeria/Ristorante Italiano* sign with a familiar surname in rustic lit up letters. Cattaneo's. The letter O in Cattaneo blinked off and on, a clear sign it needed to be replaced. Other than that, it looked like a popular pizza joint from all the people waiting in the seating area for their order. Unsure of where to go, I went to the ordering counter as a man with mostly dark hair and a few rebellious grey streaks yelled out, "Order number thirty-seven!" Some dude rushed past me, barely excusing himself, as he approached the counter to pick up and pay for his order.

When I finally made it to the front of the counter, the man I assumed was the owner hung up the nearby phone, hooking a pen behind his ear as he greeted me. "What can I get for you, young lady?" he asked in a thick Brooklyn accent that hinted he wasn't originally from Rochester.

"Ummm... I'm here to meet an Evan Cattaneo. I'm supposed to be tutoring him and he told me to meet him here so..."

His thick salt and pepper eyebrows rose as he turned around to the door and yelled to someone in the back. "Son, get out here. There's a pretty girl here to see you!"

Despite my toasted caramel brown skin, my cheeks flushed, and I wished I could crawl into a wall and die. This man I assumed to be his father had no regard for anyone's embarrassment, shouting for the whole Monroe County to hear him. I wasn't some ugly duckling but pretty was never a word people, besides my family, ever used to describe me as. Weird, maybe. A loner, definitely. But pretty? Not unless you thought being compared to a Black Wednesday Addams was a compliment. I most certainly didn't because no one thought of Wednesday Addams as someone they wanted to date, but the most annoying thing about the comparison was that I wasn't even gothic. The color black just became more of an obsession than it should have.

Knowing Italian-Americans could be just as intense and loud as my straight-from-the-DR Dominican family, I couldn't help but be disappointed for Evan's sake that it was me waiting for him and not some pretty girl as his father had referenced. Now, he was expecting some girl from his high school fan club and all I wanted was to get this five-week tutoring term over with.

"Just take a seat over there, sweetheart. Evan will be with you in a second. Number thirty-eight!"

Making my way to an empty seat in the back corner of the restaurant, I unloaded our study materials for a speedy start. It took him a few minutes to materialize from the back, but when he did, he donned a stained smock as his fingers ran through his thick, dark messy hair. It was hard to describe his looks without starting with his eyes first. They were pale sage green with light brown specks that made them sometimes appear hazel. That, along with virile crafted full lips and symmetrical features, made it understandable why people found him to be a poster boy for attractiveness. I was as tall as most boys at five feet eight, but Evan was the only guy I felt petite next to. Too bad he didn't have enough substance for me or else my name could have quickly been added to his list of fangirls.

"Hey, I'm sorry to keep you waiting. I was hoping for a better outcome than last time; it's just that I help out my family's restaurant when I don't have practice. My dad says it's okay, though, since he knows the tutoring is vital for me in order to stay on the team. Thanks for coming," he said with an almost genuine smile as if his plan wasn't to convince me to just do his Calc homework for the rest of the semester. That's how most tutoring sessions with athletes went. They had no intentions of doing the work; they just wanted to wear the letterman, hook up with the hottest girl in school, and score mindless points on a court. Studying, course assignments, and while we were on the subject—*thinking*—were never in their set of skills.

"Do you mind if we start with a few practice tests? Just so I can see where you are level wise."

"Sure." He nodded and proceeded to solve consecutive equations until a few had him scratching his head. The ones he wasn't sure about, he skipped and rushed to the ones he could easily complete. What surprised me, however, was that he went back to the ones he hadn't finished, to at least attempt them. It was obvious he wasn't as uneducated as I thought he'd be and after he handed it back. I could see where he at least went wrong. Nothing a few math drills couldn't fix.

"I mean, *clearly,* you know this stuff. Why do you need a tutor?" I asked, my curiosity piqued. He rested his elbows on the table as his inviting green eyes and upturned smile peered into me.

"Because Calc is the only class I'm tanking in. It's easier to fall behind in it because it's my only class that I don't have to write papers for. I don't prioritize it, but I need to get a B+, hence why I need a tutor."

Confused, I asked the first question that popped into my head. "I thought you only needed a C+ to play?"

He shrugged. "Yea, that's for everyone else, but I'm trying to keep my GPA up because things happen. My dad is always reminding me that we can't get into a good school unless I get a decent scholarship. I just want to be judged on my grades first because I know sports might not be forever."

His candidness surprised me. I wasn't sure why he told me that, but it at least made me feel better than starting from scratch with a person who never learned to open a schoolbook.

"I have some worksheets that have a lot of similar problems as the ones you struggled to solve. It helps to keep going over them until you get it. It's the only way to learn."

He waved a hand to indicate he understood me, and I was beginning to realize in the short time he sat down that he spoke with his hands as if it was a part of his speech. Maybe that was an inherited trait.

"Actually, do you think I could sit next to you? It's just easier for me if you can point out what I'm doing wrong at that moment. You know, instead of after," he clarified as he rubbed the back of his neck.

"Sure," I gulped, not sure if I wanted to say yes but not having a reasonable reason to say no. As innocent as it was, sitting that close to people I found even a sliver of attraction to had the habit of sending my heart into a marathon of palpitations. I prayed that he smelled disgusting and sweaty, the way I expected him to after having spent an afternoon in a hot kitchen restaurant, but it was much worse.

He actually smelled... *heavenly*, like a load of fresh laundry with a hint of Irish Spring. As long as I didn't meet his eyes, I would be safe. That's right; I just had to avoid his glare, but it was the moment he reached over to grab a pen and his pale hands lightly grazed mine that I knew if I wasn't careful, I'd end up on that list of fangirls I thought were brainwashed into falling for the hype.

———

In just a half hour, he had impressed me with his ability to soak up my preferred way of solving problems, detailing his work into definite B- territory. It would probably take the whole five weeks, but I could see him ending with a B+, maybe even an A-, if he worked hard at it. Even someone who was taking it all in needed a break when their brain hurt, so when he asked me if we could take a quick break before starting back up on some other components, I gladly agreed, wanting to take some time out to read if he was going to go off and do other things.

"Hey, about earlier. Sorry about my dad being obnoxious. He's just the kind of person that says exactly what he's thinking. It's an Italian thing," he explained with a wave of his hands.

"Not a problem," I said, taking out a magazine from my Kuromi messenger bag. It was clear that the moment I did, my student wasn't going to let me just sit there. Nope, he was going to talk to me the *entire* time.

"It's Luz, right? I've been wondering something. Are you Spanish?"

Was I *Spanish*? I swear there wasn't a thing I hated more than that question. It was that or either *Why do you speak Spanish so well?* To most ignorant people, Latin Americans only came in two complexions, Jennifer Lopez and Christina Aguilera. Yet, here I was, this brown-skinned girl who no one ever accused of being mixed or biracial. I was this black girl with a Spanish name who often confused even other Latinos because, in their minds, I was too dark to be Dominican. If I was in a good mood, I'd often provide a history lesson explaining how *most* of the enslaved Africans who were stolen from their West African homelands in the Trans-Atlantic slave trade were brought to the Caribbean and South America and not the USA like most people assumed. But today was not one of those days, and I was *not* in a good mood.

"No, I'm not *Spanish*. My parents are from The Dominican Republic. Are you *English*?" He held up his arms in a surrendering plea, a warm grin forming on his face as he went into apology mode. "Okay, my bad. It's just that's what everyone at school calls themselves whether they're Puerto Rican, or Colombian, or whichever Spanish-speaking country their ancestry is from. I wasn't trying to offend you or anything; it's just that you look Black and your name Luz sounds Spanish. Is it okay to say that?"

I rolled my eyes. "Latinos come in every race, and I just also happen to be Black. It's not an unusual concept," I explained, ignoring the cute way he correctly pronounced my name. Most of the teachers at our school pronounced it like loose, which I can't say was wrong but super Anglo. When Evan said it, however, it was all relaxed and sultry like *Looze*, as if he wanted me to know he knew my name.

"And besides, I don't care what everyone else is calling themselves. I'm not everyone else," I huffed proudly. I was the girl into

J-Rock and Shoujo anime, the girl that could spend hours of my free time playing RPGs and watching wizard movies for the hundredth time. Only the nerdy kids at our school knew what those were, and even *I* wasn't on their radar. I was the girl who could never have a crush on a boy like him.

"I'm just trying to start a conversation with you, but it looks like that magazine is doing a better job at entertaining you," he said as he pulled the magazine over to his side, my gut reaction kicking in to grab it back, only to put me in a compromising position that I tried to avoid.

His unavoidable line of vision.

"Modern magazine?" he asked out loud, examining the cover.

I didn't bother reading teen magazines, not when I was a mere four months away from turning eighteen and practically a woman already. The things I loved reading about were women's issues, not little girl stories. Modern, hands down, was my favorite magazine. I stalked my mailbox every four weeks awaiting the next exciting issue.

"I mean, the cover model is cute but the headlines are ridiculous. *Make a guy fall for you in six easy steps?* I only have one. Be yourself. And if he doesn't like it, fuck him. There are no six steps to make a guy like you. You can only be you."

He spoke with a sliver of sincerity. That was the best advice in the world—*for people like him*. People like me *were* ourselves, and no one was lining up to be my Percy Jackson new release buddy. Being yourself only worked when you were popular.

"That's easy for you to say. People already like you. You don't have to make an effort."

"Yea, but I'm sure if you smiled more, more guys might find themselves drawn to you." I could feel the steam escaping my ears like a whistling teakettle. This time, I actually *was* smiling. But it wasn't a warm smile. No, it was an "I can't believe a guy could ever be that sexist" kind of smile. In 2005, the male-identifying gender should've been progressive not stuck in the 1950s where they proudly operated Stepford wives to control their emotions via levers in their backs to smile on command.

"Okay, that was so sexist. You can't go around telling girls to smile, especially if you don't tell guys to do the same."

He shrugged. "Okay, so maybe it is a little sexist, but most guys won't approach a girl who looks mad—"

"*Unless it's telling her to smile?*" I interrupted, which only provoked him to laugh. "Unfortunately. Like, I hate to be the one to say this, but it's probably one of the reasons guys tell such corny jokes. We're just trying to see what makes a girl smile so we can keep making her smile. It's like we feel compelled to do so."

Maybe what he said made sense. There had to be some logical reason guys were so unoriginal. Still, there wasn't a single person entitled to your laughter and good mood. Why didn't men, "*ahem*", Evan understand that? Gosh, did his nose always look that cute when he scrunched it up when he looked confused?

No! I refused to be one of those girls. You know, the girl who no one noticed and was infatuated with one of the most popular boys in school. After these five weeks, he would most likely forget my name. And after this year, I'd forget his too.

"It's hard to approach girls that you think won't like you."

"Yea, well, if guys gave women reasons to smile instead of threatening their existence, then maybe we would smile more," I admitted, not expecting what he said to me next. It felt like an episode of Punk'd.

"I wonder if I gave you a good reason to smile, would you go out with me?"

Was he joking? Like, literally fucking joking? Now, I knew Ashton Kutcher was around the corner somewhere because there was no way he said what I think he just said.

"To make it fair, if I gave you three reasons to smile, all on separate occasions, would you let me take you out on a date?

"Umm... no." I pushed the idea far out of my mind because nothing like this ever happens to weird girls like me.

"No, because you don't think I can manage it, or no because the idea of going out with me disgusts you?"

I couldn't give him the reason why because the real reason said more about me than it did about him. I wasn't looking to be anyone's scapegoat. There was no way a guy like him could ever get a real honest-to-God smile out of me. He was not that charming.

"Honestly, we are from two different worlds. I've accepted the order of things. You've got your role to play, and I have mine."

"That doesn't answer my question. If I gave you three reasons to smile, would you go out with me?"

I shrugged. "I guess, but—"

"No buts. It's either a yes or no," he interrupted. This time, I was sure the way the smile slowly creeping up the left side of his mouth was breathtakingly adorable.

"Fine then; yes," I blurted out, knowing what he was up against. I was a hard cookie to break, especially for some guy who most likely got everything he wanted.

"Cool," he said before he suggested we get back to studying before the late afternoon rush would force him to head back to work. And just like that, he didn't mention it again, not even when he offered to walk me to my bus stop.

CHAPTER TWO

Now

Luz

"It's that time again people," my editor sing-songed as her infectious aura entered the conference room, lightening the heavy moods of the room filled with worried colleagues. I wore my light knit printed blouse adorned with hearts because for one, it was my favorite shirt, and two, it was the only top my editor-in-chief never failed to compliment me on no matter how many times I wore it. Today's staff meeting wasn't just any staff meeting. It was the one all the staff journalists dreaded each year.

"I want to hear some great pitches today. We still have time, but I look forward to locking in some ideas for our favorite, I mean *my* favorite, issue of the year," she corrected. "Don't let me down, people."

The words left her mouth with an exuberant cadence, but it just induced fear in the writers who presented the shakiest ideas. And that was where I, Luz de Los Santos, never had anything to worry about. Not to brag, but I was killing it at my job. I never offered anything "shaky", and I sure as hell never presented my editor with a bad pitch. She sat down at the head of the conference table, looking like a boss in her high-end designer clothes and natural hair slayed to the gawds. Even with a mask on, she looked fly.

Antoinette Durand was a queen in her own right. She was the first African American woman to *ever* hold the title of editor-in-chief of Modern magazine, the country's leading magazine for women, femmes, and feminine-presenting identities between the ages of eighteen to forty-five. Modern wasn't just a magazine to me; it was my entire life. I remembered growing up in my mother's hair salon and diving into all the magazines geared toward the young, adventurous, professional woman sprinkled across several coffee tables while the clients waited patiently for their weekly ritualistic blowouts. Sure, there were others I liked to read, but none were as inclusive as Modern, and none had an editor-in-chief who looked like me.

Y'all do not understand. It was this magazine and this magazine alone that made me want to be a journalist. The passionate stories centered on women's issues. The glamorous fashion spreads that were the first to feature plus-sized models larger than a size fourteen, and last but not least, the incredible financial advice it provided for the everyday femme. This magazine had been the equivalent to the best friend I never had growing up. The second I graduated from the coveted NYU, summa cum laude with my B.A. in Journalism and wrote my first freelance piece, Modern was the first publication I submitted it to. I was inexperienced and unable to thread together a concise thought so it didn't surprise me when they passed on it. I took courses to improve my writing which paid off big. With a piece on femicide in the Dominic Republic, they were huge fans of the next one. And the next one. And the one I pitched after that. When I learned there was an opening for a journalist position with the digital magazine, I was Ariel ready to sign my voice away to the sea witch for a more permanent title.

The original position of news/politics had unfortunately not been right for me. I loved giving voices to the unheard but my university minor had been based on gender and sexuality studies. With much luck after years of consistent pitching, with all the traffic my freelance sex and relationships pieces got, when the Sex and Relationships director stepped down, Mrs. Durand personally reached out to me to offer me the job. That was six years ago and ever since, I've been a slave to learning just how important sex is in terms of relationships and dating. If there was anything to know about the latest new sex toy, your girl Luz took one for the team. Questions about the kink scene? Guess who got to attend the most exclusive, top-secret sex parties? I had no inhibitions, and while I wasn't calling myself a sexpert, I was open and unashamed to say that I had a pretty bomb sex life.

As a woman who prided herself on not limiting herself to the cisheteronormative dating pool, I wasn't just the ideal candidate to cover in the department; I was the *perfect* candidate. Sex was my favorite topic to write about, and while we were being candid, my favorite pastime to partake in. I loved helping women and femmes improve their current sex lives, and as long as I could help it, my position was going to be filled for a long time. My editor loved everything I contributed, and with the cost of living constantly rising in the city, I had planned to keep it that way.

"I know some of you that are new to the company are gasping that it's only September. And questioning why we are already planning our February issue. However, our seasoned staff will be proud to inform you that our 'Love' issue has been our bestselling issue ten solid years in a row. It takes the most planning and the most work to ensure its flawless execution.

I'm giving you all a month early to cultivate those pieces. The deadline's November, guys. Especially if we want to drop it on time for January. I know everyone hates talking budgets, but I'm happy to announce that the board approved that everyone gets a ten percent increase on whatever materials you'll need to make this issue an even bigger success than last year's."

There was a sudden perk in the room, followed by a few "Thank Gods" and clapping. The moment Antoinette announced the pitching portion, however, it was as if all the life had been sucked out of the room again.

The fashion department had it easy. My girl Genevieve had the pleasure of booking models and putting together romantic collections for editorials, but securing a cover model had the potential to be stressful considering talent could back out any minute. Still, it had to be the best part of the job. Hiring a photographer to capture the Black Brazilian popstar IZA with all of her melanated greatness was going to be amaze-balls. That girl could make the color pewter look romantic, but I longed to see her in soft pinks and pastel purples.

The lifestyle director had a harder time suggesting their "twenty places you've overlooked to meet your future valentine" proposal, not because it was terrible but because it was unoriginal and already done under a different headline.

"Original, people. Give me original."

Told ya.

"Remember, this isn't just about the Annual Love issue. It also marks our fiftieth year of publication. I want to see something especially mind-blowing. Luz, you're up! What have you got for me?" Her wine-stained lips pressed together as she raked her fingers through her expertly tapered kinky curls.

The pressure that came along with being Antoinette's prized mentee had never gotten to me because she always loved my ideas. Even if she wasn't a fan of my pitch of sexing my way through Valentine's Day with fourteen scheduled dates, I had a feeling she wouldn't shoot down my "How to improve your friendships with a thoughtful Galentine's Day part. Easy peasy.

"Okay so... I was thinking about a story that focused on sexing your way through Valentine's Day with a new date every day leading up to the day," I emphasized the day with finger quotes. "Our average readers between twenty-five and forty remain single by choice and hardly ever make time for dating. Fourteen dates with fourteen different people could potentially resonate with the percentage of our readership that's more concerned with just being out there in the dating scene than actual relationships."

Antoinette's hands formed a steeple, her long, manicured nails tapping each other as her lips pursed and her eyes drifted upward.

"Eh...what else have you got for me?"

Wow. This legit has never happened before. My boss always went with my first proposal; now I had to scramble with Plan B.

"To reiterate, most women and femmes are single by choice in 2020. I thought that we could have a story about abandoning the pressures of being in a relationship altogether and taking part in a Galentine's Day. People you're dating or trying to date shouldn't hold precedence over the people who get you through the hard times and breakups," I finished, feeling impressed with my counterpoint.

I never planned dates past date number one. Multiple dates implied that I was open to giving my heart to someone, and I, for one, wanted no part in that. Every woman, femme, or enby (nonbinary) that I knew in a relationship right now was miserable or settling because a good portion of them weren't even having their basic needs met. Though I was a sex specialist, I often passed the relationship aspect of my job onto junior journalists on my team. Writing about the fun stuff made my job easy. So, it was an unsaid truth of mine that I was the last person on earth that would have considered falling in love *fun*.

"I hate to call you out Luz, but I expected more from you. I can't believe I'm saying this, but I'd even go as far as saying I disliked your presentation."

She didn't hold back. For the seventeen years I had been reading Modern magazine, I never once doubted the woman sitting in front of me. But now, here in this room, her rebuke of my pitch casted doubt in all the faith she ever had in me.

"This is our 'Love' issue." She emphasized the word love. "Your first pitch is only about sex, and while I understand the intentions of your second one, it would've been a better fit for last year when we did that gift guide feature about what to buy your girlfriends when you're all single and loving life. You're missing the key component, and that's love. What have you got that centers on that?"

What the hell did love have to do with it? When Antoinette hired me, I never stressed that I knew more about love than I did sex and relationships. Relationships whether platonic, romantic, or sexual, didn't always factor love into the equation. Love didn't have to be the key element for relationships to be validated. Sure, those promises of deep, passionate emotions were a noble concept but weren't always realistic. As lazy as it was, I didn't have any other pitches, but with the entire room staring at me, all collectively waiting for me to fall flat on my face, I had to pull an idea out of my ass and I had to do it fast.

"I want something that revolves around the act of falling in love," she stressed, breaking the brief silence between my empty thoughts and lost voice. I hadn't experienced this feeling since my first pitch, and I never wanted to feel this level of embarrassment again.

"Okay," I started with a chance to give my brain the time to process another story. With all eyes on me, I blurted out the dumbest, most unrealistic idea that popped into my head, "can the number of times that you have sex contribute to the art of falling in love? And by the number of times, I should clarify. Is it possible to fall in love with a person by, say, the third time that you have sex?" The culture was different now. Couples were falling in bed with each other sooner because of hookup apps and Netflix and chill. So, was it likely people were calling it love quicker than they were calling an Uber?

"I mean, what is sex, really?" a colleague from the astrology department questioned with a turned-up nose and a roll of her eyes. "Some people consider sex to be penetrative sex. Others define it as getting to third base. How do you define it so that most of our readers are satisfied?" she asked with a flip of her crispy, colored-damaged ends. She could've kept the commentary to herself. Best believe when it was her turn to pitch, I was going to be throwing out tons of questions to poke holes in her little raggedy-ass ideas.

"Yes, that may be true, but to me, I define sex as all acts that end in mutual pleasure. Any kind of sex can be fun, but not all parties usually leave the encounter satisfied. Given the chance, I'd delve into this story, letting all parties in on what is expected of both partners." I provided more context to support my theory.

"Okay, just so I'm understanding you, do you want to explore if we can develop love, even with a stranger, after only three sexual encounters? That story would require not just a willing participant but a high level of honesty and communication. Communication *even* my partner and I don't always have," Antoinette ended with a joke that had half the room fake laughing and the other half in one way or the other looking at the clock. She had already spent long enough dissecting my ideas. Everyone else just wanted to move it along to hear someone else speak.

"I know I can pull it off." I faked confidence as Antoinette's dark doe eyes peered at me with uncertainty. She pointed at me with a manicured finger and a calculated nod of her head. "Believe it or not, it intrigues me. It's out of your comfort zone. Hook-up culture differs vastly from when I was a woman your age, but a piece like that could encourage our readers to voice their needs and wants early before anyone gets hurt. I like it. Let's go with that," she finalized. Everyone with half a mind knew that once Antoinette said she liked something that you had better deliver your best performance. While I faked appearing cool and collected on the outside that my boss finally took interest in one of my ideas, on the inside, I was freaking the fuck out. Who in the hell was I going to meet in the short time that I had to test out this so-called theory?

"Oh, and Luz? I like the top. Very topic-appropriate."

While my heart-adorned blouse made me look like I was the woman for the job, love, for me, had always ended in heartbreak.

For the first time in six years, I was not looking forward to starting a project.

CHAPTER THREE

Before

Evan

She needed to smile more? What the hell was I thinking telling her that? Not only did she strategically avoid me in the hallway the next day, with games and practice, I hadn't put forth any effort toward my ongoing quest of getting that genuine smile out of her.

I wasn't sure what it was about Luz that had me swearing off the promise I made myself over the summer that this year I was going to stay focused. All I knew was that when I saw her, I knew I wanted to get to know her. It was just dumb luck that she was one of the smart ones, giving me a free window of time to make my move in our five-week-long tutoring sessions. Whether she loved or hated me, she was never going to *not* show up to one of our sessions. She was too responsible for that. So, when she walked into the library at 3:10 on the dot, I knew today was going to be my first shot at turning her reluctance into a conceivable chance.

"Thanks for being on time today. I'm in a rush because I have to be home by five thirty so that my mom can pick up a few extra hours at work. I lost my keys earlier this week, so until she can get another set made, I have to be home before she leaves." She slunk down into her wooden chair, not bothering to look up or acknowledge how she'd gone out her way to avoid me all week.

"I'm great, Luz. How are you?" I took the worksheets out of her hand as her soft, black eyes met mine in her usual scowl. Her usually bare face was replaced with playful pinks across her eyelids and a full, sensual pout complimented by lip gloss. It wasn't too much or too little, but it was enough for me to notice the difference. While she wore black every day, I couldn't help wondering how cute she'd look in a tank top the color of her eyeshadow. Or a dress. Girls with darker skin looked hot in all those girly colors.

"I'm sorry. I'm just eager to get started because I don't have time to waste. Can you just pretend to care?"

I laughed; the situation so clear I can't believe it took me this long to figure it out. She liked me, but the thing was she hated herself for it. Dodging me in the halls and giving me the cold shoulder was her way of putting up her guard because, in her world, she wasn't supposed to be into guys like me. She knew if she gave me a chance, she wouldn't be able to stop smiling. I almost felt tempted to crack my knuckles. This was going to be easier than I thought.

"I do care. If you're that much in a rush, how about I just give you a ride home when we're done? You only live twenty minutes away from me. There! Problem solved. Now, can you tell me *why* you're wearing makeup today?"

She groaned, accompanied by a rolling of her cat-lined eyes. "Because I want to."

"So, it's not because you were meeting with me?"

Her eyebrows shot up to her hairline, appalled that I would

even suggest such a thing. Getting a rise out of her was the only way to get through to her; otherwise, all we'd be doing was studying.

"You're not that full of yourself, are you?"

I shrugged. "I'm not full of myself; you just don't wear makeup a lot."

"And you know this because?" Her eyebrows squished together as her shoulders met her ears in a hard shrug.

"Because I'm always looking at you," I blurted out before I realized how creepy it sounded. I noticed how her straight, dark hair was always parted on the same side and stopped fuller at her shoulders. Out of the entire school, she was the only girl who wore tights when every other girl opted for the bare look even as the chilly winter season approached. She had the cutest laugh and the prettiest smile. I just knew it. But I'd need to lay the charm on thick to get it out of her, and I was trying to save my best material for emergencies.

"Okay. That doesn't sound creepy at all." She brought her Calc book up to cover her face to hide from me, but I was almost positive it was to hide that she was blushing.

"What I meant was I don't look at you to stare at you. It's just I notice you. Ever since you started here. I've talked myself out of starting a conversation with you because I know girls like you are intimidating."

"Right. I'm intimidating because I don't smile at you. Got it," she chastised.

And right then, I seemed to beat myself all over again for ever telling her she needed to smile more. That was going to keep biting me in the ass until I found a better way to explain myself. Looking at the clock that now read a quarter of four, I didn't exactly have long to do so.

"In all fairness, you don't smile at anyone. I don't see you talk to anybody. In the rare case that you do have a conversation with someone that's not a teacher, you sort of just look the way you're looking right now. Like you want to rip their head off," I admitted, but she surprised me when she turned her chair around to better face me, crossing one sheer polka-dotted stockinged leg over the other.

"You want to know what happened the last time I smiled randomly at a guy waiting at a bus stop with me? He followed me when I tried to walk to the next bus stop because I was so tired of how uncomfortable he was making me feel. But wait, it gets better. When we got on, guess where he sat? Right down next to me. And because I was so sure he was going to follow me home, I walked into a Wegman's, trying to lose him, but surprise-surprise, he followed me there too. The only place he didn't follow me was the bathroom. And if one of the employees hadn't been in there to help me and call the police on him, he could have done something way worse. The guy looked old enough to be my father. So, you want to know why I don't smile? It's because I don't want men to misinterpret it as me being approachable and asking for it. When you live where I live, it's more of a defense mechanism than anything."

Now, I felt like shit. Here I was accusing her of looking mad all the time when I hadn't taken a minute to walk in her shoes. She was a girl who probably crossed the street when a bunch of guys were gathered in one area; whereas, I didn't worry about that at all. Running outside at night rarely crossed my mind as dangerous. I was athletic, six four, and not a woman, but I'm sure girls who shared the same fear as Luz just didn't feel safe. By telling her to smile more, I was threatening her protective instincts. If I didn't feel like an absolute bonehead...

"Luz, I'm sorry. I could've spoken better; it's just..." I raked my fingers through my thick hair, my nerves getting the better of me as if I'd never asked out a girl before. For the record, I'd never faltered asking a girl out. Flirting was like breathing to me, but with Luz, she took the confidence right out of me.

"It's not easy telling a girl you like her when most of the time that she looks at you, it's to tell you to get out of her way. I like you. *There*. I said it."

And like that, it was as if a pin had dropped. She turned her chair back, avoiding my gaze, and shuffled through her papers like she finally remembered this was supposed to be an hour and a half long tutoring session.

"Don't bullshit me, Cattaneo. If this is some kind of joke to get me to like you just to see if I'm easy or not, you're wasting your time. I don't put out, and I'm not going to be some jock's experiment," she spat, tucking thick strands of hair behind her pierced ear.

I could've called it quits there. It stung to hear her assume I couldn't genuinely be into her, but with the drive and ambition my coach and parents instilled in me, I wasn't a quitter. When you wanted something bad enough, you fought long and hard for it. That something I wanted was a girl named Luz.

Without warning, I hooked a hand around the leg of her chair, pulling her closer to me as I turned her to face me. With a comment like that, I had to be sure. "Okay, Luz, you wouldn't be some experiment for me. I actually like you. Why is it so hard for you to believe me?"

When she finally looked up at me, her lips were tucked away, her eyes giving away traces of sympathy.

"Because I see the girls you normally attract. They're all short, blonde, and cheerleaders. I look or act nothing like them. And I'm okay with that because I like who I am."

"But that's not fair. Most of those girls are just girls who hang around my friends. I've been single this whole school year. And not all of them are blond; half the cheerleading squad are your complexion or darker. I can't exactly help the height thing. Most cheerleaders are smaller." To even suggest I had a type based on the girls who hung around me didn't seem fair, but I had to remember that I had no control over one's perception of me.

"According to you, I'm not allowed to date girls that deviate from my social circle, but I don't have a type of girl I'm always attracted to. I just like girls who are cool, smart, and funny. You just happen to be all of those things—while also being pretty," I admitted. If she wasn't into me, that was cool, but I loved that she was honest and unwilling change who she was just to get you to like her.

"I'm sure underneath all your hard exterior there's maybe a hideously goofy smile you just don't want me to see, and that's okay. Maybe I'm not worthy of it today, but I know it's in there somewhere. You wouldn't have gone through so much trouble to make your lips look all kissable if the only thing your mouth was capable of was sneering and trash talk." The tip of her tongue traced the plumpness of her full lips, toning down what looked like a grin developing into that of a fool's smirk. But then her laugh, her unmistakable chuckles, had revealed the emotions her covert lips were so good at concealing. She had not only smiled but also laughed at something *I* said.

Maybe in her head, no one was counting, but for me, that was one.

CHAPTER FOUR

Now

Evan

Watching a bunch of teenagers throw around the ball on the court reminded me just how much I loved it growing up; it also reminded me of how much I listened back then when I had to be a team player at that age.

Juan Carlos—or J.C. for short—was the most like me at that age, only he is ten times the player I was. Despite his six two frame, he still had the baby face that could convince people he was still sixteen. There was a lot of pressure for him to use basketball to his advantage. I knew firsthand how helpful athletic scholarships had been at securing my financial future.

The AAU league that I coached for wanted to strengthen my players, especially J.C. for basketball season, but it became more challenging watching how J.C. played. He had many chances to pass the ball and despite overall liking his AAU teammates, he wasn't much of a team player. Maybe he didn't have to be a team player playing for his high school team, but by the time I was done with him, he'd be one here.

Yousef, on the other hand, was improving. He'd been open twice, but I know he didn't always take opportunities since he stayed close to his brother Kyvon. Doing so meant he missed opportunities to be more open. I hated to make him feel as if he were doing something wrong, especially since he used to be a lot worse. He was only looking out for his brother, but Kyvon had shown he was more than capable and could hold his own. Guess you couldn't help being an older brother.

Despite running a little late with practice, I tried not to rush the boys when they were horsing around. They came to the community center to have fun or stay out of trouble, and since so many of them came from working families, my goal was never to rush them out the door if they only had empty houses to go to or nowhere at all.

"Hey, guys," I called out, cutting into their scrimmage thirty-five minutes past schedule. Within thirty seconds, sixteen kids huddled around me, many needing to get showered and dressed to prepare for parent pickup.

"I just wanted a quick chat before you all go." I fought the natural instinct to talk with my hands (an unspoken law growing up Italian-American) and relaxed my body language so I could reserve my hands for ASL.

Technically, only Kyvon was Deaf. I had learned some ASL in college but hardly ever worked in industries that allowed me to use it like my first language, English. However, ever since Kyvon and Yousef signed up for the AAU basketball team, Kyvon's navigation and making new friends brought unique challenges to his plate.

They could both play well enough to warrant them on the team, but the other boys, besides his brother, couldn't communicate. Despite taking out four weeks to get to know them before allowing them to play, I found it best that I spent that month helping his hearing teammates learn basic ASL. Even now, I admit my signing wasn't perfect. However, Yousef had spent most of his life perfecting ASL and didn't mind correcting us all in improving our skills.

Now, I never let the boys say anything unless they could sign it too, and it's greatly affected how all of them responded to one another. Plus, it's useful. The fact it's not taught in schools in 2020 is asinine.

"J.C., too much showboating. Pass the ball when someone is open." J.C. shined that signature grin that let me know he'd heard me but intended to only listen to it fifty percent of the time.

"Also, something I noticed. Everyone plays hard. I know this is helping you in your off-season, but play to have fun too. Don't always worry about how good you play. Most of you won't become professional athletes, but all of you can enjoy the game," I advised but also simplified in sync with my signs. I tried to make this known every practice so that no one would be mad if they lost.

Though most or all of them had strong paternal figures in their lives, I wanted to be an influence that would count for something. I didn't need to be a stand-in father or uncle, but at best, I wanted to be that cool older brother most of them could talk to about anything.

It'd taken several months to even get here, but slowly it seemed like I was breaking through. Emmanuel raised his hand, but before he could finish the question, I corrected him. "So, if we lose, do we still go out for—?"

"Emmanuel. Sign it so Kyvon can understand it too. He understands your ASL is not perfect," I signed and spoke at the same time.

Emmanuel, like most of the kids, did best when they sounded out what they could remember. Yousef hesitated before throwing out a word or two that would make him more understood. I already knew what he was going to ask; I just thought it'd be better to familiarize himself with signs he didn't know. Yes, we'd still be going out for pizza whether or not we won. Typical teenagers.

Kyvon smiled, happy to know no matter the outcome, pizza was still an option I'd be treating them to. He gave Emmanuel a handshake for remembering to ask the *important* questions.

"We're forty-five minutes over, but a few of your parents were running late, so take advantage of that. Hit the showers, guys. You all stink."

My last comment was met with tailor-made, rapid-fire insults that if I weren't from New York, I'd say were too clever to have been come up with on the spot.

Their candidness meant that they were comfortable around me, which is more than I can say about my presence when I'd first started coaching. I was aware of how threatening my presence appeared to a dozen and a half kids that didn't look like me. My goal has never been to force either of them to like or interact with me. There were enough things to feed my ego, and this was no white savior movie. My only goal was to help mold them into better versions of themselves.

It required the work past coaches had done for me, and while it had taken time, the trust and respect they gave I'd earned, not even the least bit ashamed it hadn't happened overnight. A long time ago, a girl I had loved showed me I was in a position not everyone had, and if I wanted to be better, I not only had to acknowledge it. I actually had to *be* better.

Even if my impact on their lives were small, I knew every one of them knew they could come to me with anything, even if it wasn't basketball-related. A few of the parents started rolling in when Kyvon approached me to help him with his locker again. With the way this kid forgot locker combinations, I was considering investing in a smart key lock for him.

"You forgot again?" I signed.

"I only use here. Nowhere else," he jovially signed back, leading the way to the male locker room. I admit I should have seen it coming, but I was too busy to care about celebrations that weren't family-related. I had reached the heart of the locker room before I realized "The Birthday Song" being sung was regarding the fact it was my born day.

Chants of the obnoxious tune filled the room as Emmanuel and Randall reappeared with a cake that had two number three candles. Gosh, time flew by so fast. Was I thirty-three already?

By the end, they expected me to blow the candles out, but as grateful as I was that they remembered, I couldn't help thinking this was too much. "Wow, guys. I'm touched, but you didn't have to do this. A greeting card is more than all right next time around," I joked and signed.

"We wanted to show you how much we appreciate you," J.C. defended. "You've helped a lot of us in the last couple of months. My mom's grateful you helped get her that job. Now, she can afford to pay off her student debt faster."

In all honesty, all I did was give her a good reference. Her degrees and years of experience got her that job. It just didn't hurt I'd went to college with the CEO.

"We knew you'd never ask for it, hence the surprise," Yousef added. "And we knew you'd never accept our gift if we hadn't surprised you."

"So, I'll accept the cake because who takes back a beautifully crafted personalized dessert, but if you guys spent money on tangible gifts, I hope you kept the receipts because I can't accept anything from a bunch of out of work teenagers," joking around.

"To be real with you, we didn't use our own money. We raised the money through a GoFundMe campaign. So, it didn't cost us a dime," Randall chimed in.

"Well, if it didn't cost you anything, then bring on the gifts!" I encouraged, prompting several of the boys to fight over who was going to hand me the decorated envelope first. Kyvon ended up doing the honors as a few minutes of arts and crafts could explain the scrapbook cut out of my name on the front from what looked like old Sports Illustrated covers.

"Just so you know, I prefer NBA store gift cards," I joked and ripped into the envelope. There was a letter from the boys and an online printed ticket with email instructions on how to redeem the certificate. Not wanting to show my confusion, I was quick to thank the kids despite not understanding what I'd just gotten but wanted to appear appreciative.

"Thanks, guys. I'm sure I could use one or two of these."

"You didn't even read it!" many voices spoke at once, forcing me to unfold the certificate and reveal what the gift was for by reading the invitation out loud.

"Dear Evan Cattaneo,

Thank you for your interest in Elite Match, the premier bi-monthly speed dating event in NYC for hopeful applicants looking for love—

Did you guys crowdsource to enroll me in a speed dating service?"

Though many of them tried to speak at once, defending the decision, Randall eventually took the lead. "I mean, it was that or consider a six-month subscription on Tinder Plus or Match.com, but we know you don't do well with hook-up apps."

"Plus, with the crowdsourcing copy we gave, people kept throwing money at it. It probably didn't hurt that we put your most pathetic looking picture up there. Women seemed to be compelled to donate after that!" J.C. said.

Even though a part of me didn't want to know, they soon confirmed which picture they'd thrown up there to gain funding. I quickly regretted asking. "Guys, the thought was nice, but all of you are too young to know anything that goes into dating—"

"Well, you must be too if you're still single." Just like J.C. to be ready for a roast.

"Evan, we put a lot of research into where to pool the

proceeds. We know you like giving us your time, and we appreciate it, but, bruh. You have too much time on your hands. Your IG page is full of landscapes and dog pics. You can tell you need a date." Yousef took a stab at roasting my love life.

"You guys sound like an Italian-American mom right now."

"Well, my mom said—her words, not mine—for a good-looking Italian man, he's too fine to be single."

Okay, things were getting a little too personal. "How about this, guys? I'll give it a lot of consideration. I'm hesitant to accept your gift but knowing you didn't spend your own money into considering it for me, I feel obligated to use it."

A group of sixteen adolescent kids knew that was about as much as they could get me to agree to when it came to their generous gesture. I put it out of my mind, thanked every one of them as I addressed their waiting parents, and made sure the remaining few caught their subways on time.

I hadn't even realized until they were all gone that I hadn't even read the entire invitation in full. With less pressure on me to react, I read the entire letter out loud to get its full meaning.

"Dear Evan Cattaneo,

Thank you for your interest in Elite Match, the premier bi-monthly speed-dating event in NYC for hopeful applicants looking for love. Your application has met the necessary threshold of time for us to reach our decision and with much consideration, we would like to cordially invite you to our bi-monthly event.

We offer dating coaching, one-on-one relationship coaching, and endless resources to ensure you get the most out of an event such as this.

We cannot guarantee you'll find your perfect match, but we pride ourselves on helping each individual address their unique challenges and encourage them to discover what they're seeking in a long-term relationship.

Our success rate of sixty-five percent matches made speaks for itself, but we hope that in your journey toward seeking a potential partner that you take advantage of all we have to offer. Text Elite Match now to keep your reservation for our upcoming event.

In the chance you find yourself ill-prepared to attend, your invitation voucher is redeemable for any event in the next four months of this calendar year.

Thank you for considering Elite Match, Manhattan's premiere speed dating event!"

CHAPTER FIVE

Now

Luz

After an hour's commute, I finally made it into Newark. I needed something to put me in a better mood, and nothing did that better than rocking a new do. Growing up in a salon and despite finding comfort in the hours it had taken to straighten my 3C-4A curls bone straight into my former signature silky bob, I'd realized how lazy I was with my hair since reverting back to its natural state. I rushed at any protective style that saved me that hour of prep time my typical wash and go took, and heading to my Tía's shop was the best spot to go.

Newark was a semi-special place, considering most of my extended family lived there. We weren't a perfect family, but in small doses, being around them wasn't so bad—especially when I couldn't get my hair braided anywhere else at a fifty percent discount as I do at my Tía's hair salon. Or should I say the hair salon that she co-owned?

My Titi Zahira was the black sheep of the family. Even though she wasn't born with the elegant poise of her sister—my other aunt Noelia—or had adhered to the traditional domestic role typical of Dominican-born woman like my mom, Danyeli, she was the first to co-own her own business.

Titi Zahira's salon was impressive; it was in the deep trenches of the neighborhood and even though I wasn't in love with all the catcalling, beggars, and hustlers that I encountered to get there. It stayed packed on the weekends, so it was right where it needed to be. A sigh of relief escaped me the moment Eloho + Zahira's sign came into view.

If Titi Zahira hadn't been so tough growing up, I would've said she was auntie goals, but being the eldest of four siblings meant she'd experienced the brunt of the criticism, misogyny, and anti-blackness of growing up Dominican, and I was trying my hardest to make this the last generation to take part in that. Even though my mother was the darkest daughter, she was the first. In most families that was a target on your back; unfortunately for Titi Zahira, it made her unbreakable like steel.

Walking into her salon, which specialized equally in natural hair, African hair braiding, and Dominican blowouts, reminded me that even though Black Dominican-Americans weren't the poster for the mainstream Black-American family, clocking in all different shades of brown, we still could have passed for the hood Huxtables.

Titi Zahira tossed her multi-colored, micro-braided hair and shot me her signature "¡Hey, Luz, ¿qué lo qué?" Dominican greeting.

"Nada aquí, Tía; pasando el rato," I answered back in my best attempt to keep up with her island Spanish. Despite speaking it fluently, I was still insecure about speaking it around my aunts and uncle because they criticized small things. Never mind that people my age spoke Spanglish half the time and we got around just fine.

"What do you need, girl? Is it something I can do for you or a job for Eloho?"

Remember when I said my Aunt Zahira co-owned her salon? Well, Eloho was not only her business partner but also her husband's sister. So, Eloho was my aunt by marriage.

Titi Zahira was brown-skinned, like me, so people always thought I was her kid growing up instead of Demeter, her eldest daughter. Titi was a stallion and blessed with the thickness I wished hadn't skipped me, which meant despite being married once or twice (or thrice), even at fifty-five, she was still beating off the men who tried to holler. It wasn't the attention she was still used to getting in her forties, but she wasn't insecure and she had still retrieved the bag.

I hated to describe her this way because it didn't do her justice when it was by choice not to adhere to the same boxes as her sisters, but she was a proud hood princess and didn't let anyone shame her for it. That was her most admirable trait. She was living her best life and didn't give a damn what anyone thought of her.

She kind of got saditty over the years after marrying my Uncle Jidenna, a nice and too humble Nigerian man to her prideful nature, but ever since they got married, she's been embracing Afrocentrism. It was why when she saw a need for a natural hair Dominican salon instead of your run-of-the-mill fixer of *pelo malo*, she answered the call. They still offered their signature Dominican blowouts; they just didn't partake in crappy hairstyling practices of relaxing your hair without your consent.

"I'm getting my hair braided today, Titi, but the next time I need a trim I'll come to you." I made my way over to Eloho's side of the salon and hoped the wait wouldn't be too long.

"Damn, you can't say hi to nobody," a hostile voice made me jump out of my seat. Demeter, one of my baby cousins, popped out the corner of the nail station.

"Chill, I peeped you in the corner; I was just trying to secure my spot," I argued back before giving this tiny human a hug. Demeter wasn't blessed with the height many of the women in this family had, but if you were a colorist and texturist and couldn't get down with a sista who had tighter than 3B hair, you'd confirm she was a knockout.

Which she was, but it wasn't because she was light-skinned or had the long, curly hair I used to wish for. Like her mother Zahira, Demeter was a no-nonsense kind of girl, even at twenty years of age. I wasn't jealous of her, but I envied how her demeanor was viewed differently in Dominican spaces even though she had the stereotypical appearance of a mixed Black girl for sure.

Things she did or said appeared fiery while I was just angry. She was petite like my mom, so no one ever accused her of "fighting like a man" or being masculinized for her height growing up. Not to mention that even though Uncle Jidenna wasn't her biological father, he still treated her like a daughter. Which meant she spoke conversational Igbo and other similar dialects from her summers spent in Lagos.

She was cool, though; everything I thought I was at that age but wasn't. She did nails and makeup at her mother's salon, but based on her small YuVube following, she wanted to be a makeup artist for the celebrities. She had a mom that supported that dream, so it was likely it would happen, no matter how long it took.

We shared a light embrace before Eloho, my extended auntie, came from the back looking stunning in her off-the-shoulder, Afro-centric Dutch wax print top and dark jeans that brought out the jewel tone of her deep brown skin. Her hair was enviable, falling in thick, back-length 4C coils. Now that I was used to my bob, I'd never let my hair grow that long, but I wouldn't mind braids that length. Imagine me come time for wash day. I'd take my twelve little inches of stretched out coils any day.

"Luz, is that you?" she asked in her light Igbo accent.

"Girl, you know it's me."

"No one sees you anymore. It is like you are a ghost," she joked before asking if I knew what I had wanted before I sat down.

"I'm kind of in a box braids mood." I made my case, hoping to walk out this salon feeling fierce, confident, and beautiful after a day like today.

Having one of the owners in your head was a privilege. Auntie Eloho made my favorite tea and was honest about the colors that would flatter my caramel brown complexion. We ended up going with a bronzish-brown, a shade that matched my dyed hair perfectly. She even bothered to ask if I were a talker or preferred a more introverted approach while getting my hair braided. She respected the fact that being confined to a seat for twelve hours wouldn't put me in a mood for talking, which was more than I could say for Titi Zahira.

Speaking of moods, when she turned my chair around to part my hair in the back, I noticed at one point my Titi Noelia and cousin Mikayla had sneaked in unannounced. Mikayla was the least toxic person in our family, aside from my mom, but that wasn't the only thing they had in common with one another.

Mikayla had that beautiful dark brown skin, matched only by my best friend Candice, and she had managed to make use of her statuesque frame by following the footsteps of her mother as a former pageant queen.

Mikayla was a walking extension of her mom, Noelia Morales, née Cruz, who had become the first Black Dominican to place in the Miss Universe pageant (Trust me, she never lets any of us forget it either). We used to be a lot closer when we were younger, especially since we'd been about the same height despite our eight-year age difference.

Inheriting her mother's high standards of performative femininity had been one reason we grew apart. I had grown a bit into a misandrist after college, so I didn't even want to attract these raggedy cisgender men who had so little to offer but ok-peen and a handful of problems. But Mikayla was in the business of attracting high-quality partners as a dating coach based in the Tri-state area.

I'd since grown out of my habit of hating men for no reason, but I wasn't afraid to hold these fools accountable when necessary.

Not that I was measuring our beauty against each another, but if I had to say which of us focused on the best ways to attract people, I'd give that banner to Mikayla. It was a trait definitely inherited from her mother who, at one point, had that it factor too.

I always embraced Mikayla growing up because looking at her felt like looking at my mom in her teenage years. She and her mother Noelia were physical opposites. Of a modest height, full lips, and light brown skin, Noelia used to joke that Demeter had to have been her daughter switched at birth, followed by Zahira being my mom, and my *actual* mom having birthed Mikayla. Sometimes, Dominican families worked that way (especially with that good old-fashioned mejorar la raza, the practice of being with someone lighter than you to avoid having dark-skinned children being instilled generation after generation). You could give birth to a child that had a different skin color, phenotype, and racial identity than you had.

While my aunts clowned me regularly, I was fortunate to have been part of a matriarchal family that had shown me three different reflections of Black beauty in my formative years. That was more than I could say about any Spanish-language television station or Latinx-based magazines.

Titi Noelia was nosy, so there was no way she was going to ignore me, but sometimes I wish she would because she sucked at giving compliments. Good ones were only reserved for her eldest child.

"¡Ay mira, Luz! I thought your mother told me you were

getting your hair done." She pranced over in her stiletto heels the moment Auntie Eloho was grabbing another pack of hair. This close up you could see the fresh face of Noelia's freckles, a trait she'd been forced to conceal during her old school pageant queen days.

"I *am* getting my hair done," I defended, neck strained from keeping the back of my head up. "There are these things called box braids." I'm not even going to pretend that I didn't hide a little sarcasm in my tone.

"But you already have such pretty hair." She fingered my braided hair, already complete near my ears. When she said *done*, she meant straightened. That was probably just the type of torture Titi Noelia and Mikayla were on their way to get their hair sleek and manageable. I wasn't trying to deliberately shame them, but I felt they looked prettier with their natural hair.

Noelia switched to Spanish when Eloho came back, likely so she wouldn't understand what she was about to say. *"I guess when Danyeli texted me you were getting your hair done, I thought it'd be a deep treatment or a blowout. You already have that pretty hair. I don't understand why you would hide it by getting braids."*

"Well, my hair will be pretty once the braids are in because I'm pretty. Don't push your insecurities on me," I answered back in English, not even trying to hide the sarcasm this time. Titi Noelia shrugged, defeated in her attempt to make me feel bad about my choice, but she was a champ at handing out those backhanded compliments as if it was a part-time job.

I know by her definition, pretty hair meant anything but 4C. I tried to understand that she came from a time where hair texture diversity wasn't celebrated, but I loved my 3C/4A hair as much as I liked my homegirl's 4C hair. Unintentionally, I had supported texturism as a girl, choosing to never wear my hair curly until my last year of high school, but now that I loved myself, I would not participate in that behavior.

"Stop picking at her, damn," Titi Zahira chimed in. "Gonna run away my customers actually paying full price."

That was the best it was going to get when it came to defending me when it came to Zahira. She knew the consequences whenever you went too hard on Noelia.

I did my best to humanize Noelia's experience in dealing with all the bullshit that had been thrown her way in her pageant queen days, without her contributions. None of my aunts, uncle, or grandmother would live here, let alone to have been gracious enough to have all their children born here. Noelia couldn't be critiqued without her bringing up the fact that her pageant days brought her path to US citizenship and that had aided in bringing them all here, and if it weren't for her, they'd still be living twelve to a house in the Dominican Republic.

She was right in a way; based on the gains of living in the states, only immediate family expected to live under one roof, and despite living in poverty most of our lives, we still had things to be grateful for.

It was just that it was always her secret weapon to gaslight you. On the outside looking in, the only person who didn't seem to be affected by her toxicity was Mikayla. But even that was a stretch. I couldn't imagine what it'd be like to grow up dark-skinned with a light-skinned mother who had a bit of a superiority complex. With the soul-crushing things that she said to us, I couldn't imagine Mikayla was immune.

"Plus, you know since she came out the womb, it's been her sole mission to be *different*. Just like Danyeli," Titi Zahira teased. "Don't get the feminist started, Noelia. Especially a woman who ain't even trying to catch a man."

There it was, their main ammo for teaming up on me and ignoring the fact that I'm queer and that cisgender men weren't my only option. As I mentioned earlier, when many of these family members weren't in large doses, they weren't terrible. However, when their like ideas got together, it was often me who was the object of ridicule, a cum dumpster for all their unwanted opinions.

Sometimes, if you ignored the flame, the hens stopped burning. With my luck, they had found something else to criticize in solidarity with one another that didn't include me. As Eloho painstakingly parted what looked like an inch worth of hair into twenty pieces, I noticed Mikayla admiring her appearance in the mirror while fluffing out her week-old supermodel blow out. Watching her retouch her makeup, I was just realizing she was the only person I hadn't spoken to since I got here.

There had been a time we were so close, and now, we rarely spoke when we were in the same room. We had bonded through similar hobbies growing up, but now it just seemed like we inherited our mother's internal rivalry with one another. It had been so stealth, I couldn't even pinpoint when it happened.

All I know was it started with small things and ballooned to things beyond our control. By the time we were both adults, even becoming the first person to go to college in our family hadn't felt like an accomplishment because Mikayla had to one-up me and attend a prestigious Ivy League university.

She'd even studied something nearly identical to my psychology of sexuality major in college, only she had applied her knowledge from it to start a business as a dating coach. Even my dream job couldn't compete. She was a perfectionist, and while I'd gotten incredible grades in school, I started feeling average in comparison. It didn't help when her Type-A mother couldn't wait to compare us.

I wasn't green with envy of all the gains Mikayla made, but sometimes I wished our carefree days as kids had translated into our adulthood. She looked like she was about to leave and as awkward as the situation felt, I didn't want her to go without me saying anything to her.

"Girl, you look cute. Where you off to?"

She straightened out the collar to her jacket and flashed a

casual smile. "Just off to meet with some clients. Nothing special. You know how it is when you're trying to start up a business."

I nodded, having no clue what it was like to start my own business. Relief set in when she had to run so we wouldn't have to fake at small talk. I was proud of her, even if I couldn't say it. Sometimes, I hoped we'd squash whatever got us here. As sappy as it sounded, I missed our once sisterly bond.

Ding!

Speaking of sisters...

Candice: Hey hoe. Long day at the job. Trying to wash this stress away with mojitos and Long Island iced teas. Please tell me you'll be around.

Candice was my bestie. That one non-blood related person you wished was your actual sister or cousin. Finding a friend like her was a hard find as a teen, let alone an adult. She was the person I could count on to help me bury a body, be an alibi, or light a person's car on fire—*if* I needed those things. She was the kind of friend you held onto as long as you could, and if we ended up as two spinsters, it was my goal to get buried next to her with matching tombstones that read *Brujas For Life*.

I wanted to wind down after a whole-ass work shift's worth of getting my hair done, so I thought it best to text back as fast as possible.

Me: A little busy at the moment, but I should be free by happy hour. Text me the address and I'll come through...

CHAPTER SIX

Luz

My eyes darted to the time on my phone as I ignored Candice's call for the third time. I was running a little later than planned, but her calling to yell at me wouldn't get me to that Upper East Side bar faster. She knew better than anyone that coming from Jersey wasn't a ten-minute train ride, and taking a Lyft wasn't any faster. I sent her a quick I'll-be-there-in-a-minute text and turned off my phone until the driver pulled up to the restaurant.

With Candice and me, there was this unspoken rule that in order for us to have a good time, we only had three options; Go to a place where we loved the music but had to fight unwanted attention all night. Hit up happy hours where we hated the music but could relax and spend the night uninterrupted, surrounded by nothing but hipster white people, or spend the night crashing at one of our places. Candice's spot was more ideal. She had a door-man, a full bar, and an endless amount of Nollywood movies at her disposal. Amenities weren't my place's strong point but my apartment had heart and better restaurants nearby to satisfy our

Caribbean palettes. The place she'd chosen today was the one where we hated the music, but hey, it was her invite so her choice. Next time I had a say, we were going to a spot in Inwood. Much. Better. Food.

After a day like yesterday, I didn't care where we drank. I just needed my bestie, a rum and coke, and the rest would work itself out. Luckily, it was a slow day with no playoffs or games to make the bar crowded, so spotting Candice sitting down was a cinch. I mean, she was the only other Black girl in here. Ignoring the dirty looks of confusion of what we were doing there from a couple dude-bros in white collars and pressed suits, I squeezed through the modest crowd to meet Candice at the bar and sat down in the seat she saved for me.

Candice Ayala was the friend I should've had in high school and in college. In an interesting turn of events, she's been going to my Titi's salon since she was a teenager and we had both been too anti-social to approach one another then. By college's end, we bumped into each other at a club and the rest was history. She was arresting, blessed with rich dark brown skin that mirrored my mom's. When most people looked at us, all they saw were two Black girls, which was fine by us. By way of Santiago, both of her parents were from Cuba. You'd never know it, but she was my first real Latina girlfriend that I bonded with based on our cultural and racial identity. As much as it hurt to admit it, other Latinas I'd befriended had excluded me from their plans because I didn't fit their "going out" aesthetic or referred to me as the Black friend. I used to think I needed them, but all they ever did was make me feel like I was being divisive when I brought up real life shit that I went through as a Black Dominicana.

With Candice, I could be me. With Candice, it was a real sisterhood. With Candice, I'd embraced being Afrodescendiente in a way that the term Afro-Latina no longer compared. Maybe the term started as a way to uplift Latinx people of African descent, but it did what every movement does; anyone with a slight curl to their hair claiming Afro-Latinidad while the dark skinned visible negras like me and my homegirl, who'd spent a lifetime fighting anti-blackness and fighting for visibility, got pushed to the back of the conversation. All I knew was that her friendship made me proud in this skin, and I hoped she felt the same way about me.

Although judging by the way she eyed me up and down and from the look on her face, she had already determined that my hair was the culprit of my tardiness.

"So, you don't know how to answer your phone?"

Giving my head a quick pat down before regretting it due to the tightness of the install, I sat down next to her as she took a tuft of one braid and flung it to meet the rest of my hair.

"You lucky you look cute. A good hair day is worth making your best friend wait."

So glad we agreed. When it came to manes, Candice was the queen of switching her hair up. Her kinky curls were her pride and joy, and only after growing it out her entire life, she got her first real hair cut that consisted of more than a standard trim a year ago. Mind you, she only let them cut six inches of it, but she learned the wonders of how transformative a great cut can work for your natural hair.

"So, what brings you to happy hour today?" she asked, flashing that part angelic, part mischievous smile of hers.

"To be real with you, these tight-ass braids."

"See, that's why I crochet more than I do full installations. That fake hair on top of my hair be too damn heavy," she said, making me take a better look at her full, lustrous, and kinky textured hair in a full faux blowout of mermaid waves. Now, this was a woman that could rock long hair without even blinking. It was down to her butt when she wore it stretched out, and through a lifetime of healthy hair regimens, it was all hers.

"¡Pero mira la sirena! *Okay,* inches."

She playfully whipped her hair over her shoulder and blessed me with a coquettish smile as she signaled to the bartender to whip up some signature drinks.

"But I know your arm stay ready for all them white people you work with that always want to reach out and touch your hair," I joked, karate chopping the table in front of us. Candice was the bougiest girl I've ever met. Her hair and nails were always professionally shaped; her clothes were always designer and her interview voice was posh and perfected to where it was hard to tell she had grown up in Camden, New Jersey. However, when it came to her hair and personal space, you saw the Camden come out *real* quick.

"Mama, these people I work with know not to play with me, but I checked this one girl who started working at my talent firm for just looking like she was two seconds away feeding her curiosity."

Speaking of talent firms...

"Hey, how's work? I feel like you have this exciting job, yet you never share the deets." My friend was a top talent agent for one of the largest firms in New York and has met *all* the celebrities. Because insta-famous people were changing what the word celebrity meant, it also meant that many of her clients were obnoxious Tik-Tok'ers whom she often had to babysit and stay on their asses to make sure they met their obligations. Despite breaking her goal of a six-figure earning potential, she hated her job and never failed to remind me how much she did.

"Ugh, I don't know. I've been trying not to bring work with me everywhere I go. Let's just leave it at that. I *have* taken out some more time for my hobby. You like what I have on?"

An olive green, drop waist jumpsuit adorned her curvy figure in a way that made her waist look snatched and her dark brown skin appear like she was some earth goddess.

"Don't tell me you made that?" I marveled, reminding her that I wore a twenty-six tall in pants and a six in dresses. "Many of the pieces you've shown me have been nice. Why don't you start your own boutique? There are women who would die to wear any of your designs. Hell, tell me what that cost to make me one in blush and you've already made your first sale."

She covered her face, attempting to hide the smile that formed, her deep dimples on full display. "You think it's that good? Because I've been having a lot of self-doubt in, my skills, and even my therapist can't help me understand it. This damn imposter syndrome. Why don't we talk about your job? What are you writing about today, Ms. Sex and Relationship Director of Modern Magazine?" she added playfully as I took a sip out of my blue colored cocktail.

"I mean, I didn't want to burden you with my problems, but since you *asked*, I have this story I have to write for work, and it's some bullshit." Knowing I had to tread lightly because when it came to relationships, no hay color. We were like night and day. She loved the idea of being in a long-term relationship, meeting her Prince Charming and riding off on a white horse. I just wanted the straightforward part. The part that ended in orgasms. I wanted that for her, though. She was too amazing to not find what she was looking for, and I know she often felt overwhelmed with the assholes in her tax bracket and underwhelmed by the men who were well below it. Why couldn't I write this thing about her?

"So, the magazine is preparing for our love issue, right? And I had these dope ideas, but my editor shot every single one down. I panicked, of course, and suggested this dumb that I've regretfully dubbed the love bet."

She shrugged, taking another sip of her drink. "Okay, so what's the problem?"

"The problem *is* that I don't think I have the story in me. In my proposal, I have to meet someone and determine if it's possible to fall in love after the third intimate encounter. But you know me; I'm not the second date kind of girl," I explained, knowing I liked no one enough to even get to a third date, let alone a third fuck.

"Mama, you're a writer. You can't just make the shit up?"

Maybe it was the two cocktails and one shot in me, but I slapped the table, outraged that she could ever suggest something like that. "Bitch, I'm a journalist. I can't just fabricate the truth." At that, she rolled her eyes and gave me a taste of that Jersey girl still inside of her.

"Alright, puta. Don't start."

"Anyway, there's always been this level of authenticity to my writing because I don't write about what I'm not willing to do." I've visited sex clubs, dungeons, tried the poly thing, performed every kinky or vanilla sex act worth doing, but love? That concept seemed as foreign to me as Iceland.

"Well, the point is to meet someone, right? Who you can discuss with what you want and expect and see if falling in love by the third time you're intimate feels like love? You're making it seem as if you have to approach some random person off the street or choose someone you're not attracted to. Pick someone fine, get acquainted under the covers, and see if it works. What's hard about that?"

What was hard about that? The truth was I didn't think there was a human being I could ever be vulnerable enough to fall that hard for just because they were good at making me come.

"I think there's a story here, but I'm not sure the best one could come from me. I should've never told her I would do this thing."

Candice's eyes reduced to suspicious slits. "You have been in love before, right?"

Curling my upper lip, I shook my head in disgust. Sure, I've liked partners. I'd even go as far to say the few times I've found myself infatuated with a person. Maybe I fell too fast, too soon. But love? I could only think of one time I may have been in love, and it was a time in my life I was so thrilled to be so far away from.

"So, you're telling me you've never had this one person in your life that you couldn't stop thinking about. Someone you couldn't wait to see every day. Someone that made you smile just for no damn reason." I took a deep gulp swallowing the lump that formed in my throat. Fuck, I did have someone like that. But, I was a kid, and teen love affairs didn't count to me as real love.

"Gosh, it seems like you're speaking from a personal experience," I challenged, but all she did was keep to herself, spinning the mini umbrella in her rum-based cocktail.

"Okay, girl. Details!" I demanded as she rolled her eyes and flailed her arms around like an adolescent.

"Luz, it was a long time ago. I almost feel silly for harboring feelings for someone I don't even talk to anymore. Chile, I haven't even Googled him."

"Well, have I met him?" I shot back, suddenly feeling offended. I thought Candice told me everything, and I knew nothing about this person based on how she described her feelings.

"No, and you never will." She described this privileged, rich white boy she met when her mother brought her to live with her while she worked for his family. We'd had similar upbringings, but my mom had always been more lenient than Candice's mom, based on the horror stories she'd told me. But when you're seventeen, the heart wants what the heart wants. I guess we had both had our share of teen love and drama.

"So what happened with that?"

"We just grew apart. Probably better for the both of us. His dad was like this British diplomat or something, and my mom worked for his family as the housekeeper. We were from two different worlds, you know? But he made me feel so seen, which is more than I can say for the men I've dated as an adult." Candice still had hope that what she longed for was still out there, but I knew her well enough that she wasn't willing to settle. I knew she had her qualms regarding her parents' marriage; it was an uncomfortable fact that her father had been unfaithful multiple times. However, it never stopped her from believing that her Mr. Right was out there. I guess now I knew why.

"So, you're saying you've *never* felt that way about a person before? I mean, we're not talking the last one because we both know how that ended, but what about before that? No one ever gave you butterflies?" she probed suspiciously.

"No." I said, knowing that was a bold-faced lie. Only one partner had made me feel all of that, but then he turned out to be just what I thought he was—a jester in Prince Charming's clothing. But man, that was so long ago. What you feel as a kid just doesn't translate when you go out and face the actual world as an adult.

"Well, mama, you agreed to it, so you're going to figure something out. You just need to surround yourself with people whose main conquest isn't sex. Opportunities like that don't come cheap."

I craned my neck. It sounded as if she already knew what I needed to do. "Well, Ms. I-have-all-these-connections, what are you suggesting?"

With a side bop to her head and a bite to her lip, Candice was being tight-lipped about something.

"Candice!" I snapped as her shoulders caved and she let out a deep exhale.

"Okay, so I have this agent friend. We interned together straight out of college, and while she's intense, she's always dropping these suggestions to me because she knows I'm out here looking for something serious. You always joke how I'm bougie, but this bitch makes me look like Cardi B."

Waving my hands around growing impatient, I begged her to get to the point. "What? Is it like a party where ballers hang out?"

"Not quite, but it will cost you." She began telling me about this mixer-like event and the people that show up there. I was kind of reluctant. I can deal with not seeing any papis, but when she said brothas would not be in attendance, I kind of wondered why she suggested it to me. "I can only assume that the sistas and mamis that you like might be non-existent as well, but what I can tell you is none of the attendees will be broke."

Ugh! So, I'd have to code switch for a night. I did that enough at work. I had this mantra that if I had to alter my true authentic self with a suitor, then that person wasn't worth being with. Candice worked in a male-dominated field, so she was used to suppressing her Newark charm until she was well away from the fake people at her talent firm. But, I was out of ideas and desperate. Whatever she was suggesting, I had to at least hear her out.

"It's more or less a speed dating event that they host every month up in Soho. The price tag is steep, but it filters out the potentials that are just looking for sex." As if reading the uncertainty on my face, Candice countered with, "If you find someone on a dating app, you might get someone who'll prove your theory on love not being the real deal, but if you're hoping on someone who'll be patient and honest, what do you have to lose? I mean, how many speed dating events do you know that are LGBTQ friendly?"

Damn, she was right. I didn't have a man or woman in mind for this experiment of mine, and the so-called cost meant I wouldn't have to deal with any busters. As much as I hated to admit it, I was interested.

"So, good news is I'm open. Think you could text your girl and find out more of the details?" Without a second to waste, Candice pulled out her phone and texted her friend, but before she could type out a second message, her screen lit up with a Facetime notification. When she confirmed it was her friend Zozi, I insisted she answer it. Having her explain over the phone with her own words was better than delivering responses over text.

When her face streamed in, it appeared as if she was in the

middle of a face routine, not that she needed it. Her light brown skin was as flawless as any A-list celebrity's.

"My friend, are you for real this time? Because every time we discuss this matter, you always flake on me." She spoke in a raspy but prestigious South African accent. Her curly hair met her toned shoulders in defined ringlets as her dark brown eyes looked at the screen in confusion when she saw Candice wasn't alone.

"Actually, Zozi, I was asking about that event for a friend this time. She's surer than I am, but she's too overwhelmed with the thought of online dating."

On the other end, she shrugged. "Who wouldn't be? It's all pictures and profiles. No one will tell you who they are in a two hundred-word bio. Is it possible you two can find a quieter spot? I'd like to explain some things and I'd rather not yell."

Candice and I left our cozy spot at the bar for a table that wouldn't have been our first choice, but it was in the more discreet section of the bar.

"Candice, will you be a dear and show me your friend's shoes?"

With a sense of discomfort, Candice aimed her phone down at my feet, which I had no clue what that had to do with the dating event. Her face pinched as if she'd just smelled the inside of a trashcan.

"Ugh, it's worse than I thought. I'm not sure what your friend told you about me, but I don't give poor advice regarding these things. If you're looking to attend one of these, please don't wear anything like that. Sneakers might be cute on commute, but with that attire, you'll only look frumpy."

I know this chick did not just insult my brand new Cortez's. I just got out of the beauty salon. Did the woman want me to wear my heels during happy hour?

"Otherwise, you're a beautiful girl. Just make sure you play up your best attributes. The event Candice is speaking of is Elite Match. There, you're expected to look as if you have a career and not a job. What is it you do..." she trailed off, hinting that she didn't know my name.

"Luz."

"Right. Luz." Candice shot me an unsympathetic look as if saying, Hey, don't look at me. You asked for this!

"Well, Zozi, I run the Sex and Relationship department for a popular women's magazine," I said through gritted teeth, half expecting her to say something else demeaning. This woman was like Whitley Gilbert, Lisa Turtle, and Regine all wrapped in one package. How in the hell did she and Candice get along?

"Great, then you have access to a more eye-catching wardrobe. What you have on right now is *cute,* but the women that get the most attention at these events dress sexy. Classic but not without showing the appropriate amount of skin. If you're serious, it might help to attend more than one. No one finds their ideal match on their first try. The attendees there always seem more drawn to the women who are the pickiest."

Welp. That sounded like her in a nutshell.

"When you arrive, there's a ninety minute vetting process that matches you with what they refer to as your soul match. Ignore that. Enjoy your entrée and work the room. They use that as a gimmick to match you up with people whose answers match closely to yours, but we all know that opposites attract. Be honest. Say you're looking for love, but if what you're really after is a partner with deep pockets, I'd suggest altering your answers a bit. Just so you don't look to obvious."

This was getting a little more complicated. How could I be sure this was what I wanted? I didn't even know how much the damn thing cost. That could make or break my decision of even trying this damn thing. "So, Candice mentioned it being on the pricier side. What does that look like in a ballpark range?" When the words seven hundred and fifty dollars left her pouty lips, I swear I almost fainted. Seven hundred and fifty dollars? For a date? Just what kind of people showed up at this sort of thing?

"I should also mention that $750.00 doesn't include the fifty percent discount for women attending for the first time." Three hundred and seventy-five was still steep but far more doable. After picking her brain about what she got out of the events, she gave this heartfelt story about how after two relationships she found her way out of, she just couldn't do the struggle love thing again. She wanted to date men looking for love and wanted to get married. But in New York, where women outnumbered quality men three to one, she started taking measures into her own hands. Hence, a dating event with a price tag of most people's rented rooms in the city. I wasn't as serious as she was looking for love; I just needed someone who would take my project seriously.

"I should also probably confess that this is for an article I'd planned to write for work."

Her curls bounced as she shook her head and explained that it didn't matter. "Elite Match won't promise to find you the partner of your dreams, but it will get you in contact with fewer people willing to waste your time."

That settled it. While I still had her on the phone, I booked a ticket. Guess I was going on a speed date.

CHAPTER SEVEN

Before

Evan

One of the positives to my current schedule was that the one class that all my friends and I shared was the easiest to get an A in. Even with my lowest effort, I'd managed to get a B- on my last project, so it was safe to say it was the class we all goofed off in before we busted our asses in the grueling practices we had after school. The teacher was nice and the overall vibe was chill, but the real reason I had excitement written all over me was because it was the one place I had endless amounts of art supplies available at my disposal. With Valentine's Day coming up, I was going to surprise Luz with a handmade valentine. One she'd never forget.

"You know this project doesn't require glitter, right? And what's with the tissue paper? Wait, Cattaneo, are you making a love letter?" Before I could stop him, my buddy Terrence snatched the makeshift fold-out card I was working on, waving it around for everyone in our corner to see.

"Dude, c'mon! I'm not making a love letter. It's more like a valentine. Now hand it over." Not bothering to get out of my seat. Without her name on it, no one would know who it's for and besides, I didn't exactly want people to *know* I was into her—in case she turned me down. It was bad enough when someone in your social circle hit you with rejection. Given that Luz was virtually unknown at this school and what others would call weird, my friends would've never let me live her lack of interest in me down.

As my teammate recited the lyrics of *L' is gone*, a Musiq Soulchild hook I'd written in the right flap of the folded-up heart, I was reminded why the song had made me think of her. Conveniently, the song featured the first letter of her name, something I knew my friends weren't quick enough to piece together, but the line about a girl having caramel skin could bring on questions I wasn't necessarily prepared to answer. I thought it was sweet; I hoped she thought so too.

"Caramel complexion? Who are you giving this to? Rochinique? Because you know Cotton hit that shit sophomore year, right?" There was no other reaction than to roll my eyes. Even if that sort of thing mattered to me, it was safe to assume my friends only expected me to pine after another cheerleader. I didn't have to do anything to get one of those girls to go out with me. All I'd have to do is shoot one a smile and she would perform the predictable rest of the work. That's just how easy it was to hook up with someone in your circle. But Luz was the one I wanted to do backflips for. She didn't make things easy by admitting she liked me. Call me a glutton for punishment, if you must.

"I know it can't be Stacy because she's more chocolate than caramel." They debated back and forth like I was going to break at any moment and confess. If there was one thing I learned from my dad, it was that you didn't kiss and tell. No respectable man would talk about a girl to his friends unless he was a total scumbag. Luz and I got off to a bad start, but I knew if I could prove to her I wasn't playing any games, she'd come around to confessing her true feelings for me.

"Cotton, it's not a cheerleader. You don't fuckin' know her," I argued, my friend handing me back the card after he didn't get the reaction he wanted to get out of me. For now, I was just going to stay on my side and mind my own business as I added my sparkles and colored glue just as I intended.

"She must not go to this school then because me and Cattaneo got the same taste in girls, and I don't see any at this school I'm trying to smash."

With Cotton, it was always a competition with him. Who could bag the most? Who could smash the most? It was fucking annoying, considering any time I had showed even a slight interest in a black girl, all of a sudden, the guy liked black girls again, despite the awful things he said about the ones that didn't look mixed race. I just liked girls. I didn't care what their hair looked like or how light or dark their skin was. As long as they had traits I admired and looks I found attractive, who really cared about that other shit?

"Dude, you and I don't even come close to having the same taste in girls. Maybe in looks but not in substance. I like girls who can think for themselves, who hear what I'm saying instead of nodding and smiling."

Cotton shrugged. "So, I like chicks whose main interest is me. Who wants someone they have to work hard to get?"

What's sad was that just a summer ago, I would've thought the same thing. The truth about having a hive mind was that until someone challenged you on your mindset, everything you knew about things always seemed right. Now that I'd felt what it was like to work for something, *for someone,* there was no way I was going back to my old way of thinking. Cotton snapped his fingers, a look of sureness awakening his sharp features.

"Oh, I know who it is now! It gotta be that theater nerd. The one with the overbite but has the big titties," he said, getting a laugh from everyone in our corner except me. "You guys are assholes. Besides, it's not her. And with all that bad guessing, all it tells me is that you have no idea who it is." And for now, I wanted to keep it that way. At least until she agreed to go out with me.

———

I had a hard time stuffing that thing in her locker, especially given the effort I put in the last-minute felted hearts I decided to add. But as soon as that break bell rang and the hallways flooded with students, I knew any second she was going to come and grab her AP English book like she always did just in time to make it to her next class. From a distance, I watched as she put in her locker combination, bending to the ground as the card fell to her worn-down dark red patent leather Doc Martins. She looked hella confused, but there was no mistaking the smile finally breaking free when she thought no one was looking. Making my way toward her, I brought my index and middle finger to my lips and blew the number two in her direction, that smile turning into a scowl when she realized I was rubbing it in.

Card in hand, she came after me, spewing her regular rhetoric about how foolish I was for pursuing this. For pursuing her. "You can't possibly be serious about this? Stuffing love letters in my locker? Do you know how bad this looks for someone like you?"

Turning around to add to the hallway banter, I walked backward to measure her reaction. Words could lie, but body language couldn't. "And they say guys are oblivious. Am I not making my interest clear enough? I like you. Why is that so hard to understand?"

Her eyes narrowed as she pursed her lips and stomped the ground. "Because this is fucking weird. The popular jock. The social outcast. I feel like this is a cheesy 90s movie just waiting to blow up in my face. I don't need that shame or humiliation."

As the halls cleared with students anxious to get to their next class on time, Luz and I were now alone in an empty hallway, on the one side of the school that was safe and secluded enough to be the craftiest make-out spot. The two classrooms down that hall were reserved for music and theater, but for half the week they were empty since the teachers that held classes in them had spread themselves thin providing the same programs to other schools in the district. When the clicking of a third party's heels grew closer in the distance, Luz surprised me by pulling me in the closest classroom and shushing me to not blow our cover.

Being this close to her, her hair smelled good. Like, *really* good. Like I've got the world on a string Sinatra good. Every time my mom was in a good mood, she would throw on some perfume that she rarely wore and put on that song from Frank Sinatra. I used to think it was silly, but now I felt like singing and dancing about how lucky I was to be here right now. "The coast is clear. I think she's gone."

Luz turned to me with her long lashes and dark eyes, sweet and sparkling. Only when she remembered who she was with that her face transformed back into its usual disdain for me. "Why are you sending me corny valentines? You know people were around to see you, right?"

Wow, she was really frustrating. "Luz, who gives a shit who saw me with you? It's my senior year. I want to date who I want to. Whoever has a problem with that can jump off a cliff for all I care. I've never had a girl be the way you are with me. You don't care how it looks calling me out or holding me accountable. You set cut and clear boundaries and don't pretend with me. I really like that about you." I didn't look at girls as hard or easy, but having people treat you like a god amongst men got irritating sometimes. I was tired of going after the ones who laughed at my dumb jokes for my sake or offered me things to get me to like them. Plus, I felt like she actually listened to me when I talked to her.

"If you don't find me attractive enough or don't want the pressure of dating a jock, just tell me and I'll lay off. But if there's any chance that my feelings were mutual—"

To silence me, she put her hand over my mouth as she pressed her opposite index finger to her full lips to shush me. "Don't talk. Just listen. Even if I do share your feelings, which I'm not saying I do, but if I did, it's not like anything could come from it. My mom is extremely protective about me dating people she doesn't know, and I can almost guarantee you that she doesn't know anyone in Northland-Lyceum. Even if you could muster up another smile from me, that's the obstacle you're faced with."

She lowered her hand from my mouth, finally giving me a chance to respond to her so-called *challenge*. So, her mom didn't want her dating strange people. Was that all? If I prided myself on anything, it was that moms loved me. Dads I weren't so great with, but moms? There wasn't a mother alive who could resist the Cattaneo charm. This was going to be a piece of cake.

"Luz, I don't know if you've realized this, but I eat obstacles."

Rolling her eyes, she let out an exasperated sigh. "See, this is what you don't get. My mom is Dominican. Like fresh off the boat Dominican. Dominican moms aren't like American moms. No means no. Maybe means no, and you hardly ever hear a Dominican mom say yes." She stomped her patent leather boot. Clearly, she had never dealt with an Italian mom from Jersey. They pretty much prepared you for the world when it came to being faced with disappointment. All it meant was that I would have to adjust my strategy.

"We'll see."

CHAPTER EIGHT

Now

Evan

"I just want to bench one more rep. Mind spotting me?" My work buddy Broderick positioned himself underneath the bench press, moments after upping his press by twenty-five pounds. Making sure he lifted safely, I stood above him, encouraging him on to meet the next set. Broderick was an acquaintance who doubled as my gym buddy from time to time. We worked on the same floor but rarely ran into each other unless it was to use the company-owned gym. We went out for beers every once in a blue moon, and while I'd only met her twice, if he ever invited me to grab some drinks with him and his fiancé, I was never in poor company.

Hanging out with him was a little easier than some of my college buddies; most of them were married with kids, and half the time, I wasn't sure their wives liked them spending time with a bachelor—unless they were trying to set me up with every single friend they had. My friends' wives weren't aware how little influence I had over their lives. When they wanted to go, I couldn't stop them, and if they needed more time to themselves, I wasn't convincing them to stay.

"Hey, Broderick. I wanted to get your opinion on something," I said, taking down my mask.

"Can it wait?" His dark brown skin glistening with sweat from the challenge of added weight. He managed his set before I picked his brain. Waiting for him to refresh his palate, he took a sip from his water bottle and probed my request. "Yea, bro. What's up?"

"What is your unabridged opinion on speed dating?" As Broderick pointed to himself in a state of confusion before I redirected the question back on me. "I meant for me, genius."

"What do you need that for?" he asked in a forced shrug. "You don't seem like you would have much trouble getting dates. If you do, let me know because Janine got some fine ass—"

"Eh, let me stop you right there. It's too damn awkward to keep getting set up with my friends' wife/girlfriend's single friends. When we don't like each other, they take it personally. When we do, they expect us to planning weddings. It's a lose-lose," I interrupted.

"Okay, but you just said you were considering online dating," he sarcastically countered my defense.

"Speed dating. But I'm not considering it for myself. My kids went through all these lengths to save up for this elite event for people serious about an actual relationship. They did their research. It's expensive, and has a high success rate of finding people serious about long-term relationships. I don't know, though."

I had nothing to lose, not that I had much to gain either. But I'm sure if I didn't at least try not to waste my kid's hard-earned donation, there would be less hard feelings if I decided it wasn't for me. They would live if I refused the situation altogether, but giving it more thought, it felt like a missed opportunity. Like a time in your life that you didn't plan but turned out to be a blessing for you.

"I think if it were me, I'd be reluctant," he huffed out a breath of relief. "I didn't meet Janine that way, so the old-fashioned me thinks the execution is a little cheesy."

"It's not that I disagree," I started with this sudden need to defend the decision, "but that perfect world that made me assume the woman of my dreams I could meet at a grocery store feels long gone. Especially since it's so hard to approach people after COVID-19." I had to face it; people didn't date like that anymore. We were beyond the times of finding your true partner when grabbing for the same laundry detergent or reaching for the last guava kombucha at Trader Joe's.

"Probably won't meet the love of my life at a speed dating event, but it could be fun if I let go that I have to find someone to enjoy the night. Dating profiles are the fucking bane of my existence. I would rather put myself out there than try to talk myself up in a three-sentence online profile."

My advantage was I didn't have a ton of scorned exes or toxic past relationships that left me bitter or dead inside. Even my last relationship ended calmly and mutually, as we both decided we just weren't right for one another. A woman wouldn't be inheriting any drama or unhealed trauma I hadn't addressed. So, I kept thinking, what could it hurt to not rule it out?

Broderick took a chug of his water bottle. "I think you should do what makes sense for you. Your kids care about you. You just can't help that they see you as a loser who can't get a date on his own," he deadpanned but couldn't keep up the public humiliation for long before his features drowned in a choked-up smile.

"First of all, fuck you." I threw his gym bag at him, hoping it'd surprise him last minute and mess with his balance. To my disappointment, it didn't. "And secondly, since your opinion doesn't matter as much as the company I have at home, I'm going to pretend I didn't ask you," I joked, before waving him goodbye and making my way to the gym's exit.

———

I could've used a shower and clean clothes, but I knew the minute I got home, none of that would matter to Ms. Mary Mack. After a brief stint of dating a cat lady, I knew the next animal I owned would be a dog.

Growing up with two family dogs, I loved their company. I thought I'd never get over the pain when my first dog died when I was eight, and I didn't know you couldn't bring dogs back (damn All Dogs Go To Heaven), but I was more prepared for a dog's lifespan by the time my parents inherited a newly born pup when I was fourteen.

Maybe it was why I hadn't sought many romantic relationships in recent years. Most times, Ms. Mary Mack made me forget sometimes, it was nice to have also sought human companionship.

Ms. Mary Mack had my schedule memorized by now, so even if I hadn't heard her paw steps approaching the door, I knew she would be waiting up. I knelt down and patted her, peering into soulful eyes. "Hey, girl. Sorry I ran a little late."

With Ms. Mary Mack, I paid for it when I wasn't around for her when she was awake. It wasn't my first time caring for a dog, but it had been my first experience with a cane corso. I had adopted her when she was four years old, which made her about my age now in dog years. Since she was already mature and developed her own habits, it took a while to re-establish boundaries and teach her how to respond, not that she wasn't the chief person in control.

Ms. Mary Mack was a rescue, and after her last owner, she required a little extra care to get her to trust me. I fell in love with her on the spot, especially after I learned her breed was as Italian as I was. I considered calling her Onyx, thanks to her beautiful slick black coat, but since she had a few white spots on her tummy, in that instant, I was reminded of the schoolyard clapping game and after a few days of getting her to answer to it, it stuck.

It took a while to ease her separation anxiety once she got attached to me. Cane corsos were a smart breed but naturally destructive. If left alone too long, she knew how to make me pay for trying her patience, but all it took was figuring out a way to cane corso-proof my apartment, and it was a match made in heaven.

"Ready to go on that run, girl?" As her tongue hung out as if to signify an enthusiastic yes. I was already in my gym clothes, so after retrieving her collar and leash, we were on the beat for an evening run.

Nothing like fresh air to get your mind off things like dating events and apps. Would I consider the damn thing or not? It's not like I was up to anything new, and my designated days to volunteer or errand run weren't giving me the opportunity to meet new people. Ms. Mary Mack stopped mid-run to sniff and take a well-needed bathroom break. Seemed like a good time if any to bring up the event.

"So, what would you think if I started dating again soon? Think you might be okay with that?" I asked as she went about her business, leaving me to scoop up her mess and throw it out.

"My expectations are low, but my kids? You remember my kids, right?" As I described in better detail what each of them saved up for so I could make a habit of going out more, if even just one night. Ms. Mary Mack didn't seem impressed. Her holier-than-though expression was written all over her face, but I suspect if she could talk, she'd deny it.

"It'll probably be a waste of time, but who knows? The least it might do is get me out of the house. I don't want to do anything without you, so I want your honest opinion. What would you do?"

CHAPTER NINE

Evan

After an hour-long debate with my main girl, I determined that I had her blessing to go through with this. Dating should've been simpler, but hook-up apps were the only way to meet someone these days. Although I had never found myself one hundred percent invested in meeting women that way, I now saw that being thrown into something that knocked me out of my comfort zone was good for me.

I had nothing to lose by going, and the worst that could happen was that I'd meet someone I liked. All I needed to do now was confirm with my dog sitter that she would be by to check up on Mary in the rare case that the dates went well and I was turning in later than expected. Either way, it was nice to go out in a social setting where people wanted to...I don't know...socialize. I told myself earlier that it didn't matter what I wore, but as time drew closer to me to leave, I went back to my closet and changed into something more "date" worthy. I wore enough suit and ties during the week as required at my firm. Tonight I wanted to feel approachable. A slim, dark crewneck, jeans, and some dressier boots gave me that vibe without second-guessing myself. Plus, it didn't hurt that my arms looked impressive without having to flex them. Before I could talk myself out of it, I was off to the closest subway station and on the E train to Soho an hour early, the quick walk to the upscale bar being just what I needed to calm my nerves.

Upon entrance, the hostess enthusiastically greeted me by introducing herself. "Hi, my name is Anna Mae and I want to welcome you to our fourth quarterly speed dating event. I assume this is your first time doing this sort of thing?" she spoke soothingly with a rich southern accent. With her vintage style and rockabilly pinup hairstyle in a bright shocking purple, she looked more like a 1950s Black burlesque queen than an event planner. Stunning, but not my type since I wasn't into so many visible tattoos, but given her sweet personality, I'm sure I could've made a brief exception.

"My name is Evan Cattaneo. I'm a little early, but as you guessed, this is my first time doing something like this. Since I wasn't sure what to expect, I wanted to make sure there wasn't a check-in," I admitted. She gestured for me to follow her, leading me to a room with half a dozen workstations. Turns out, I wasn't the only early one. In the corner, another attendee typed away fiercely on the computer's keys as if they were writing a bestselling novel.

"Actually, Mr. Cattaneo, it's a good thing you came early. Our event requires you to enter your invitation number to unlock the questionnaire that's going to pair you with the first match of the night. You're allowed to mingle if after the first ten minutes y'all don't have that 'it' factor you're looking for, but the entire point of the questionnaire is to match you with someone who shares your values and interests. We call it your soul match."

I nodded, trying my hardest not to laugh at how silly this all felt. I hadn't taken a test on a computer since I was an undergrad, and this was a lot of what that felt like.

"To make a long story short, depending on your answers, you'll be assigned to a room where your soul match will be. It'll be you and perhaps twenty others. Your first soul match will wear the same color wristband, so make sure it's visible to the eye. Looking at those guns, I'm sure that won't be a problem for you, handsome." She winked as she pulled out the chair for me and helped me input the invitation number that unlocked the questionnaire.

"There's no need to call me when you're done. This device I have here lets me know when you finish. When that happens, I'll be back with your bracelet and will show you to your mingle destination. Don't worry about mixing up your soul match. We don't use another wristband shade twice. If you get something like a deep purple, look for someone with a deep purple wristband and not lilac, comprende?"

I nodded with understanding.

"Great! We're ready. Happy matching." She left with a big smile and a perk in her step, clear in every click of her heels made with the floor. I cracked my knuckles and formed a steeple before beginning with the first batch of questions. They all started basic enough. Age, gender, race, sexual orientation, religion, political view and if any of those things contributed to the person I wanted to be paired with. I didn't have any racial preferences, nor did growing up Catholic mean I wanted to end up with a Catholic girl. I preferred to meet a woman closer to my age, and while I leaned more toward conservatism, I wasn't so tribal where I couldn't side with a liberal woman who could make me look at issues objectively in dealing with what was the right thing to do. On to the next set of questions. Interests.

For the next section, I was glad to see that you could pick more than one option. As far as musical tastes went, progressive and hard rock had always topped my faves, but I was open to anything as long as I was in the mood for it. With movies, I was adamant that I only enjoyed action and historical dramas. In the ten-minute portion, topics involving travel, sports, languages, and hobbies came up as I flew through the section in less time than recommended. The next segment took some time to consider my responses, as it was more of a what-would-you-do collection of questions. Maybe it was more of a character test? Why else would someone want to know how you would handle an uncomfortable situation? More people were filling up the workstation as I hit done on my browser, and as promised, the purple-haired hostess was there within seconds to collect me and slap a bright teal wristband on my willing right wrist.

"So, it looks like you got the green room. People are already beginning to pour in, so you may even meet your soul match right away," she explained as she led me to another private section of the restaurant that was full, considering my early arrival. Guess everyone had the same idea.

"Quick update on your soul match. I just got a confirmation that you matched eighty-five percent with someone. This is *good*! It means she's already here and that you have many things in common. Most of the people in this room are your close matches, so if fireworks don't fly, you could still have chemistry with any of these people. Your entrée is included in your invitation as well as a two-drink ticket. Any additional drinks you can start a tab for." She winked, holding her hands out in a presenting-like demonstration. "I'm just going to leave you to it. Good luck out there," she said as she headed back through the double doors as I got a good look around the room.

Every single woman in this room was a knockout, ranging in body types, hairstyles, skin tones, and styles. If I had just been dropped off in this room with no context, I would've mistaken it for a modeling shoot over a dating event. Blondes, brunettes, curvy women, and everything in between. Many of them were already chatting it up with other attendees, and from what I could tell were wearing matching wrist gear. It wasn't until I looked toward the bar that I noticed a woman with these back-length copper braids that almost blended in with her deep, sun-kissed complexion.

The blue and white striped romper she wore hung low off her silken brown shoulders, a matching belt showcasing her slim waist. When I made it down to her legs, I couldn't help but admire how toned and long they were. I loved every inch of a woman's body, but I was definitely a legs man. Her wrist was adorned with a bright teal band identical to mine that helped me fork up the confidence to go over and introduce myself. With a body like that, there was no way there wasn't a sexy face to match it. Maybe this speed-dating thing wasn't so bad after all.

"I like your bracelet," I announced, giving my match enough distance to feel comfortable but still be aware of the matching wristband I wore on my wrist. It was clear from the glimpse of her side profile that she was top tier in attractiveness, but there was something familiar about her feline-shaped eyes, pierced nose, and full, sensual lips. Her evenly arched eyebrows furrowed as the single word leaving her mouth helped paint that missing piece to my past life. She wasn't a stranger but a *friend*? I wouldn't go waving that flag any time soon.

"Cattaneo?" she said with gritted teeth and a level of disgust reserved only for me. This had to be some kind of joke.

"Luz?" The name left my mouth without thinking, along with the memories of our high school relationship. Some good, others bad, but nothing that made me angrier than waking up to having my car keyed along with four slashed tires, something to this day she's denied doing. I knew in my heart that she did it but had to cut my losses when I couldn't prove it. After forty-five minutes of questioning, this was whom fate matched me up with?

Tonight couldn't get any worse.

CHAPTER TEN

Before

Luz

Why did someone as cute as Cattaneo claim to like me? He was practically every high school wallflower's dream. Despite what I wanted to so desperately deny, he was freaking hilarious. It took everything in my power not to let him penetrate my funny bone, and then there was that adorable small cut in his left eyebrow. Imperfections like that were only to remind you that the rest of us were just plain and uninteresting. I'm also sure this didn't matter to most girls who liked guys, but the fact that he was taller than me and didn't make me feel like a freak was a bonus.

Being five feet eight wasn't a big deal for most girls who longed to be taller, but growing up in a Dominican family, I was already taller than every girl in my family with the exception of Titi Zahira. Dominican girls were always tiny, under five feet one, like my mom, but around other girls I felt like a beanstalk, and it didn't help that lots of guys I knew were my height or shorter.

Ay negrita, you better not wear heels if you want to find a boyfriend.

Ay nena, you can't wear anyone's hand-me-downs because your feet are too big.

Those were the everyday comments I heard from my family, and some of them were way worse than that. There was no way a guy like Evan could just fall in my lap.

It wasn't for a lack of confidence. When I looked in the mirror, I liked my warm brown skin and the dark, soulful eyes that stared back at me. Perhaps, I wasn't what the majority people would call drop-dead gorgeous, but it was rare when I didn't feel my version of attractive. I just wasn't comfortable with just anyone accessing my softness and femininity. In some odd way, I'd always felt like femininity was so exhausting and performative, but for the first time in this brand new school, I felt compelled to do something different to my looks to get Evan to compliment me.

I was becoming a slave to his attention, and I didn't want the attention to stop. The nail in the coffin was that my mom was barely okay with me having my first girlfriend when I was sixteen. I was sure that having a boyfriend at seventeen wasn't going to make her day either. She wasn't overly strict, considering she could have been worse since we were Catholic, but it had been years since we stepped foot inside a church. Yet, the second I brought up dating, she worried herself to death that maybe she was being too lenient. I didn't want to give her a reason not to trust me. Going behind her back to date a boy at school would make her change her entire schedule, and all I did was watch TV and write. Until I left for college, that was probably all I was ever going to do.

Who was I kidding, though? I was going straight home from school after Evan canceled our tutoring session today. His leaving early forced my mind to enter my negative space. If he liked me as much as he said he did, why wasn't he up my ass like all his team-mates were on all the other girls they hung around?

Ugh, this is why I didn't want this guy getting in my head! One afternoon to myself and already I had decided that guys like Cattaneo were the masters of playing mind games.

———

As I walked through the hallway of our apartment's building, I couldn't stop thinking about what I'd say to Evan the next time I saw him.

Look, it's obvious you don't like me, so why don't we both do ourselves a favor and go our separate ways?

After today, our next session would be our last, so it was a chance for a clean slate with no hard feelings. Entering the door of our apartment, I was met with the delectable smell of some-thing warm, fruity, and sweet. The Monchy and Alexandra track that played in the background had been one of my favorite bachata songs, a tale of adoration and love sung in a tropical blend of Dominican Spanish . My mom was always cooking, but it was rare that I came home to the smell of her cooking desserts and loud music.

Her favorite bachata playlist was usually reserved for Saturday cleaning, and the only time she ever made for sweet foods was when we were having family or guests over. Stewed meat over white rice and habichuelas was all she ever made time for before she was off to work, but when she entertained, she pulled out all the stops.

"Ma!" I yelled over the music, hanging up my coat and kicking off my boots by the door so I didn't track any dirt from outside into the house. By her many sets of slippers were a pair of over-sized Nike Cortez's that out-measured my mother's chanclas by several inches. Did my mom have a guy over here?

When she didn't answer me back, I just followed the voices

and laughter to the kitchen, only to drop my book bag, my heart diving out of my chest when I saw him.

There he was. All six foot four inches of gorgeous jock with powdered sugar littered across the tip of his nose, mouth, and fingers. *Wait.* Was that a dedito de novia in his hand? "Oh, hi Luz. I was just hanging out with your mom, and she offered to make me these pastries. I've never had anything with guava paste in it before. These are *superb.*"

My mom, a five-foot munchkin with flawless dark brown skin and dark, shiny hair that spilled to the middle of her back looked like a shrimp next to him. And for someone who's English hardly ever got tested, she sure was finding a lot to say to Evan with the little English she did know.

"Ay, negra. Your friend from school is so nice. He says you're helping him get good grades like you."

I walked further into our box of a kitchen, my eyes growing mortified that there were photos albums and pics of me looking like a Chia Pet with my unruly mass of hair. Okay, maybe he hadn't given up on me, but did my mom have to show him pictures with my hair looking all wild?

"Your friend was also wondering if it was okay to take you out this weekend. I said it's okay. That's what boys should do. It's how they did back home."

She spoke that last part in Spanish. "*Negra, I told you the liking girls thing would just be a phase.*" She also said this in Spanish.

My mom wasn't what I'd call old school, per se. It made her uncomfortable that I had a girlfriend, but she never mentioned conversion camps or that I should go to service more to pray the gay away. She just chalked it up to being a phase.

"*He's a nice, handsome boy who wants to go to college. He's Catholic, and best of all, he wanted to introduce himself to me before taking you out. When I'm not home, I like to know where you are and who you're with,*" she spat out in her rapid-fire Dominican Spanish. Evan, visibly uncomfortable, leaned in to whisper to me.

"She's talking about me, isn't she?" Contorting my face into a grimace, I nodded, embarrassed. "Good things, I hope."

"Just peachy."

"Are you upset to see me here today?" His pale green eyes accessed me. I wasn't sure "upset" would be the word I'd use, but at the moment, it wasn't something I could easily express. I didn't think he'd go through all this trouble to date me and asking my mother for her permission. Who does he think he is? A *gentleman*?

"I'm not upset. More like surprised she opened the door. The only white people that come around here are from the church of Latter-Day Saints, and they are one-hundred-percent fluent in Spanish now."

He mouthed a "wow", his expression transforming uncomfortably into a smile.

"That is hilarious. But yea, I told you I was serious about this, and you told me you didn't want to bother your mom, so I figured it couldn't hurt to talk to her."

He picked up another baked finger-shaped pastry, politely asking me to open my mouth. The warmth of the molten guava paste almost burned my tongue but was still mouth-wateringly delicious. Before I knew it, I was smiling with victory as clear as day on his silly, cocky face. That was three.

"Negrita, I have to get ready for work soon." She put the dishes she used to make the pastries in the sink and turned on the stove to heat the rice and chicken from yesterday. "*Why don't you pack your boyfriend some dinner and walk him to his car.*"

I rolled my eyes. "Ma, he's not my boyfriend. At that, Evan laughed. Novio was the one word in Spanish he did know.

"It was nice meeting you, Evan." My mom came into hug him as he dwarfed her in his frame. She disappeared into the bathroom as the water turned on and provided the much-needed cover from my mother's nosy ears.

As my mother requested of me, I scooped out a hefty serving of her stewed chicken into a small plastic container, filling another small one with day-old white rice. "When my mom offers you food, you better take it. Turning down her food is the fastest way to get on her unpleasant side."

"Thanks."

I handed him the containers as I opened a lower cabinet to grab a small plastic bag to make it easier to carry. He lowered the contents into the bag, our fingers lightly brushing as I pulled them away fast to tie it shut. "Shall we?" I led Evan back to the living room to collect our shoes as he followed me out into the hallway.

When we made our way out of the building and out of view of our apartment, he pulled me off to the side as I noticed his dark blue Subaru parked only a few houses down. "So, I wanted to ask you how come I had to look at your baby pictures to see you had naturally curly hair?"

Easy. No one ever noticed me with my natural hair texture, but the second I got that wash and set, it was all, "Your hair looks so nice! Where do you get it done?"

I shrugged. "I don't know. Probably because everyone in my family thinks I look prettier with straight hair. I come from an enormous family of women who do hair, so it's not a big deal. As long as I wrap it every night, it stays like this."

He tucked a loose strand behind my ear, blessing me with his clean fresh scent. "Well, how about this time, you just don't get it straightened? When I pick you up Saturday, I want to see what your hair really looks like. I think it looks pretty."

Um...let me see. Choose having my mom rip and pull at my already-tender-headed scalp, followed by an absurd amount of heat or just taking a shower and wearing a wash and go? I wore my hair straight because my mom usually helped me, but if I wore it in its natural state, all I needed was some shampoo, conditioner, and a good leave in. I shrugged.

"Yea, I guess I can do that. But just a quick warning: Don't expect my hair to look when I was five. It's all bigger and kinkier now. It won't feel as silky as it does straight." I tucked the other loft of hair behind on other ear.

"Well, everything about you is soft. I have a hard time thinking your hair won't be the same. Besides, I'm sure you'll look cute with your naturally curly hair. And while things are going so well, can I put in a request to see you in lighter colors?"

With my index finger, I wove tight circles in the air as I considered his request of me.

"Okay, Cattaneo. Now you're pushing it!"

A laugh lit up his already handsome face as he held his hands up in defeat. "Just thought I'd ask."

With a satisfied smile and a prominent chin, I reminded him that some things were non-negotiable. "Can I put in a request for what you wear?" I asked sarcastically.

"It won't matter what I wear. With you on my arm, no one will be looking at me." The corner of his lips tugged up in a confident smile that almost made it hard for me to look away. "See you on Saturday."

And with that goodbye, I knew that I would obsessively anticipate the stroke of midnight come Saturday morning.

CHAPTER ELEVEN

Now

Luz

Aw hell nah.

Was this all an elite dating service had to offer? State of the art matchmaking my ass. The results lead me straight to my ex!

I should probably rewind things and explain for clarity. The man who stood before me—the one being proposed to me as my soul match—was none other than Evan Cattaneo, the first boyfriend I had ever truly loved.

When I was still optimistic about romance, Evan Cattaneo had wooed my reluctant heart. Not only did he bewitch me into falling for him, but he also went out his way to make me feel like I was the only girl to exist. I was living every inbetweeners dream. I had captured the jock with a heart of gold, all while being my authentic self. No teen movie makeover required.

It hadn't taken long to see his true colors. For the record, at one point, I do think his feelings for me had been genuine. It just never stopped him from spreading that love everywhere else. I had blocked him before the concept of social media afforded me the privilege to and made little time for love ever since. Only one other situation had mirrored what I had with Evan in my lifetime, but all that experience taught me was how right I was to look down on love.

Gone was some love-struck girl who looked forward to afternoon cuddles and make-out sessions and in her place was a woman who guarded her heart like the gates of Buckingham Palace. Sure, the one positive thing being with him was that he had actually learned how I liked to be touched but giving my heart to him had been a complete mistake on my part.

"You have got to be kidding me." Evan rubbed his face in a sign of defeat.

"Now I know why Zozi suggested I ignore the whole soul match thing," I retorted, emphasizing soul match with some sketchy parenthesis. "I was picturing this night to go so differently, but I'm seeing that this was a mistake."

"Tell me about it," he added with faked a smile. "By the way, you look amazing." His thick eyebrows furrowed with loathing in his green eyes.

It took everything in me to resist the urge to curl my lip in disgust. Who cared if he thought I looked amazing? I didn't live for him, but damn if he didn't look good himself. Who told him he could get grown and sexy and grow a beard?

Tonight's voucher covered two cocktails, the suggested maximum for enjoying the night without embarrassing one's self, but I could tell I'd need more than that to get through the night. The bartender prepared one for each of us, stating we could order another a half hour from now while he fulfilled other orders.

"I'd say the same thing about you, but I'm sure you have a fan club of women in an iPhone thread stroking your ego regularly," I drawled, making sure the comment was laced with sarcasm.

"Would I be here if I did?"

"It's hard to know. If you break as many hearts as you did in high school, I'm sure you have to figure out alternative options to pick up women."

"So, we're going there, huh?" He licked his teeth, pursing his lips in that way that showed I was getting on his nerves. "Because you're painting me out to be this monster when I had four slashed tires and a keyed-up car, proof that you weren't so innocent yourself."

Before the school year ended as if it were God's plan, some stranger had gone ape shit by slashing all his tires and keying his car so good that it was as if someone tried to give his hood a fade. Of course, instead of taking responsibility for it being a circumstance of the way he treated girls, I became his scapegoat. Mature, right?

"With as many girls who probably hated you in high school, there was probably a long list of them who felt you had it coming. Don't confuse me with someone who cared enough about you to waste my time ruining your car."

Evan's face scrunched, recalling details that made it hard for him to swallow his own bullshit. "That's funny because I remember that time in our lives differently."

"Oh, yea?"

"Vastly so. I remember being so in love with you that I couldn't believe you thought I cheated on you. I kept replaying it in my head; could I have done something different? But you wouldn't have listened anyway."

An eyewitness's testimony spoke for itself. What I saw on May 26' 2005, at five thirty-three in the afternoon was the person I thought was my boyfriend in a competitive exchange of sucking face.

I would have been a fool to take back a guy who humiliated me, proving to everyone I was some phase in his life until someone new in a tight blouse gave him attention. Strangely enough, I almost did want him back.

Evan Cattaneo had manipulated me so strategically, I'd broken all my rules for him. Luckily for me, I reminded myself I had options. I hadn't owed anything to a boy who couldn't stay faithful for less than a school calendar year.

My heart was broken, but come fall, I'd be surrounded by an entirely new pool of people to get to know and who were more transparent than the high school boys I was used to, pretending to be good guys. Getting over Evan had *never* been easy, but it schooled me in ways I never imagined. By college, I could no longer be swayed by small-town charm and snake-charming green eyes.

Evan and I mutually agreed not to make a scene as we proceeded to our table. Thirty or so other matched couples soon followed suit as we all enjoyed our overpriced meals and strong cocktails in solidarity. The last comment that came out of his mouth stuck with me, though. With an attempt to channel my feminine energy, my plan was to take the path of least resistance, however I wasn't sure I was going to sleep good tonight if I let something like that go.

"Well, you did cheat on me unless you're going to tell me some teenage girl's lips somehow magnetically drew her to yours." My rum and coke couldn't have come at a better time. As much as I had wanted to cash in both drink tickets, patience was going to be my greatest gift tonight. Since we couldn't sit in silence the whole night, I knew anything that came out his mouth might constitute that second drink.

"Let me stop you right there." He reached his long arms over the table, talking with his hands as he did when we were teenagers. "I know you've been hell-bent on me being the villain in this story, but I tried to tell you the truth back then—or at least what I knew as the truth at that time."

"There can only be one truth, Evan."

"But I was as confused as you were. I hadn't really known what happened until sophomore year of college."

He set the bait, but I debated whether to take it or not. "How convenient. Did your new girlfriend dump you then?"

Evan's eyes narrowed as he clenched his jaw with mild irritation. "Luz, apparently you don't remember Joseph Cotton."

"Of course, I did. He was some random jock who, on occasion, made it his life's mission to ensure I had no self-confidence. What did he have to do with any of this?"

Evan's eyebrows squished together as if he was trying to make sense of things himself. I almost regret asking if it was just going to be followed with half-truths and the retelling of events to make him the victim of all this.

"Apparently, he liked you too. He was an asshat but also my friend and teammate so, when we started dating, I felt like he started acting strange after that. He'd find any excuse to tell me how weird he thought you were or something as equally ridiculous. Obviously, I didn't know that he liked you or else I would've kept my distance, but he lived off that sort of mentality that he had to be mean to the girls that he liked. After we started dating, I noticed it more with all the dirty looks he'd give or the unsolicited comments about how we didn't look 'right' together."

None of this still explained why Evan locked lips with some sophomore.

"I won't bore you with the rest," he continued, sensing I needed him to move on, "but the short version of the story is we ended up seeing each other at a frat party, and in some inebriated rant, he admitting to getting some random girl to kiss me right when he knew you'd be around to see it." Evan stared off into the distance as if he were just as confused as I was as he explained this so-called version of what happened.

"We were friends, but I never felt like I trusted him. He was always competing with me on the dumbest things, and our friendship was probably toxic," he admitted with a sense of calm.

I sipped in silence at his recollection of the events, nunchucking my sanity through the bullshit of his lies. "So, you expect me to believe that a kid that *barely* talked to me had an infatuation so contaminated that he was willing to stage a girl making out with you, all in the effort to break us up?" I managed to say in one breath. "Do you know how outlandish that sounds?"

Evan scratched his beard, furrowing his eyebrows as if he were admitting all this stuff for the first time in his life. "To be honest, it does sound about as out there as a situation could go, but I have no reason to lie now and especially not while we're sitting a foot away from each other fifteen years after the fact. I never got to tell my side of what happened, but I get it if all that built-up resentment is giving you doubt. "

Evan's features softened, a sign he was genuinely distraught but trying to hide it. Not exactly the reaction I was expecting from someone supposedly lying.

"Even if you are telling the truth, if you were me and I told you those same exact events that *supposedly* took place, would you believe me?"

Evan sat back in his chair, his eyes widening in recognition at the thought. "Honestly? Probably not." His expression had been so genuine and cute that I found myself laughing along with him. This wasn't supposed to be happening. I was supposed to be upset. Snap out of it, Luz!

"Just about everything about all that seemed pretty out there. But then again, my entire high school experience felt as far out of the direction I thought I was going. Basketball was my life for four years straight. Until I met you."

I prayed to whatever entity was listening that some sappy Uncle Jesse music wouldn't immediately follow that comment.

"So, if you had to ask me, then yes, if it were you, I would have rationalized everything you said. I loved you too much not to. Even now, I still can't believe I lost you to something so juvenile and trivial. I wanted to kick Cotton's ass for having the guts to admit that to me, but I figured what's the point? I had lost you anyway. I would've felt better for a minute or two and then I would've gone right back to being mad again."

Watching his emotional admittance was a bizarre thing. He never once looked down or gave any clue that suggested he was making it up as he went. Not knowing what to do or say, I shuffled the food around on my plate, taking in his sincerity.

Funny thing was...I believed him. The shitty part, though? Believing him meant that the fire that fueled that energy for half my life was based on a lie. I'd allowed most of my adult years avoiding stability when it came to romance. Long-term love had proven twice in my past that it hadn't been for me.

When I invited partners into my life, it was with the understanding that we'd have fun for as long as it still felt fun. Most times, it worked out beautifully. Once or twice, love ruined everything. I would boldly remind myself of all the times where letting someone in emotionally destroyed me and in recalling those memories, Evan's face always showed up.

There had never been a time that I asked for an explanation because my eyes had told me everything I needed to know. So, to hear that my eyes had deceived me was a hard pill to swallow. What I saw that day needed to be true. Otherwise, I lost one of the first partners that made me feel seen and heard in a relationship being petty and jealous.

"Anyway," Evan shook his head, steering the conversation in another direction, "I don't expect your forgiveness. I know you don't give it easily, but I am sorry that I hurt you. I'm sorry things ended the way they did, even if, to you, it sounds less than genuine."

Evan sighed deeply, his long eyebrows relaxing until his face made no expression at all. I should hate him, but now, I'm not so sure.

"Instead of taking a trip back down memory lane, how about we share something more positive. What do you do for a living?"

CHAPTER TWELVE

Luz

From the moment Evan and I sat down, neither one of us made any effort to work the room. In fact, we had been the only couple who had matched and not flirted with other potential matches.

Internally, I was bullet-pointing all the ways his perceived betrayal had ruined me and even encouraged me to make poorer decisions in relationships due to lack of judgment, but I couldn't help that I had never trusted many after our breakup.

I had been in love before him, but it hurt more with Evan because we'd been so public with our relationship. Thinking he had embarrassed me, or worse, gotten me to fall for him just so he *could* humiliate me had killed my self-esteem and hardened me. That most of it had been a lie made sitting across from him, explaining what I did for a living, feel out of body. I was once again that seventeen year old girl who wasn't sure there was perfect fit for her anywhere.

"So, you work as a sex and relationship director? I'm assuming that's at a magazine?" he asked, proving he had swallowed nearly everything I shared about myself up to now. "Would I know it? Major publication, independently distributed, or start-up?" He took another sip of his lemon water, appearing enthused.

"Actually, it's Modern magazine," I admitted with little boost from that mixed drink, hoping there would be a sign of recognition on his end. To my surprise, his reaction satisfied my ego. His eyes widened, but I couldn't be sure if it was shock or disbelief. The laugh that he fought started to reach his eyes, and I wasn't sure if I should be confused or offended. Did he think my career path was a joke?

"Would love to know what's so funny."

"Nothing," he answered as he fixed his face. "It's just...come on. Modern magazine? Do you remember all the stuff we did off the articles alone back in the day?" His voice lowered to a whisper with the last sentence. "I damn near became a lifetime subscriber."

Evan never hid that when he initially thought of women's magazines, they were all about makeup tips or articles on how to attract the perfect man. Like most things in our past, I had to prove him wrong once again. Of course, there was nothing wrong with those topics. I loved wearing makeup and certainly didn't need someone shaming me for doing so.

I had to wonder, however, why every periodical associated with women and femmes had to be labeled as superficial. Modern magazine was a host to many resources like how to handle mental health and how politics affected everyone who wasn't a white, straight, cis man, in addition to giving tips on sexual wellness.

"Wow. Congratulations. That must be, like, your dream job."

Shrugging until I nearly touched my earlobes, I brushed it off like it was no big deal. "Sometimes, it is. Nine months of the year, it feels like I do nothing but rush home to sleep just so I can wake up and go to work again." I was silently agreeing that my job was pretty awesome overall, though. Yet, something I said must have thrown Evan off as he cocked an eyebrow, unconvinced.

"I feel like there's a major but coming."

"There is no but," I said proudly.

"But you said it was your dream job only *nine* months of the year. So, for the other three months, you're not sure?" His tone rose in pitch, still confused at how I posed the question.

"Keep in mind that most of the year for me is..." I hesitated, trying to find the right words. My job was far from a drag, but it was a magazine and every magazine had that time of the year where the workload was beyond any other time in the year. Unable to articulate things quickly, my hope was that a shift in conversation might refocus things some place other than my job.

"Let's stop talking about me. What about you? Where do you clock in and out of every day?"

"I work for an investment firm, but you didn't answer the question." His smile was coy but riddled in arrogance.

Two could play that game.

"Didn't I?"

As if I'd said something funny, Evan laughed, convinced I had more story to tell. "No, seriously. I want to know why there are brief periods of time that you don't enjoy your job."

This dude was about to make me go full on Soulja Boy on The Breakfast Club. "I never said I didn't enjoy my job during these times—"

"Ah ha," as if a light bulb clicked on in his head, "so, you admit that there are *these* times?"

"Evan, I don't know what you're trying to get me to admit, but I love my job and certain times of the year you're just dealing with a heavier load that often throws a wrench in your functioning mental state."

Fashion magazines prepped for their September issue months in advance. Teen magazines exhausted their efforts for prom season. Depending on the magazine, or if major publications wanted to highlight a niche demographic, there'd be more focus on Black History Month, Latinx History Month, Pride Month—you get the gist.

Every magazine had that issue that required more prep time than others, and Modern magazine was no different. Modern magazine celebrated every marginalization women or femmes faced, but in preparation for its Love Issue, everything else paled in comparison.

"Our February issue typically drops in January. For everything we highlight during the month of February, love advice is often our most searched keyword. The articles with the most traffic are often related to dating, getting over breakups, how to spice things up for Valentine's Day, and how to make your friends feel appreciated on Galentine's Day. Some of our highest online traffic comes from the Love Issue. Since I've started running the sex and relationship department, my editor has always been impressed with me. This year, though, not so much."

When prodded, I mentioned the assignment I had found myself in after having each of my pitches rejected. Even though we hadn't seen each other in years and I spent ninety-nine percent of that time hating his guts, strangely enough, I trusted him with this.

Without making it sound as if I was looking for a test subject, I softened the piece to appear that it was no strings attached but could lead to more. Up to this point, it seemed as if Evan understood everything.

"So, the point is to not fall in love?" he asked, confused.

"I didn't say that, but I'm a realist," I defended.

"Maybe I didn't make myself clear. From the sounds of things, you were already doubtful of the pitch, correct?"

I nodded, unsure of where this would go.

"And you're willing to pay a $375 price tag just to ensure you'll find a genuine person, only to expect what's essentially a friends-with-benefits situation."

That wasn't true. The event was a segue to weed out all the busters only looking for a hook-up. "Just because I'm a realist doesn't mean I want a fuck-person to taint the tone of the piece. I could have found someone on Plenty of Fish or Tinder, but I wouldn't mind meeting someone, whether we worked out or not, to be serious about looking for love."

His eyes narrowed as if he was trying to figure it out in his own head. "But you personally aren't looking for a serious relationship. So, my guess is that you expect it to fail?"

Gosh, why was he trying to poke holes into my intentions? I was already struggling with the idea as it stood. I couldn't change overnight that I had such a low expectation when it came to being vulnerable and giving too much of me. Technically, he was forgiven, but just the perception of a bad experience created a domino effect.

"Evan, I already told you. Dating sucks when you're a woman. People will lie and act their way to the Academy Awards to get the things they want from you with giving very little in return. I've had my share of bad relationships, so, yes; I don't go into relationships with the same optimism as I used to." Even in casual encounters, people often told you what you wanted to hear.

"And if we both don't know what we want, I don't see why I can't find someone who isn't going to play me and will at least prioritize my pleasure. Cuz you know y'all cis men ain't exactly batting a thousand."

Evan's eyes widened, offended that I would accuse him of such a thing. I had to remind him I wasn't talking about *all* cis guys but them as a whole. That didn't stop him from reminding me when I called him on his past toxic masculine behavior and how it affected me; he had made every effort not to fall into that category. I couldn't argue with that.

I hadn't only been looking for men at this event. Following the advisement, I opted to wear a rainbow flag pin, just to let others know I wasn't specifically looking for a cis-het relationship. From all the rainbow enamel pins, necklaces and even nail polish I saw around the room, it was clear that at least a third of the room was queer too.

"Anyway, those were my intentions for the night before we sat down together. I just didn't count on seeing someone I knew, so, I guess one less person to include."

"Whoa, so I'm just automatically out the running?"

Was he serious? He actually thought about putting himself up to something like this? Not that I minded. I had to keep ignoring ol' girl Zozi's voice in my head from reminding me it was best to ignore the person I matched up with. That it might take a few events to find something special, so I should never take the first available, even if it was tempting.

However, none of her advice took into account that I'd not only be inches away from one of my first loves, but that I'd also get the closure I'd wanted for years. All it would have taken was a conversation and back then and I would have had my answers, but alas, I was too young and impulsive to need another explanation.

"I didn't think you'd be interested," I nervously chimed back.

"It's one thing to exclude me because *you're* not interested but a whole other monster to exclude me because of false bad blood or because we dated and it didn't end well."

"I'm not excluding you. It's just…" I couldn't think of an extravagant way to say it, so I said it plainly. "You don't think it'd be weird?"

Evan straightened in his chair, rubbing the palm of his hand on his beard and cheek. "Of course, I would. But it's not any weirder than not seeing you for fifteen years and then being matched with you at a premier matchmaking event. It could just be that it doesn't still ring true for you, but I'm still heavily attracted to you. For the entire forty-five minutes we've been talking, I haven't even wanted to meet new people because no one here would have compared to talking to you."

It was nice to know you still had it when it came to the ex you hadn't given much thought about over the years. As much as I hated to admit it, talking in-depth about things people usually reserved for a second date had felt easy with him. But if I had answered just a few questions differently, I could have been sitting across from that girl with the shaved sides along her 4C natural mohawk and sexy sundress.

"And I can take a hint."

"Don't put words in my mouth, Evan. Ya girl never said you weren't fine." I normally kept my man-stroking to a minimum, but he was putting out ideas and words I hadn't spoken and I was just setting the record straight. "It's just weird. Don't shoot me for being honest."

"I get that. I just can't help thinking about something from our past. A certain smile bet that if I won got me a date with you. Recalling it now, it was pretty childish, but all I can remember thinking was how much fun I had trying to keep that smile on your face."

Hearing his words, I hated admitting that a sliver of his appeal was penetrating. He sounded sincere, as if he was least interested in the sex and more about the actions that lead up to it. That was too bad. All that sexiness molded into each inch of his lean, muscular frame had me reconsidering my excluding him altogether.

Our reconnection required some level of patience; I had to keep reminding myself that he hadn't intentionally hurt me all those years ago, so all the animosity I was holding onto was going to affect how we moved going forward. I wasn't usually one to hyper-focus on the good times when it came to failed relationships, but he had been sweet. Teen shows and movies always showed the wallflower getting the popular guy, but that wallflower had never looked like me.

Even if Evan hadn't been popular, I still would've felt validated having someone so handsome think I was pretty. As a teen, I'd been so used to hearing "You would be so pretty if you stayed out of the sun" or "You're so pretty for a Black girl" that for someone who outgrew half the kids my age by the seventh grade, it was just nice not having to force myself to shrink or alter my appearance to feel seen.

I could totally see myself fucking a guy like him three times, satisfaction guaranteed, with the possibility of walking away with no hard feelings. Assuming we came to the decision to walk away.

Urgh, I had to stop thinking about it. I was trying to look at it with optimism, so it wasn't healthy to expect it to fail before it started. At least I would be testing this theory on someone I knew should we go through with it.

"I'd have to give the idea a little more thought," I broke the silence with every effort not to sound thirsty.

Evan nodded. "I respect that. Maybe we should take down each other's numbers. I would love to call you, even if it were just two old friends catching up."

We entered each other's digits into our cell phones as he asked if it were okay to work the room. "It was nice talking to you, Luz. I'm glad to see that the things I'd always loved about you hadn't changed."

He smiled his goodbye, but I wasn't so sure I wanted him to leave. Was I comfortable with him potentially chatting up other women who could convince him they wanted the same thing? Would I regret it if he left right now but by the time I came to a decision, he came up with an opposing one? Less than an inch away from leaving his chair, I reacted. The biggest heartbreak of my life was a lie, so letting him walk away felt like a mistake.

"Wait."

Evan turned to me, an intense stare softened by kind eyes. "I'm not playing hard to get; I'm just precautious. This is going to require more than a two-hour sit-down, and I'd have to know we plan to be adults about it. No ghosting, no gaslighting, no games."

A wicked smile etched across his face and at that very moment, I realized the severity of what I was getting into. "You've got yourself a love bet, Luz De Los Santos." He extended his hand to mine in a mutual shake. "But I warn you; I'm used to winning."

CHAPTER THIRTEEN

Evan

This shit was so surreal. One day, I'm bingeing documentaries on '70s rock and roll musicians with Ms. Mary Mack and the next? A woman from the past is offering me the chance to make love to her three times to prove that she can't fall back in love with me. Twenty-twenty was the year of *the* clusterfuck, but it was at the point where I could no longer process anything.

That woman in question was not just *a* woman. Luz De Los Santos was *the* woman. Most might use the phrase *the one that got away*, but to put that out into the universe would be saying that the height of my romantic relationships peaked by the time I was seventeen.

Whatever terms I used to describe her wouldn't make it any less true. Luz had always been the girl I considered my first real love. The first girl who dated me for me and not for some superficial reason that had to do with my inflated ego. She was just...my girl.

And without even knowing it, she had shaped my entire life.

It was safe to say that by the time I reached my senior year of high school, I knew basketball wasn't enough to fuel my future. I knew it could grant me access to scholarships and financial aid I couldn't get without it, but of all the girls I fell for, Luz had been the only one who encouraged me to have more than sports.

When it came to what I could do on the court, there was no question I had talent, but between college scouts and recruiters, my name rarely came up in the whispers or talks of the minor league like a few of my fellow players who dedicated nothing but time crafting their court magic. For years, I questioned what my life might be like without basketball. In a matter of weeks from knowing Luz, for the first time in my life, I considered more than one backup plan.

You would never be able to tell, but despite being what I'd described as full-fledged bravado, I was secretly insecure. Before her, girls gravitated toward me because I was handsome, tall and popular but I never got a sense that they liked me beyond my outer layer. Before Luz, no girl could ever admit there was something she liked about me aside from my height, jersey, or pale-green eyes. Half the time, girls didn't even listen to me or cared when I had something to talk about beyond sports, so I played up those attributes out of fear I wasn't interesting beyond those things.

Luz got me to open up about things *other* than sports. She listened to my fears about the future as well as the anxiety I felt being an only child, which was amplified, being the only boy to traditional Italian-American parents. I had to make them proud. I had to go further than they did or it didn't count. I didn't have the luxury of being an embarrassment.

In return, I got a cute little bookworm to come out of her shell. I learned to be better at listening when the subject didn't pertain to me and—let's face it—a much better lover than I had been in my head.

There had been a time in the distant past where I'd let a

bunch of teenage idiots convince me that performing oral sex on a girl was gross, and unlearning that ideal was the best take away from our time together. I took pride in knowing that if love-making was an actual profession, then my oral skills would earn me top dollar.

There were definitely worse teenage guys than me, but I became a better man after Luz. It took a long time to unlearn all the harmful behaviors I participated in and all the misogyny I turned a blind eye to. Luz held me accountable, something I wasn't accustomed to growing up with old-fashioned parents.

In Italian-American homes, it wasn't uncommon to raise your daughters but love your sons, meaning, much of a girl becoming a woman centered on her being a good wife to her future husband, but rarely was there any preparation involved when it came to grooming sons to be a good husband.

Not that I had been thinking about marriage in high school, but the faster age hit, the greater efforts I made to be better than the average man. I didn't want to be the kind of guy a woman was settling for. Much about the way Luz had made me feel contributed to that.

There probably wasn't a single thing I regretted more than losing her. Back then, she was a girl who trusted her intuition, which I loved about her, but I always wished she had allowed me to explain myself more. In real time, I hadn't even been sure what had happened. All I knew was everyone thought that me losing the girl I loved was somehow funny.

It made it that much easier to drop all that dead weight after high school, even more after college. The people who needed to be in my life were there, and the people who weren't? Let's just hope for my sake, Luz fell into the former.

I couldn't wait to get home so I could tell someone; Ms. Mary Mack was definitely in for an earful. When I relieved my neighbor, I was still wired so I changed into my sweats to take her for an evening run. Before we left, she'd been warned. There was about to be some hefty competition for the leading lady in my life.

———

It was a quarter past midnight by the time we got back. Ms. Mary Mack hadn't likely taken a nap waiting up for me, and my neighbor had less expertise with keeping a cane corso tame, so it took a little longer than usual to get her to use up all that energy. It was all good, though. I skipped a workout at the beginning of the week so all this did was make up for that.

Heavy pitter-patters echoed throughout the hall as she scratched the outside of my bedroom door after a much-needed shower.

"I don't want to disappoint you, Mary," I cooed, inviting her inside as she hoped on the bed, "but sooner than later, you may lose your bedroom privileges." Ms. Mary Mack wasn't concerned or phased one bit. If anything, I was wasting her time by not having the door readily open for her. She already had it in her mind that she intended to be a bed warmer and anything else was below her.

Ending my day in a pair of lounge pants and t-shirt I laid out before showering, I joined Ms. Mary Mack and cuddled up next to her. "Now, where were we?"

Ms. Mary Mack hadn't given me her undivided attention since the minute I got home, but now, she couldn't avoid me. "Remember when I said I had a date tonight? Turns out, I got a little more than that." I rubbed under her neck, warmed by the fact her ears still rose whenever I pet her there.

It made her that much more susceptible to hearing me explain my run-in with Luz. "I'm not going to lie to you, girl. I really missed her. I just can't believe someone hated me so much that they sabotaged my entire relationship with someone I was happy with." A stupid prank had ruined my relationship, but I couldn't help recalling all the growing up it had forced me to do. Not to mention all the emotional immaturity I had to toss to get to where I was today.

While I had missed our late-night phone calls, the kissing, and the sneaking around whenever her mom wasn't home, pessimism would have found some way to screw things up if I didn't have to examine myself years prior to even needing a service like Elite Match.

I couldn't help thinking we came back into each other's lives for a reason. Maybe the opportunity was presenting itself because we were both emotionally ready for love. Luz had mentioned she had been cynical about love; I wonder if this moment meant she was ready for a change.

Change was inevitable, but I needed to prepare myself for it too. The Luz I fell in love with back then might not be the same Luz that I reconnected with this evening. I could end up falling in love all over again or find we're not as compatible as we once were.

Then again, we had an eighty-five percent *soul match*. I didn't believe in stuff like fate or destined matches, but I believed in love. I can't ignore how strongly I still feel for Luz, even after all this time.

"She's just, so pretty, Ms. Mary Mack. Beautiful brown skin. Gorgeous smile. Cute, curly hair." Ms. Mary Mack drowned her face underneath my pillow, her tall-tale signs of jealousy on display. "You're pretty, too, in your own way. I just like human beauty too," I defended as that seemed to make her feel better about me bringing up my adoration for someone else.

I bored her with the story of how Luz and I met for the first time, only to be interrupted by the sound of my phone notifications going off. My notification center was getting full.

Two messages from Luz De Los Santos.

"Holy shit." If the external me reflected half of what I felt internally, I was about to be an emotional wreck. Luz was texting me. I had gotten home so late that I hadn't wanted to text her so she didn't get any creep-vibe ideas. I wanted to ease in and send a proper text like "Good morning beautiful". Clearly, she had other plans.

"Mary, I am freaking out. I know you spent the last thirty minutes listening to me showboat, but I'm freaking out!"

Ms. Mary Mack wasn't interested in showing me an ounce of sympathy.

"Fine. Be like that."

My notification center lit up a second time. I now had three messages from Luz De Los Santos. "Shit, this is the third one. Should I read them? I don't want to read them if I can't text back a meaningful reply."

Ms. Mary Mack soulfully bore her stare into me, and I took that as her silently telling me to read the damn texts.

Luz: *Not to be weird, but are you up?*

Luz: *This isn't a booty call text btw*

Luz: *If you're asleep, sorry to bother you. Just hit you up when you're awake.*

I read each message carefully, hoping I wouldn't miss any hidden meanings—nothing too salacious or sarcastic. There was little that could get crossed in the reading of these messages.

"Quick, Mary, what should I text back?"

CHAPTER FOURTEEN

Evan

Me: You sure this isn't a booty call? A hi, sup could have had me scratching my head but a "you up?" text is barking up booty call territory. Don't want to give me the wrong idea. I'm impressionable

Within seconds, the thought bubbles next to her name appeared followed by a much-deserved clown emoji reply. Good. So, she knew I was joking. Not everyone always got my sense of humor, but Luz had always seemed to.

Luz: If it's too late, we can always try for tomorrow.

Me: No. Now's a good time and coming from you, it's never too late or early. I'm actually glad you reached out. I planned on texting you first, but you beat me to it.

Luz: So, how was your day earlier?

Me: If you're going to text me first, at least give me the decency of asking how your day was before mine. As a charm school dropout, you're flying past all the lessons I actually paid attention to.

Me: And with that being said, how was your day gorgeous?

The next message didn't come as quickly as the last, but when her reply finally came in, the length of it explained why.

Luz: My day was good actually. I'd been feeling pessimistic about this one particular story but after hitting up a group thread with a few of my co-workers, it actually motivated me. They all seemed eager to read my love issue piece. Especially when I told them I'd already found my test subject ;) I mean the worst that can happen is bad sex.

When I read the text back, I knew I wouldn't be satisfied with writing back words that didn't have the same emotional influence as spoken words. Reading back the words "bad" and "sex" made me doubt that I hadn't been the lover I thought I was when we were seniors in high school. Either way, texting wasn't cutting it. I wanted to hear her voice.

Me: Do you mind if I call you? Texting is okay when communication and boundaries have already been established but it feels like we're starting over. I prefer a real conversation over acronyms and emojis. If we can Facetime, that would be better. But I know it's late and you ladies usually have a night routine that you don't want us men all in on. A voice call would also suffice.

Luz: I can do Facetime.

Without hesitation, I went into her contact info and hit the Facetime icon and waited patiently for her to accept the request, which she did on the third ring. As her end streamed clear, the sight of her in a slinky red chemise had my cock standing at attention. She looked sexy as fuck in red. I whistled, followed by a cheesy hubba, hubba that resulted in her flipping her collection of intricately plaited braids over her shoulder, accompanied by a cocky grin. She was so fuckin' adorable. That was the one thing that stayed the same.

"So what's this thing about the worst thing that can happen

between us is bad sex? Did I leave a bad impression on you?" I
wasn't entirely arrogant. I understood that the boy I was at seventeen wasn't the man I am today. But Luz had been the first girl I
made love to that taught me patience and how important it was
to prioritize a partner's pleasure over my own. Maybe it wouldn't
be the same today, she never hesitated voicing her concerns. She
had no problem articulating at seventeen when she wished I'd
take my time instead of being in a rush to orgasm. And before you
ask, yes that was her at seventeen.

"Fifteen years is a long time to be set in your ways. I'm not
saying I expect the worst, but I don't want to be hopeful and
expect the best either." She shied away the question.

"Luz, that's not what I asked you. Did I ever give you a reason
to think I can't satisfy you after we started hooking up?"

She rolled her feline eyes at me, finally admitting that while
we had a rocky start, when we became more comfortable as a
couple, my performance was sexpert level.

"Yea, you were actually one of the fun ones. The way you'd
make me laugh with your come faces, I actually missed that about
you."

"I mean, could you blame me? It got worse after that cock ring
you bought me for winning against that prep school of trust fund
kids. When I actually would be ready to come, I was delirious." I
am also proud to admit that I no longer needed a cock ring to last
longer.

If she wanted to use one for fun, though, that was a different
story.

"I forgot how it feels to make you laugh and see you smile,
knowing I'm the reason. I love it," I said, watching her laugh her
ass off on the other side. As if sensing Luz's presence putting me
in more than a good mood, Miss Mary Mack jumped into my lap,
covering my face in territorial licks and later looking in the screen
like, "He's mine, woman. Get your own."

"C'mon girl. What did I tell you about when I'm on the

phone, huh? What did I tell you?" Her marble brown eyes regarded me and huffed as if she knew she was in the wrong but wasn't going to admit it. She was so damn spoiled.

"I like that you have a dog. I've always liked animals but have never considered owning one," Luz admitted. Wrestling Ms. Mary Mack to calm down, Luz laughed on the other side, her loud, resonating chuckles causing Mary to bark at me. "It's easy. They show up at your house and you don't tell them to leave. That's what I did. Turn around so I can introduce you to someone."

At the mere suggestion of her sharing the spotlight with another woman, in a dramatic exit, she jumped off the bed and headed straight into the hallway.

"Honestly, Ms. Mary Mack is a rescue. She gets anxious and irritable when the attention isn't all on her. She's easier to warm up to when you see her in person."

Her brows shot upward. "I bet," she replied dryly as she fixed the slipping strap of her nightgown to the center of her shoulder.

"Looks like we've got slippage. No wonder my girl was acting all jealous. You see, she's Italian just like her father. She probably thought you were going to flash me," I joked as the smile on her face transformed into something more curious when I proposed my next question.

"So, now that I'm alone, I wanted to ask you. This whole experiment that you want me part of, what exactly are your expectations? I know I'm the subject of your piece, but is there a chance there could be something beyond sex? I only ask because after catching up after all this time, it's hard not to feel something could be there between us. Correct me if I'm wrong."

I'd been in three serious relationships, four if I counted my young love with Luz. She was the only one of my exes I still thought about and talked myself out of looking her up on social media. Now that I was talking to her, it almost didn't feel real, as if I was dreaming this was all happening. That when I woke up I'd have to type her name in a search engine just to see if I'd get any results for my Luz De Los Santos. Even after our falling out, she was still my Luz. Could I really be that lucky to call her mine again?

On the other end, she took a deep and heavy sigh, which only flared up my doubts that beyond sex and her project, we'd never be anything more. A past love affair and a three-page Valentine's Day story where all the names would change.

"So, the thing about me is there have been some things in my love life that have made me unenthusiastic about promising anything serious. I'm not saying no with finality; it's just that I've been single for a long time due to some partners who left me broken."

"Am I one of those partners?"

She shook her head, only to confuse me seconds later by nodding. "What I'm trying to say is that you're not the main person but maybe you're the start of my distrust in people."

I nodded, taking responsibility of what she found to be her truth. It wasn't the whole truth, but it was how she felt about things and I wasn't about to sit up here and question that. The only thing I had the power to do was to change her mind by proving her wrong.

"Sometimes, I brought a certain energy that I'm not proud of to many of my past relationships. Based on the outcome, I've decided it's just easier to be single sometimes. It's just easier on the heart and mind."

In a way, I understood. Relationships these days were tough and, in a way, limiting things to just sex often felt simpler. Sex with Luz would never be simple. She was my first love and now reuniting with her had made me certain that I'd never gotten over her.

"Listen, I'm going to be honest, Luz. This game? This little experiment you want be to be part of? It's going to backfire on you. So, be careful what you wish for," I playfully threatened because I knew for a fact this was not going to be like any relationship that she'd ever been in.

"Be careful what I wish for?" she questioned, her eyes widening waiting for an explanation. "What is that supposed to mean?"

"It means you want to know if it's possible to fall in love with someone by the third fuck, and maybe the answer would be no with another test subject, but this is me we're talking about. Someone's who's already done the impossible before. You mark my words, I, Evan Cattaneo will make Luz De Los Santos fall in love with me all over again. That and we'll have incredible sex," I added, provoking a roll of her eyes but not before I caught that she was totally smiling.

"Cattaneo, you are off the hook, but it amuses me, so do your worst. Seventeen-year-old me ain't thirty-two-year-old me. Just sayin'. Back then, the slate was damn near clean."

She was right. Before me, she had only dated one other girl that got to be her first everything, but firsts didn't matter to me as much as lasts did. And I was planning to be her last.

CHAPTER FIFTEEN

Luz

My next venture with protective styles would be twists. As much as I loved rocking box braids, they were too much to keep for the four weeks I had originally intended. Not to mention, I missed my curls.

Since an emergency uninstall was in order, I knew just the person to call. I'm sure Eloho wouldn't have had any issue taking them out for me, but then I'd have to deal with Titi Zahira judging me for wasting Eloho's time for a seven-day hairstyle when I wasn't even a full-paying customer.

Me: Hey Candice, you busy?

So close to the weekend, I wasn't sure if I should expect an immediate reply. Candice's schedule wasn't always jam-packed with events or dates, but one thing I could always set my watch on was that it was rare for a Friday or Saturday night that she wasn't watching her niece or nephew. So, imagine my surprise that, even with her hands full, she managed to reply.

Candice: Cornrowing my niece's hair. Why?

By cornrow, I'm sure she didn't mean the two convenient Dutch braids I donned when I was short on time and skill to do much else. Candice had inherited an enviable skill of being able to recreate—if not all—at least seventy-five percent of most hairstyles that worked for natural hair. Her niece's hair would probably be nothing short of an intricate pattern that could rival any West African hair braiding shop.

Me: Well if you're already in the mood to do hair, think you could help a sista out with an uninstall?

Candice: If you have a few hours. I'm only half way done, so you'd be waiting on Gina.

Me: Girl, I got time. Plus I have juicy gossip. Too much to say over the phone. But it'd kill two birds with one stone.

Candice: Assuming Elite Match went well?

She didn't know the half of it.

Me: Too much detail to not describe in person.

I hadn't made the text sound nearly as exciting as the news was, so it didn't surprise me when the reply wasn't immediate. I also knew divulging too much would make her guess, and with this kind of tea, I was certain she wouldn't want to wait for another day.

Candice: If you can promise pumpkin ice cream, jalapeno puffs and a box of puff pastry, I might be able to fit you in my schedule...

Bartering with me for a trip to Trader Joe's. She ain't slick. She know damn well how long them lines be. It was a weekday so my hope was the wait time and shopping experience wouldn't take too long. What I asked of Candice was a lot out her day; the least I could do was provide snacks.

Me: You drive a tough bargain, but I think I can handle those terms.

Candice: See you when you get here.

Me: See you...

———

"Can I watch TV now?" Candice's adorable niece Gina asked in her newly braided updo made to look like a mini-crown. Regina, or Gigi as Candice referred to her, was the daughter of the sister she'd always known about but didn't connect with until they were nearly adults. Candice always resented her father for being messy and having an affair outside of his marriage to her mother; but she acknowledged that she wasn't mad at her sister or her sister's mom.

Sadly, due to some of the trauma Candice had dealt with in the past, despite her estrangement with her parents, she had developed a decent relationship with her sister's mom. I wouldn't say she'd call her a second mother, but they were civil enough to put past feelings aside to strengthen the relationship between two sisters.

I've hung out with Gina's mom a couple of times, and JouJou was cool people. I could relate to her in that single moms had raised us both, by no choice of their own, and it was nice of Candice to watch her to help her out from time to time. The only weird thing about their relationship was that Candice's older sister, Marcie, had absolutely no relationship with Joujou, which meant, in order to create less conflict, she watched both her sister's children on opposing weekends so they wouldn't run into one another.

"What did I tell you I wanted to see before you turned on the TV?" Candice was a cool auntie, but she made them kids work before she ultimately gave into their every request. She wasn't hard on her niece and nephew, but one of the only things she required of them when they stayed over was to prioritize reading a book.

It could be a picture book or a novel, but as long as they spent some of their time reading something that aided in their development, the rest of their stay was full of spoil-them-rotten vibes.

"You told me to pick something and read it for an hour."

"So, what are you going to do before you approach me again while I'm doing Titi Luz's hair?"

"Finish that book I started last time I was here?" Gina guessed before disappearing into another room so we could get to some grown folk talk.

"How long have you had these again?"

"Probably a week, more or less. I was feeling myself at first, but I think I went too long this time. They're too damn heavy and too long for my taste to workout in."

Candice chuckled to herself, but I could hear the subtle shade. "Maybe I'm more used to box braids than you. When you do them yourself, they take longer but they're never as tight as someone else doing it for you," she teased, bragging about how that was her whole aesthetic back in high school.

Despite how fast Candice's fingers pieced through each strand, I managed to release the first twenty braids or so closest to my ears and forehead. My booty was already feeling it as it set into the hard, cold floor that when we took a break, I was going to grab a pillow next time for my aching bum.

"I was living that teenage love affair vicariously through you, girl," I said, singing the lyrics to said song before she missed her chance to.

"It's funny you should mention teenage; that reminds me that I found a subject for my piece."

"He's an adult, right?" she warned, leaning over to mean mug me...*hard*.

"Yes!"

"I mean, like, adult-adult. Not some twenty-three-year-old figuring out his life?"

"Girl, are you telling this story or me?"

We took a snack break, twenty minutes in because information just didn't sound the same without junk food. Puff pastry just hit different when you combined it with cream cheese and guava paste. Once everyone convened in the kitchen and had our fill, curbing our sweet tooth, I was right back down to sitting on the floor with a pillow to sooth my sore behind, watching the synthetic hair fall to the floor.

"You'll never guess who I met at the speed dating event because I've never talked about him. I never thought we'd cross paths again after high school, and for the longest time I hated his guts." The most challenging part of the conversation was making it sound child-friendly, just in case Gina was ever within earshot. For now, though, I was committed to keeping the reveal simple.

I stuck to the basics first and explained how and when we met, the effort he had put in to catch my attention, and how a misunderstanding had forced us apart. Since Candice had grown up far *more* religious than me, I knew most of her questions would center around whether we did more than kissing. We had rarely shared war stories of our decorated pasts before college, but given how strict she had been raised, I always assumed she didn't have one.

"But did you really date or did y'all just *date?*" By her emphasis on the word date, I assumed she meant fool around.

"It started out as just dating, but then it turned into *dating.*" As I explained for that time, it had been some really good *dating.* Candice kiki'ed under her breath and Gina was none the wiser.

"Was he your debut?"

I stood there, proud that she'd adopted my progressive moniker for describing one's loss of their virginity. "Technically, no, but he *was* the first Ken doll I owned," I admitted, strategically placing a played-out, yet iconic, toy as a stand-in for cis-guy.

"So, now you just want another dip in Barbie's dream house?" Candice joked, making me that much closer to hitting her in the knee for her corniness. Then I remembered she was in charge of the back of my head, and if she wanted to, she could have me out here looking wild.

"So, why'd you guys quit each other?"

"If I have to explain that part again, I'm going to crawl into a hole and hide. Just know that after a civil chat, we cleared the air, and he seemed hell-bent on being my test subject. And with as fine as he got with age, ya girl might be considering a month-long vacation at Barbie's dream house."

Candice collapsed into the pillows behind her, accompanied by the cackling and foot stomping no sista could resist once you got her going. She'd brought so much attention to herself, even her niece had to come in and ask what I'd said that had been so funny. This girl was about to get me in trouble with somebody's mama.

"No, but seriously; is he tall? Is he scruffy? What are we working with?"

Words felt too simple to describe how handsome Evan was. His features weren't uncommon, but he made them look uncommon on him. "He actually is tall, even for me, because there is a certain standard when you're not five foot three." If Candice wasn't rolling her eyes in the back of her head, that pause she gave sure suggested that she had. The girl preferred men over six feet when a guy five ten could've still satisfied her height requirement. It wasn't a bad thing that she preferred her men with a little height, but I made it known how hard it was to date men when they preferred petite women. Needless to say, every time I brought it up, she was not amused.

"He's a little tan. I wouldn't quite say olive, but he has decent color after a summer of record rising temps. Let's see, green eyes—"

"Is he a papi?" Candice interrupted. While she didn't have a preference, Candice always seemed the most interested when I brought up a Latinx man, especially when he looked like Rome Flynn.

"Um, no. Italian-American?"

Candice tried not to sound too disappointed when her only reply was, "Oh."

"He's cute, though. If he were Latinx with the same exact look, I'm sure he'd be up to your standard."

Seeking proof, she demanded I take out my phone and confirm with photographic evidence. On paper, Evan hadn't been the easiest sell for Candice, but one couldn't deny how hot he looked in pictures.

"*Okay*," Candice acquiesced as she nodded her head in approval.

"Now, I know this isn't very feminist of me," she warned before she'd even posed the question, "and you don't have to confirm with pay stubs or W-2s, but is he in a higher tax bracket than you?"

Candice sounded just like my dating coach of a cousin sometimes—asking all the wrong questions for all the right reasons. "I don't want to go in specifics, but the dude works in finance."

Without saying a word, Candice let out a sigh of relief, proceeding to work her fingers through my hair. For me, it was hard to say it out loud, but as a Black woman, I was just more comfortable with dating a cis-man who made the same or more money as me. I considered everyone's access to wealth in their situation but I've been in enough situations to that forced me to financially take care of someone, and I wasn't sure I could do it again.

"What do you think is so special about him that makes you want to take a chance on him now?"

I had a mile-long list of things that might interest a woman like Candice. Wanting to focus on the juiciest details, though, I omitted some of the things that would only matter to me.

"For a white boy, he made effort. When he didn't know something, he didn't pretend to. Whenever I held him accountable, he'd feel some kind of way, and instead of holding onto it, he'd reexamine why I felt that way and tried to do better because he actually cared. Reconnecting with him now shows me that he's stayed consistent with seeking growth and not being stuck in the same mindset that he grew up."

It was no secret that we didn't agree on every subject, but the fact he wasn't racist, colorist, homophobic, or transphobic. With my influence, he was also a lot less sexist than he'd been cultured with. Even though he did nothing at bare minimum, at his least, he was more reflective than most men I knew.

"Plus, he was so good in bed."

"Girl, I know that's right." Candice leaned in for a high five and a laugh.

"I'm prepared to walk away once things reach their conclusion. It'll be nice to know there won't be broken hearts or resentment leading up to things reaching their natural ending. Until then, you know about as much as I know."

No longer able to keep her boredom at bay, Gina approached the living room, hoping to use her adorable sweetness to take advantage of her cool aunt. "Auntie Candice, can I watch Avatar now?" Gina asked in an adorable pout.

"Did you read any of the books I asked you to?"

Unable to lie to her suspecting aunt, she told the truth. "No."

"Well, when you go back and do what I asked of you, I'll let you watch an hour or two of TV."

With that demand, Gina dragged her feet all the way to the kitchen table and opened a book. If I remember correctly, it looked like it was one of my favorite authors, Veronica Chambers, who was practically the godmother of Black Latina authors.

"Damn, you won't even let the girl watch Avatar: The Last Airbender?"

"Ugh, that's all she watches when she's over here. Real talk? I just need a break from it sometimes."

"Have you ever sat down and watched Avatar: The Last Airbender?" I asked, swiveling around to make sure she heard me. No one actually paying attention to Avatar would make such inflammatory comments.

"It's a kid's show with kid jokes. What's there to watch?"

My neck damn near did a complete 180. "You about to make me go home and do this ish myself. I ain't know you felt like *that*."

"Luz, will you turn around so I can finish this shit? Damn. Plus, it's not like I'm asking her to do homework. I'm asking her to read things that will expand her understanding of herself. So, she ain't damn near thirty like we were before we saw a Black Latina reflected somewhere. That silly show is going to be there when she gets back—"

"See, now you just being disrespectful," I interrupted.

"I'm trying to figure out how you expect me to do this head when it's constantly looking at me." Candice squinted her eyes in protest before moving my head back to its former angle. "Back to your little high school sweetheart. Are your intentions to fall in love? Or just the part that's fun to write about?" she teased in a singsong manner.

It was a valid question. I ignored her oh-so-subtle-shade, but it did highlight how she saw me in the pursuit of romance. Non-committal. Casual. Easy going. For whatever reason, all those qualities tended to attract the complete opposite—people who sought monogamy. Individuals longing for commitment. Partners seeking long-term commitments but somehow finding me. She once compared me to a character in a romance novel who never looked for love but was always lucky—or in my opinion, unlucky—to always find it.

We had different ideas on how we approached our romantic relationships but for whatever reason, she attracted the energy of people who were better for me and in a twisted irony, I attracted the people with expectations more similar to her needs. Neither one of us had ever conquered that thing called love; the only difference between Candice and me is I never wanted to.

To fall in love? To fall in lust? I knew the outcome of falling in either but not many prospects prepared you for both.

"We haven't even gotten past a few texts and phone calls, but we're going to be transparent when the vibe changes—when things aren't working out well, knowing it won't hurt anybody's feelings. That's more than I can say about my longest adult relationships." For now, that was all I was comfortable admitting to. Yet, there was one thing that needed to be addressed before the night was over.

"Now, Imma need you to put that Avatar: the Last Airbender on and pay attention to every detail. 'Cuz if you ain't a fan by the next time I see you, there'll be problems."

CHAPTER SIXTEEN

Luz

Simple tweaks to your daily routine to help you have better sex tonight.

That had been the subject line I ultimately went with when it came to the piece I ran by my editor for today's daily content for the sex and relationship online vertical. Daily articles were required of every department to keep the magazine's online presence as relevant and engaging with readers as they were with our print issues.

It was a nice change of pace from all the extensive after-hours research I typically poured into when it came to my print articles. I wasn't trying to brag, but unlike the other nine departments that dished out web content, my posts typically garnered the most engagements from readers.

Likes, retweets, and comments were the types of engagement more valuable than gold in this digital era. Sex sold; there wasn't any argument about that, but what really made it worth it was the comments section. I could pop some popcorn and literally live in the comment's section of any one of my popular posts.

Replies were nice too. In another world, I could have seen myself being in charge of social media. They had the responsibility of helping things go viral and making articles a whole-ass mood on Twitter.

For now, I would just have to be content that the hundreds of thousands of impressions Modern got on social media was totally my doing, and *that* was worth bragging about.

My phone buzzed with close to a dozen notifications at once. Was I a total idiot for only noticing the ones that came from Evan? After a long conversation last night, I was stalking my phone well into the day, hoping for a Cattaneo fix. Tempted to text him when I woke up, I resisted the urge to come off as thirsty and decided against it. Who would've guessed a higher power would answer my prayers?

Evan: Good morning beautiful.

Evan: Sorry about keeping you up last night, just wanted to let you know I had a great time talking to you.

Evan: Was wondering if today you were free for lunch?

Internally, I battled with the idea of accepting an invitation so last minute. It went against everything my cousin Mikayla taught as a dating coach to never be a person's last-minute plans. Sure she was younger, but as much as I hated to admit it, a lot of her advice made sense. If a person was feeling you, they'll take out the time to plan something in advance.

Me: Not sure. Don't do well with last-minute plans. Especially dates.

Even though I typed it, I instantly regretted turning him down. I knew damn well I wanted to see his sexy behind, but there were rules to this dating game, and if I showed that I could be convinced to always do things a certain way, there might never be room for compromise.

But then I had to remind myself how we'd spent a night

catching up that seeing him in person was the only way to make it feel real again. I couldn't stop thinking about him. The way he made me laugh. The smize in those unusually pale green eyes every time he looked at me. I could even admit that his cocky brand of sarcasm worked on me, no matter how hard I tried to fight it.

Evan had an effect on me I thought I'd never feel again. To think everything was riding on a simple love bet. Could I even handle knocking boots with someone who had made such a crucial impact on my formative love life?

Evan: I'll have you know this would not be a date.

Evan: I agree, dates take planning. Something I've already taken time to consider places I'd like to take you this Saturday. When our REAL date happens.

Evan: I'd just really like to see you and Saturday's a long time from now. Can I have the pleasure of treating you to lunch? That's allowed, right?

Me: It is and yes, I can meet you for lunch. Just don't expect any happy hour quickies 😊

Evan: Well, I would like to take you out for a late lunch if you're able to get away for that long. But we haven't even gotten to the sexting phase of whatever you want to call what it is we're doing. So, there's still plenty of time to change your mind about happy hour quickies 😄

Me: You're so cute

Evan: But you're cuter

Me: Where should I meet you?

Evan: Don't be silly. I'll pick you up. Text me the address. I can't risk someone else stealing you on your way to me.

Ugh. Why did he have to say shit like that? Not only was I ignoring my cousin's advice by giving into spontaneous plans, but I was also going against my own rule by letting a potential suitor pick me up at work. In the six years I'd been employed at Modern magazine, I'd never let someone come to my workplace. Some of my fellow employees liked showing off their hot partners, even if it was just for bragging rights.

But me? I was too private a person and had never shared anything serious enough to make a spectacle of who I was seeing. In less than forty-five minutes, Evan would be on his way here, and I'd be one step closer to knowing if sex and love can stay friends long enough to test falling for someone in a short period of time.

"Hey Luz, do you mind stepping into my office for a minute? I won't take too much of your time."

Antoinette took me out of my Evan daze as I answered his texts to the best of my ability before dropping the phone face down on my desk as the wheels to my chair squealed and trailed behind her to meet her in her glass office. Giving it more thought, I was rarely directly summoned to Antoinette's office. Sure, I'd come to ask to leave work early for a family emergency or when I wondered if the piece I sent could afford for me to add some tweaks before she went through it, but to be put on the spot? I really hoped she wasn't letting me go.

The sound of her stiletto heels clicked with each step she put between us, and I couldn't help thinking she was made for those heels. An unsaid law around these parts was if Antoinette sat down in her office before you stepped inside, you were moving too slow. So, I made sure I kept a steady pace before she could turn the corner of that neatly filed executive desk.

"So, I haven't heard any updates from you. How's that piece coming along? It's not like you to not have brainstorms and rough drafts at least by the first week. It's what I've always admired most about you. Always ahead of the game."

All the while, every nerve of mine was set aflame as she continued to click the base of that retractable designer label pen.

"It's funny you should ask that," I began, thinking of ways to buy some time so I wouldn't haven't to admit I haven't even started a first draft. I'd been too busy obsessing over all those sweet-ass texts Evan sent me over the last few hours. She was right; that wasn't like me but after I left her office, I was really going to get started on that initial draft.

"Why is that funny?" Antoinette followed with a hardness that suggested she saw right through the bullshit. Like a kid caught sneaking cookies from the jar, it was best to fess up about the little progress I had made so far. She knew I worked best under pressure, and I still had until November to turn in a final draft for Antoinette to approve come February's issue. A whole three months.

"I'll be honest. It is coming off a little slow but only because I met someone. We're in the negotiation stages of the process, so things haven't played out long enough to test my theory yet." It felt good to be honest, but I couldn't help biting down on my bottom lip and squeezing my thighs together to squelch the nervousness at not living up to my boss' expectations.

"Hmph." A look of disappointment lined her genetically blessed features. "Do you like this someone?"

Did I like this someone? *Like* was an understatement of how I felt. I was physically, sexually, emotionally, and mentally attracted to the boy I once knew, but I was certain it was too early to call it love, especially when I hadn't jumped those bones yet.

"It's complicated but I'm sure I'll find my answer soon enough. I apologize for not updating you sooner; it's just with a subject this unpredictable, I assumed it was too early to make assumptions on what the outcome would be. I'm processing things on a week-to-week basis, so my approach might be different than all my other pieces." There went my pessimism flaring up again.

Leave me alone messy pessy or at least go away long enough to tell my boss everything she wanted to hear. "I can guarantee a rough draft by mid-October, though. Even if the results don't work in the favor you might want them to, I can promise I won't disappoint." I smiled warmly.

"I trust you, Luz. You do always deliver."

Like anything she deemed worthy of pulling me away from my desk, I could always count on a big *but* coming.

"*But* I was especially looking forward to this column because it's coming from *you*," she stated, emphasizing the you.

"Do you want to know why that is?"

No, but she was probably going to tell me. The worst part was knowing it'd be a direct critique that I needed to hear but might be resistant to listen to at first. I credited her enthusiasm when it came to my pitch, but I was stumped as to why this piece meant so much coming from me.

"Luz, your columns are typically thrilling. Adventurous. Entertainingly compelling. They're why I never regretted hiring you. You remind me of me at thirty-two."

Confused by her comment, my brows went into a furrowed frenzy that I feared she'd take my befuddlement for taking offense. Antoinette was goals for anyone with big dreams. There used to be times where people assumed a woman like her could never be sitting on that throne she occupied. Since I dreamed of being editor-in-chief of my own magazine someday, I hadn't seen that as anything but a glowing compliment.

"Luz, you're so beautiful—and bright and ambitious. You show me just how much you value your career with the work you create. I hope you don't let work run your life to the point you never genuinely stop and really give love a chance. I've always respected your choice to highlight some of the unique challenges you face when it comes to female sexuality in Dominican culture as a Black woman.

I know that's a very different perspective that I can't give but I still see myself in you. Sex is nice but even if you have it every day, it never replaces love. I'm sure you know that already. I get that sex is exciting and highlighting ways for women to become sexually liberated in their own way is influential, but I don't want to live in a world where love doesn't contribute to that. You *are* the Modern woman, and the Modern woman falls in love too—even if her heart is often too guarded to know when it's happening."

That was so *not* how I was expecting that conversation to go. I had been scolded, critiqued, and criticized, but I had never been evaluated on how I conducted myself in my private life. I prided myself on being the type of woman who saw her value first. I had learned the hard way not knowing your value was the easiest way to be taken advantage of in a union that didn't serve you. Was it really such a bad thing that I protected myself when no one else would? I respected her concern for my well-being. Most people didn't have a boss who cared so much, but this was one of those times I wish I could voice that I had the knowledge to make the right decisions.

"I know I'm probably crossing a boundary that seems unprofessional, but I don't want you to get to my age before you open yourself to real love. It still exists. Sometimes, we just need reminding, that's all."

She made sure to throw in that it was also ok to go the spinster route, but that she was sure there was someone for everyone and that a career can only take one so far. For now, all I could promise my mentor was that I would do my best. Luckily, for me, my best went above and beyond most people's definition of their best. I was determined to make the most of my love bet and show her I had layers.

There was already something there with Evan, but I didn't think I could fall back in love with him just to save my job. "Thanks for checking in with me, Antoinette. You've giving me a lot to think about."

In a rare casual exchange, Antoinette nested her chin in her hands, the opaque white of her manicure contrasting against her dark, velvety skin. "Just promise me that you won't let your life pass you by. Being goal-oriented is great, but it gets a little lonely sometimes. I don't want you having this conversation with someone else twenty-five years from now."

Her posture straightened as she resumed her regularly scheduled poised demeanor, her perfectly arched eyebrows lowering in a slight furrow. When I turned to see the commotion for myself, the glass office made it that much easy to paint the picture that went with the recent ruckus on the floor.

"Wonder what that's all about?" When I spotted him, I knew. Snake charmer eyes, ruggedly handsome smile, and a grown-and-sexy-beard would make anyone thirsty, but unrecognized meat was bound to get devoured by all my male-loving staff members.

"If you'll excuse me for a moment..." I made the perfect exit, marching my pastel colored pumps through the herd of wild animals. From how it looked, all my colleagues mistook him for one of the male models. Don't think I didn't peep some of these so-called happily boo'd up people trying to shoot their shots.

Relief washed over both Evan and me the second he spotted me approaching as his mouth reserved a special kind of smile for me. Once it reached his eyes, it was obvious who he was here for. He wasn't some random stowaway that wandered in by accident but a guest I had invited here just for me.

"There she is," he announced as he tugged at his expertly tailored suit. "Just about ready to head out or do you need a minute?"

"This isn't the boo you're planning to write about, is it?" Jared, one of my nosy junior writers so eagerly asked, knowing damn well it wasn't any of their business.

"If I'm allowed to say, guilty as charged." Evan reached out and shook his hand.

"Don't forget to come back, now," Jared teased, right before I pulled Evan in the direction of the elevator to save him and me from further embarrassment.

When the doors finally shut and I had him all to myself, I

could practically taste the mint on his tongue and alluring scent of his cologne. "Hi," I finally said.

With one hand firmly on his chest and the other touching the back of his waist, it wasn't long before our lips met in a delectable kiss and everything disappeared.

From the way his soft his lips came down on mine, I was relieved that I had decided earlier to take a late lunch. I now had to heed Jared's advice and make sure that I came back.

CHAPTER SEVENTEEN

Before

Luz

"I can't get over how nice you look. You're pretty all the time, but today, you're just...wow," Evan commented while taking my hand as we stepped outside of his car after a long, hour-and-a-half drive. When he said he had planned to take me somewhere nice, I half expected it to be simple like pizza at his family's restaurant and maybe a movie because that's what most people did on their first date. But no, we'd driven a whole ninety miles to an incredible American landmark that most people only visited on vacation. Niagara Falls.

I had only been lucky enough to see the historic landmark in commercials and magazines. Today, I was seeing it with my own eyes and brought two disposable cameras just so I wouldn't run out of space when I took pictures.

"Just so you know this isn't going to be an everyday thing, okay? I just wanted to try something different out," I admitted modestly. I was never one to show so much of my bare legs; in fact, I thought my mom was going to freak out when I left the house with a skirt this short. She surprised me by doing the exact opposite. Instead of telling me how tall I looked, she told me I looked like a model. She even complimented my hair, something she only did when it was straight, and told me I was beautiful. Mothers are supposed to tell you things like that, but it was rare when I actually believed it. This time, I did and the second Evan took one look at me, he had made me feel as if I was the only girl in the world.

"Well, you look hot. I'm happy we're finally doing this," he said, placing a kiss on the back of my hand as we explored the scenery. There were plenty of things to do. Like any tourist attraction, there were endless numbers of shops to get lost in, but when my eyes caught wind of this bright yellow building with orange pillars on the outside, intrigue and excitement pulsed through me when I realized it was a mom and pop bookstore. It was sort of a ritual when my mom and I went to the mall. Borders and Barnes & Noble had to be one of our stops, but there was something monumental about supporting local neighborhood bookstores. That had to be our first stop.

"Hey, can we go in there?" I asked, pulling him toward the bright brick building. As I expected, he showed reluctance, cementing himself in place and making him harder to move. "C'mon, Luz. A bookstore? We look at books all day at school. This is supposed to be a date," he playfully argued. Letting go of his hand, I crossed my arms over my chest, giving him the most judgmental look I could muster.

"Yea, but they're not school books; they're fun ones. Besides, aren't I on this date too? Do I not get to decide what we do?"

"Of course, but we can go to a bookstore anytime. We're not gonna get a chance to come here every day."

I sighed. "Huhhh...it's too bad because I always thought people who read were really adorable. Oh, well..." I said, walking off and working in a little reverse psychology. At first, I wasn't sure he'd fall for it, but no more than a second later, he took my hand and guess where we were headed? Right to that bookstore.

The sign out front read Book Corner, only the *O*s were replaced with cutesy suns. While it didn't have the sleek appearance and set-up most chain bookstores had, the pig statues in the display window were proof that it had what most chain stores didn't have. Heart.

From the outside, you would have never guessed how extensive the store's ground floor was. It was massive, like the Tower Records of bookstores. The aisles, the pillars, the walls were all exploding with books to the point where the only place you didn't see books was on the floor. "Okay, I'll admit, this is pretty cool," Evan said as we found ourselves near a bargain book bin, where he picked up a cookbook and flipped through its colorful pages.

"Hey, wait up!" he called after me as I found my safe haven in the middle grade and YA fantasy section, picking up a book from a table that suggested books for fans of Avatar: The Last Airbender. Avatar was my favorite show at the moment, so if there were books like it, I was down for the ride. "Fans of Avatar? Isn't that a Nickelodeon cartoon?" he questioned as if the word cartoon was a stand-in for child-themed. It was only in its first season and was tackling some relevant subjects that affected us in today's society. To call it just a cartoon was insulting to its fanbase.

"If by Nickelodeon cartoon you mean the best show alive, then yea, I guess," I shot back. "Plus, the banished prince is the cutest thing ever. He's all tortured and misunderstood. For an animated character, he's a ten on the scale of attractiveness," I let slip, only to be met with a question I wasn't prepared to be honest about.

"Do you think I'm a ten on the scale of attractiveness?"

I shrugged, trying not to let my true feeling show that he was beyond a ten. "I don't know. It's hard to judge real people. Especially ones staring at you."

He laughed, the creases in his forehead adorable.

"Okay, maybe that was too forward. I'm just curious to what your first impression was of me. You're so open with your opinions but guarded with your feelings. Sometimes, it helps to know what you're thinking."

I put the book I was holding back down, browsing through the aisles as my fingers lingered on the covers I liked. Mainly the ones with symbols since the rest of them had very few girls that looked like me on the cover. Close behind me, I could feel Evan's eyes take in my body, most likely admiring the way my legs looked without my usual stockings. For the first time, I didn't feel creepy when a guy was checking me out. I even sort of liked it.

"Well, I guess I just saw you as a jock. Dumb. Full of himself, maybe even a little shallow. I don't have the advantage of knowing you long since I transferred so late into this class, but most athletes I have known were assholes. I never saw you partake in anything cruel but on the flipside, I never saw you go out your way for the little guy either. So, there's that."

"So, is that your opinion of me and my entire team or only me?" he asked earnestly.

Since I was being honest, I figured why stop there? "Maybe, but I don't know; it's probably because I don't see you the same way as them. A lot of your teammates look like my cousins. Could be my brothers if I had any. Maybe I'm just easier on them because they come from where I do. I already know from the neighborhood you live in that you're upper middle class. You have your own car. You probably never worry about money, and you have two parents always looking out for you. You can just tell when someone grew up with both parents with how spoiled they act. Not that I'm calling you spoiled, but I know for sure you have good examples of what a strong male role model looks like. I can guarantee a lot of your teammates don't have that," I explained, thinking he would shut down after that because any time you made someone aware of their privilege they got defensive.

But he did the opposite of that. He acknowledged it without being argumentative and understood that there were some things he wasn't raised to think about. He even took it a step further, promising when he got older, he would find a way to give back any way he could. I wasn't sure if that was something he could promise, but it was sweet that he actually cared. Curious to what he thought of me, I asked him the same question but paraphrased it in a way that didn't make me appear obsessive about his opinion.

"Honestly, I thought you were stuck-up. Mainly because you don't really talk to many people. I remember when the first time I ever tried to talk to you, you made me feel like such an idiot, so I thought you were a know-it-all."

I remembered no such moment, but at the time, I probably thought all the guys who wore lettermen jackets looked the same. Black, White, Asian, it didn't matter. A jock was a jock.

"I also thought you were a bit of a goody-goody, which isn't bad; you just seemed bookish. On one of the first days I noticed you, I was sitting behind you and you were wearing these thigh-high stockings. There was this small part of your legs where your tights stopped, and I just remember wondering how soft your legs felt. Then when you stood up, it tripped me out because I'm usually towering over people. Even my own father is only five eight," he said, only making me more insecure that when he thought of girls my height, he thought of his dad. Why did most guys have to be so short?

"I like that you're tall. It means I won't have to break my back just to kiss you," he revealed, nearly blushing from his admittance. I'm sure I was blushing, too, but thank God, it wasn't as visible on me as it was him.

"You've never tried to kiss me," I blurted out before I could stop myself as I fought back the urge to smile at his response.

"You've never asked me to." He was just inches away from my lips as we conveniently found ourselves in the romance section. How come I never noticed how full and soft his lips were? They were perfectly compatible with his sweet face. Then there was that cut in his eyebrow, all thick and framing his features in a way that contributed to his handsomeness. Just when our lips were close enough to taste each other, the alarm on his phone went off, interrupting what would've been our first kiss.

"Wow, Luz, we've gotta get out of here. I have a surprise for you. I swear you're going to love it!" he squealed, and in just a twenty-minute walk, I discovered why.

As luck would have it, he had had booked us a helicopter ride to see Niagara Falls and not just from a bridge like most tourists saw it. I wasn't sure how much he'd saved up for this or if I was even worth all this trouble, but the excitement of it all overwhelmed me. I'd never done anything this fancy in my life.

An hour wait for our reservation was nothing compared to the anticipation I had to actually do it and with a last minute cancellation, Evan and I were able to cut fifteen minutes off our wait time. We talked about things we had in common, like how we both could both eat breakfast at any point of the day and bickered over the things that we didn't. Apparently he was a huge Keanu Reeves fan and I was more of a Johnny Depp kind of girl because Jack Sparrow was one of the best screw-ups ever written. He told me everything from how he got the scar on his face to the first time he had taken his driver's test and failed. I fessed up about my love for Gackt and Miyavi and how for a hot minute I was actively trying to learn Japanese. Talking to him was so easy that in the forty-five minute wait, I'd even brought up about all the things my dad used to teach me, a topic I rarely brought up since his tragic death five years ago. I didn't have much time with my father, but there wasn't a day I didn't want him around so I could've gotten to know him better. My mom had chosen not to speak of him at all.

By the time we moved up to the front of the reservation list, we were instructed to watch a safety video and later weighed on a scale. "Are you nervous?" Evan smiled, sensing my nervousness and trying to calm me with his sweet boyfriend energy. He helped me into the helicopter when it was our turn to board. Even though we had both been on planes before, the small crawl space of a helicopter did little to ease my nerves.

"I'm about as calm as one could be when you're about to fly above a waterfall," I joked with just a hint of sarcasm. I was terrified of flying. The last time I got on a plane I had almost had a panic attack. This wasn't like getting on an airplane but your anxiety and fear didn't know the difference.

The pilot gave us a list of foolproof instructions to follow that would not only ensure our safety but also make the most of the fifteen minute ride.

"I can't believe we're doing this!" I squeaked as Evan instinctively reached for my hand to squeeze, his rough calluses sending me small doses of comfort. The pilot soon counted down to prepare for lift-off, leaving nothing for Evan and I to do but share pained grimaces, anticipating being up in the air at such a dangerous height. This particular tour company claimed to glide closer and lower than any other helicopter tour company was willing to go. It took me a minute to finally open my eyes, but when Evan finally got me to, it wasn't long before we had a bird's eye view of the Niagara frontier. Beyond that, we could even see the Canadian Horseshoe falls and I couldn't deny how captivating the view was from here.

The powerful streams of water were as breathtaking as they were nerve-wracking this high up. Once I got over my fear, my disposable camera worked double time trying to capture as many photos as I could before I gave up to just enjoy the view of half a dozen rainbows glittering across the fall. High off excitement, I climbed on top of Evan after loosening my seatbelt to get a glimpse from the view on his side when his lips haphazardly brushed my cheek, filling my stomach with knots of tension. Before I realized what I was doing, I leaned in and kissed his lips, reveling in their soft, sweet texture providing everything a first kiss should be. For the entire rest of the ride, we behaved, but it was exhilarating having our first kiss above a waterfall this high up in the air. If this didn't go down as memorable, I didn't know what would.

———

As Evan dropped me off at my door, he asked for a hug, which I assumed was his way of asking for a goodnight kiss. It was safe to say that kissing him made my knees buckle. I didn't know I could feel this way about a stupid boy. Only he wasn't just a stupid boy. He was nice and sweet and almost too good to be true. I wasn't sure what I did to deserve a boy so perfect, but I hoped there would be more days like this as I sent him on his way. Looking at the time on the microwave, I prayed my mom wouldn't blow a casket for coming in later than promised. When I saw my mom sitting at the couch watching TV, she looked awfully calm for me to break curfew.

"Sorry I'm late, Ma." I bite my lip, prepared to explain myself, but she chimed in that there was no need to. Apparently, Evan had clarified where he was taking me and that we might get in a little later than expected. I'm not sure what shocked me more, that she was okay with me dating or that it seemed like she really trusted Evan.

"Did you two have fun, negrita?" she asked as I curled up next to her on the floor to rest my head in her lap. "It was nice," I offered, choosing not to share more than that before getting this off my chest. "I really like Evan, Ma, but I don't think that makes me feel that liking girls is a phase. Do you love me less admitting that to you?"

Stroking her manicured fingers across my curls, she switched to Spanish, something she did when she was about to get serious about something. "*Negrita, don't you ever think like that. You are my daughter. I could never love you less,*" she professed while placing a kiss on my forehead. *"I won't lie to you and say I'm one hundred percent comfortable with it. The girls back home like you were never happy and just ended up marrying men that made them miserable because the women they loved weren't as brave as you are for being yourself. I'm just scared for you. The world treats people like you so badly and it breaks my heart thinking that someone will treat you that way. I can't protect you from people's hate and as a mother that makes me feel powerless. I thought that you liking a boy would make things easier for you. I just want life to be easy for you."* She went on, showing a vulnerability I'd never been awarded before. My mom was like any foreign mom. It was hard to talk about stuff when it crossed the mother/daughter boundary that most Dominican moms weren't willing to cross. I'd never felt closer to my mom at that moment. Even if it didn't extend past tonight, I'd never forget her words: I could never love you less. I didn't know until then how much I needed to hear that.

"You know where our family is from back home, the boys always like las indias, las triguenitas, y las mulatas," she explained. That much I'd known to be true in my few trips to the DR. Las indias were the girls who were more indigenous; the triguenitas were the ones who looked racially ambiguous, and mulata was a term most people used on the girls who didn't look fully Black but were a step above Black, or in Spanish, Negra. As much as I loved being Dominican, I hated the colorism that plagued our standards of beauty.

"People told your Tia Noelia every day that she was beautiful, pero Zahira y yo, were just visions of her shadow. When I met your father, he made me feel so special. He didn't say anything bad about my hair or skin color. He just saw me," she confided, breaking her vow of never speaking about my dad. My mom was the prettiest person I knew, so it hurt hearing her talk about how she didn't always feel beautiful growing up. Fighting back tears, I sat there and listened, hoping she might share something else I didn't know.

"All I'm saying is if it's a boy that makes you feel this way or a girl that makes you feel this way, I just have to let you figure that out for your-

self. I'm not experienced in that subject. When you become a mother, there won't be a manual to prepare you for things that go outside of the culture. It's going to look like I'm not as excited when you tell me, but I still love you the same way as I always have. I always will," she said, my eyes tearing up as I looked up at her. Drying my cheeks with her hands, she whispered, *"No te lloras"*, asking me not to cry.

"Ma, I think I really like him..."

CHAPTER EIGHTEEN

Now

Evan

"Are you sure this isn't a date? Because this place is somewhere I'd expect to be taken on a date," Luz, for good reason, questioned. The stairs leading down to the underground lounge were littered with neat piles of rose petals, ranging from pink, orange, and summer yellows, and the inside scenery was complemented with rustic brick walls and low-lit lighting. Even from my standpoint, it was quite romantic. If I hadn't been in the mood for something less mainstream, I would have agreed with Luz; it could have made an amazing first date.

"I'm sorry to disappoint you but this is only lunch. Besides, I've never had Moroccan before. Figured with you, it would be a nice time to try it." Hand-in-hand, we sauntered over to the hostess, fortunate that while we arrived at a busy hour we were seated right away in a plush, cozy booth.

"Move over," I insisted as she looked up at me with a snap of her neck that was sassier than she probably intended.

"Umm why?"

"Because I want to sit next to you," I pleaded. For as long as we've known each other, she knew I didn't do well sitting across from someone—a feminine someone. I'd always given into my instinctive need to be close to my *date*. Without argument, she scooted over, looking fucking sexy and watching me get comfortable as her chin rested in her clenched fist.

"I really like your hair today, and that color looks incredible on you," I admired, using any excuse I could think of to brush my fingers along her skin. Her hair did look lovely; it was loose and curly this time, and the fall-inspired orange shade complemented her brown skin tone. What I really set my eyes on was her smooth, swanlike exposed shoulders. I knew better to keep my hands away from that area, but a man could dream. There would be plenty time for touching later.

"Can I get you two any drinks to start with?" our waitress asked, providing us with two elegantly lacquered menus to look over. Both agreeing on mint iced tea, we were left alone to indulge in some much-needed privacy.

"You know you basically made me the most hated person in my office today," she teased. "You think they'd never seen a good-looking guy before."

As weird as it sounded, admiration from women got tiresome after a while. Don't get me wrong; inheriting amazingly good looks from my parents made talking to women easier, but my gregarious nature made it easier for women to break cultural norms and ask me out. I'll admit, though; I am old-fashioned and like to make the first move. Blame my old school parents.

"Yea, well, you would easily make me the envy of my firm, too, but I'm not ready to fight over you just yet. I'm going to need an official title first," I joked as she lightly shoved my shoulder, accompanied by her laughter, which was easy to make her do.

"Evan, you know I wouldn't disrespect you like that by calling you my friend with benefits. Especially not when the term side hoe suits you perfectly."

Spreading and fanning my finger across my chest, I replied with a fake gasp of outrage, scooting away with enough distance that forced her to pull me back to her. I knew she liked being close to me.

"You know I'm only kidding, right?" she said, soothing me with a kiss across my bearded cheek. She smelled especially sexy, and edible, with hints of warm vanilla, brown sugar, and cinnamon.

"I knew you were kidding; I was just in it for the kiss," I flirted back because being that corny came easy to me when I made time for the girl who got away. She was definitely mine.

When the waitress returned, Luz went with the Chicken Tagine a la fez, as I opted for Lamb Tagine, since neither one of was familiar with Moroccan food, and the excitement came in not knowing what to expect.

"So, Mr. Lover of foreign food, I wonder if your palette matches your passport." Traveling was for people who took actual vacations, and being a workaholic, I barely made time to kick back and see my own city. It wasn't as if I hadn't wanted to, but like doing anything socially, travel was better with a companion.

"Well, I've been to the old country a handful of times," I said in a spotty Italian accent. "And I've been to Canada and spent some time in Moscow. That was an experience. Oh, and I've been to Brazil, Rio during carnival. Other than various major US cities, I'm afraid to admit that my passport hasn't accumulated many stamps. That could change, though. How about you?"

She shrugged, squinting her pretty dark eyes as she rocked her head from side-to-side.

"I'm not that more exciting. I've been to the UK. I'm not sure I can even count the Dominican Republic since it's mainly to visit family, but one year, my best friend surprised me for my birthday with a two-week trip to Europe. We went to Amsterdam; we mildly experienced Belgium for a hot second before spending some downtime in Austria. That was a great trip, but I wouldn't call myself cultured because of it," she admitted, prompting me to think of how she defined cultured. She loved other languages and had a huge bucket list of places she wanted to visit, so to me, that made her cultured by my definition.

Once our food arrived, I could already tell that this was going to be the most satisfying meals I had all week, and judging by the way Luz was scarfing down her food, she was in full agreement.

"You know, this spot is kinda extravagant. I'm not sure how you plan to outdo this on our first *official* date," she said as she took a sip of her iced tea.

By that, I was hurt. I realized it had been a while, but given our history, I figured she already knew I wasn't the take a girl to a restaurant on a first date kind of guy when you could eat any time. Dates were something I put a lot of thought and effort into, and if we did go out to eat, it would be the last thing we did for the night, not the first.

"Well, expect something outdoors—and active. No ideal date of mine starts with us sitting down across from each other at a table. Prepare to have your body worked." Because what I had in mind, we would be doing a lot of lifting.

"Sounds to me like you want to have sexy times in a public place, which I'm down for as long as it's not the beach," she added with a totally straight face that sent me choking on my iced tea. "Oh my god, I'm only kidding...*maybe*."

Duly noted.

"Not going to lie, that was far from what I was planning, but it's nice to know you're open-minded. I want to take you places that don't necessarily lead to sex. Communication is key, right? We only have three times to get this right." In reality, I saw us having a ridiculous amount of sex beyond that margin. Call me optimistic.

"You know, I'm convinced you want to write this article more than I do. Your level of investment is more than I anticipated. I'm not sure if that's a good thing or a bad thing." Maybe I was a tad obsessed with her little project. The prize at stake was something more precious to me than anything I had going on in my life right now. It was hard for me to make sense of things, but after all this time, I still had feelings for this woman. It wasn't just about helping her with her story; it was about testing if I was in love with the fantasy of her or if there was an actual shot at being successful in another relationship. If I could give credit to anyone who'd helped me see how flawed of a human being I was, it was Luz. She was the reason I offered my time and resources so self-lessly now.

"Look. It's obvious I'm the test subject of your story. I want to make sure I come out looking like Prince Eric." Because even if it was just for others to read for entertainment, I knew it would be me that she talking about. Luz excused herself to head to the bathroom and not a minute later, incoming texts came in from my lunch accomplice that made it clear by the second text that she was texting the wrong person.

Luz: Bitch! Remember the guy I told you about? Can you believe I'm actually swooning? You know my ass don't swoon.

Luz: It's like he says all the right shit at the fuckin right time. That should be a crime, shouldn't it? Can't nobody be that smooth!!!

A part of me should've felt guilty. It was only a matter of time before she realized the texts that were meant for a best friend were accidentally sent to me. The moment she realized it, she was typing out an apology, insisting that I disregard those last texts, but I was already on my way to her, waiting outside the bathroom to catch her in the fib she'd most likely tell me. Luckily, I was smarter and well-versed in the language of Luz. She would never admit words if she hadn't meant them, and her pride would never allow her to repeat them to me aloud. If I was looking for a sign to convince me my feelings weren't one sided, I'd gotten it, and I wasn't going to let her deny it.

The restroom door eased open, revealing a pursed-lip Luz looking bested by her careless mistake. I, for one, hadn't planned on rubbing it in, but it did have an effect on the moment at hand. Her face went smug as I pulled her close. "Tell me you don't want me to kiss you." Hearing a simple no would've been enough for me to stop. A simple no kept me well-behaved. All she had to do was push away from me and tell me I was moving faster than the plan she routed in her head. But she didn't. The words that left her beautiful mouth were so much worse and not what I'd prepared myself for.

"Damn it, Evan. I can't," she said as her arms snaked around the base of my neck, her fingers circling the hair that started to curl. As our mouths met, her lips were full and petal soft, surprising me with how rough and hungry our kiss had grown. Hard, then soft, then hard again when the reality of it finally kicked in. I was kissing the one girl that reminded me what it felt like to set my soul on fire. Blazing, wanton and dripping in need for her. The bulge in my slacks rose to uncomfortable hardness, compelling me to break away from her lips sooner than I wanted to because we were just meeting for lunch. Nothing was bound from one kiss.

"Just so you know, I've been wanting to do that since the speed date. Now, maybe I have enough of you to get me through Saturday," I murmured, my mouth still painfully close to hers. A mischievous laugh left her lips as one of her hands left my neck to examine the unavoidable hard-on that formed from indulging her. I forgot how horny I could get with just a kiss alone, but it wasn't just a kiss from anyone. Only her.

"Why don't we see what we can do about this perfectly good erection." A hint of a smile formed on her very sexy, pouty, naughty lips that were already finding their way back to mine.

Mmmm...pulling away a second time was going to prove harder than I imagined.

"Get a room."

An annoyed patron brushed by us so swiftly, I didn't bother breaking the kiss to look their way. This time, it was Luz who broke the kiss, her finger pressing against my mouth as she pointed to our irritated bystander.

"Get a room. Now, there's an idea."

A very, very, *very* good idea.

CHAPTER NINETEEN

Luz

Midtown hotels weren't what I'd call pricey, but they were a huge chunk of change when you planned for something so last minute. Before I could get my card out, Evan was already signing a receipt after booking the room we agreed to go half on before arriving.

"Here is your room key, Mr. Cattaneo." The receptionist smiled back at him without acknowledging that I was even there. I got the last laugh, though, when Evan took my hand as we walked through the sleek, posh lobby. As the doors to the elevator closed, I turned to face him, letting him wrap his arms around me while his hands lingered around my butt.

"What happened at the front desk? I thought we agreed we would both pay half."

"Luz, that's what you wanted to do. I never agreed to anything. I know you're independent and new age, but I'm not used to going half on things with women. Not because I don't respect you, I'm just a traditionalist when it comes to dating. Is that something you can meet me halfway on?"

If I was being honest, that was the one traditional trait about a guy I could live with. When my dad died, I went from a stable household with two parents to a single-parent home, and I hate to say that I internalized women stressing themselves out trying to do everything on their own as normal. I'd never seen anyone court my mom, let alone buy her stuff or surprise her with things she liked after my dad died. Splitting checks felt like the way of the world now, so it was nice to be in the company of a partner who didn't ration every nickel and dime they spent on you. Look at me over here calling Evan my "partner". We hadn't even gone out on a date yet. I needed to slow my roll.

"Of course. It's just, you know, how some people are terrible with money."

At that, he laughed. "I advise wealthy people how to spend *their* money for a living. Trust me, I do okay," he said without elaborating further. At least he wasn't cocky enough to throw out numbers. If there was someone I hated more than a person who wasn't in a financial position to support a social life, it was a braggart who flashed their money around like a newly signed rap artist. As we approached our floor, he backed me out of the elevator, his lips pressed to mine, only looking away long enough to capture the room numbers. When we realized we passed our room, we backtracked, our laughter filling the hallway as Evan struggled with the keycard to open the door.

As we entered the room, I wanted to appreciate how spacious it was, a huge step up from the last hotel hookup I had with a person whose name I could not remember. But I couldn't bask in my surroundings, not when I had six feet four inches of delectable Mediterranean male here for my enjoyment. As I wrestled to take his shirt off, I was in awe of his masculine physique. Washboard abs that led up to a well-defined chest, only made sexier by the layer of matching dark hair spattered across. His arms, strong and powerful, lifted me up as I wrapped my legs around his waist, our mouths conversing in a language only our lips knew. As our bodies fought each other for dominance on the bed, I had to preface our little session with some quick guidelines before we started.

"Mmm...before we go any further, I want to make sure some things are clear."

He stood up, his bright green eyes awaiting my concerns.

"Now, I know I used to have this thing about taking your time, but I have like twenty minutes of free time. Don't take this as me rushing you, but just so you know, there's nothing to prove. Fuck me good and make me come. There is no need for all the theatrics."

He rolled his eyes to the side, his thick eyebrow cocked as he considered my suggestion. "See now, that's where you're wrong. This will be our first time in your research. I have *everything* to prove. I will not be sending you back to work in a rush, so here's my counter offer. Either you're late for the office or we save this for another time. Your call," he challenged with his hands up in protest.

Ugh, why did he have to make everything so difficult?

"*Damn it.* Okay, fine! I'll be late from lunch but only if you do me one favor. Take my phone away from me and cover up the clock on the nightstand. If I see the time, all I'll do is worry about how late I am."

He nodded, taking my phone and placing it in the bathroom. As for the alarm clock, he tossed his suit vest and his button-up over it to ensure that nothing peeked through. "Better?"

"Better," I confirmed, reminding him that I had condoms in my handbag in case he wasn't packing.

"Thank you for your preparedness, and the variety is a definite plus. Let's go with Magnum Bareskin," he suggested as he returned to the bed.

My eagerness got the better of me as I grabbed him by the belt buckle and pulled him back on top of me. Kissing Evan the boy differed greatly from kissing Evan the man. His lips were hungry and persistent, gentleness mixed with roughness from the texture of his trimmed beard.

"Mmm...can I eat your pussy?"

His mouth sent my stomach in knots by the way he trailed kisses from my sensitive neck.

"If I'm going to be late, you had *better* eat my pussy," I replied with an air of confidence that came out more of a moan.

"Can I slap your ass?" he asked with kisses along my bare shoulders as he pulled my top down and commented about how he forgot how amazing my tits were. He took one of my nipples into his mouth, and I melted and damn near disintegrated when he took the second one between his teeth, giving it different attention.

"Oh god, thank you for asking first. Ass-slapping is permitted." He continued playing with my breasts. Teasing and licking. Licking and sucking. If I hadn't been so desperate to feel him inside of me, I could have climaxed off the breast play alone.

"Can I pull your hair?" His breath was ragged in my ear as he made his way up to my throat. He had this earthy scent that drove my feminine instincts wild, but even so, I did have to put a damper on his last request.

"See, if I didn't have to go straight back to work after this, I'd say yes, but I'm already gonna be looking a mess. Let's save the hair-pulling for another time." I countered and was met with an answer that made me wish we could be having that wild-ass, lost-in-the-woods sex.

"It's easy to get swept up in the moment when you don't set boundaries—which is why I wanted to ask."

His green eyes vibrantly gleamed when he was in this stage of fooling around. That was how I had remembered them, playful and lust-filled but vulnerable when we shared a connection, which was practically every time. "Let's get you out of this," he huffed in regards to my remaining clothes. His trim nails grazed lightly along the length of my stomach, his mouth reacquainting with lands he'd conquered before.

In our past, all I ever wanted was to be under Evan's lips. The way he kissed me was magical, sending tiny sparks of fireworks against my skin and setting off explosives inside my body. This adult Evan was more meticulous; patient with fine-tuned skills from years of practice. How else could I explain the mix of sensations struggling to tell my body what to feel?

In a sharp instance, he'd pulled my naked body to the edge of the mattress, causing me to shriek in surprise as he got comfortable on his knees. "Good, you're already screaming and I haven't even started yet. That's a good sign," he joked, adding humor to the moment.

"Boy, if you don't get down there," I commanded, giving him a healthy push in the right direction as I draped my legs along his broad shoulders.

"You know, you were always bossy when you were horny. I see some things haven't changed."

He lowered down to relax his full lips, overwhelming my brown thighs in kisses. I wished I could say watching him do it was a waste of time, but I was a trembling mess at seeing him cherish all those neglected spaces. My navel, my thighs, my mound, my knees; by the time he had made it to my pussy and spread my lips with his tongue, I knew it wasn't going to take me long to orgasm, especially when he looked up at me with that hawk-like gaze.

"Mmm..." he groaned into me, providing a toe-curling vibration to my clit that caught me off guard. Soaking my already wet folds, the steady stroke of his proficient tongue lapped at me hungrily. The sensual rhythm caused me to gently grind onto his face, the prickly texture of his beard providing a new kind of sensation. "Fuck, Evan. That feels so fucking good!" I threw my head back in ecstasy, knowing that if I didn't look away at some point, I was going to come faster than I intended. I didn't want to come. I wanted to savor the moment. Have you ever had your pussy eaten so good that you didn't want it to end? Fuck! That was how I felt right now.

"I love eating your pussy," he mumbled as he licked and sucked at an orgasm-inducing pace, circling my swollen clit and gripping my thighs tightly so that I stayed right where he wanted me. The sudden insertion of his fingers was my final undoing, adding that extra fullness I so desperately craved as he massaged my g-spot with an expert touch that made me want to declare his reign. Erupting on the length of his fingers, my clit was still caught between the gates of Evan's full lips and my orgasm rocketed through me and cleared my mind of any unnecessary thoughts.

"You look so fuckin sexy right now," he said, bringing me back in the moment as he stood to his full height and lowered his pants and boxer briefs to the floor. Through my incoherent, blurry vision, I found myself gawking at the gorgeous, sheer perfection that was his body. Acute awareness of his tall, athletic physique and the act of him sheathing his fully erect cock with a condom had me lucid once again. It was as perfect as cocks could be—big, thick, and deliciously vein-y but best of all, for the time being was all mine.

He teased my folds, covering himself in my wetness and emitting a heavy sigh as he pushed his heavy erection past my opening. "Damn, you feel so good," he whispered, carrying me to the center of the bed. It was then that he got comfortable with his rhythm. His thrusts were slow and deep, just what my body craved as he stretched me wider than I ever thought possible. With his lips on mine, we stole each other's breaths each time that he drove into me, rendering one another mute.

Reaching for my hands, he interlocked our fingers, his eyes appraising me with a level of vulnerability I had nearly forgotten. Most people found it intimidating to look into their partner's eyes, especially during an act so humbling, but there was something inexplicably intimate about measuring your lover's reaction to being connected carnally. To be that honest, with someone took a deep connection that until today I tried hard to deny that I shared with Evan.

"Fuck," he groaned, flipping onto his back and straddling me on top of him. It wasn't that I preferred missionary, but I loved being selfish and just letting someone fuck me. "I'm getting too close. Thought we could switch it up."

His hair was beginning to stick to his forehead from the sweat he had worked up. He'd made the biggest mistake of telling me he was close because now all I wanted to do was exploit it and be the cause of his undoing. Mouth-to-mouth, body-to-body, we moved in passionate synchrony as his hips rose to meet mine. With an animalistic fierceness, I pinned his hands to the mattress, riding him like one of those mechanical bulls at a honky tonk. His moans were now thick with desire as his strength overpowered mine to wrap his arms around my hips to prolong the inevitable.

"Fuck, Luz, you're gonna make me come." His face was straining, fighting hard to hold back his release. He looked so cute that I almost felt bad for coaxing him to come.

"Don't you think that's what I want? For you to let that cock come inside of me?" I teased, riding and grinding, his hardness so deep inside me that I could feel myself on the verge too.

"Fucking Christ!" He grimaced. "You don't play fair!" he gritted out and took a firmer grip on my hips and surrendered to my velvet prison. He filled me with desperate obsession, his hips a driving force as he hammered into me. Faster and faster, we fought to join our bodies together until a mutual euphoria spread between us. His gaze never left mine as he relaxed underneath me, letting out a deep breath followed by a gradual smile.

"So...are you in love yet?"

There he went, ruining the moment. "Clown," I groused with a slap to his chest as he pulled me for a deep, longing kiss. I could've stayed like this forever if I didn't have anywhere to be.

"Well?"

"Oh my god!" I rolled my eyes, unmounting him and heading toward the bathroom. Turning on my phone, I almost dropped it at seeing how much time had gone by squeezing in this lunchtime liaison. A few of my co-workers called, asking if everything was alright; my boss even texting me if I had a family emergency. I wouldn't have called getting my back broken a family emergency, but just to save my hide, I texted her how something had come up and that I needed to make a quick run to my apartment. Luckily, I had an understanding boss, and I couldn't go back to the office smelling like sex. A shower was in order.

Out of nowhere, Evan materialized behind me, enclosing me in his massive arms. Our clammy bodies were covered in sweat but even so, I felt at home in his embrace. "You never answered my question." He pressed a kiss against my check, giving the mirror the impression that we'd always been this close. I liked the way he looked next to me, even if to him I wasn't prepared to say it out loud.

"Listen, Cattaneo, it's going to take more than one fuck to get me to fall in love with someone. You still have two more times to impress me."

"Well, how about we get a head start on that second?"

He nuzzled against my ear as he followed my steps to the shower. As much as I wanted to, perhaps, twice in one afternoon was moving too fast. It wasn't as if we weren't going out this weekend. That was plenty of time to let things cool off and regroup with a clear head. From my silence, it was evident that he knew what my answer to that was going to be. Happy to know that there're still some men out there that read body language and signs instead of coercing you to do anything against your will.

"Or...we can wait. I think I'm just being greedy because I get one look at your ass and tits and suddenly, I'm hard again. I'm the one who said we should be taking things slow, so it looks like I need to follow my own advice."

Like a gentleman, he turned on the shower for me and even

helped me in before heading back toward the bedroom. "I didn't say you couldn't take a shower with me." And just then, I'd never seen a naked man move so fast. A quick shower was just what I needed to imprint the image of his body for my home solo sessions. Tonight, I was pulling out my favorite vibrator, praying that thirty minutes of familiar sensation came close to just a minute of how it felt to make love to my Italian Stallion.

CHAPTER TWENTY

Luz

It was safe to say that Evan putting it on me wasn't beginners luck. I mean, *god damn*. A sista was finding it hard to walk after a session like that. Granted, his skills had always been promising. Sure, when I first met him, he had known next to nothing about a cisgender woman's body; we were *all* allowed to be wet behind the ears *at some point*. Once I let him know I wasn't going to pursue a guy who couldn't please me, he whipped himself into shape *quick*. I'd like to think I could take credit for him graduating from rhythm-less thruster to full-on master lovemaker. I should be charging money for this shit.

Oh, that's right, I do. I literally get paid to nudge people into breaking their comfort zones in the bedroom. The only difference between high school me and Modern magazine me was how much more comfortable I was with my body now. I couldn't believe there was ever a time I used to hate being tall.

It was impossible to shrink myself at five eight when all I wanted to do was hide. It didn't help that all the girls I'd ever been attracted to, where the attraction was mutual, further made me feel like I was being mounted. Most girls were short especially all the girls I went out with. This wasn't the case for all bi-women, but being Dominican, there was this pressure to be small. I hadn't inherited my mother's petite frame, so I became a life-time target of being masculinized by my family members because of my stature, something that only got worse when I came out.

I knew it was wrong, but Evan being taller than me was the first time I'd understood why people liked taller men. It wasn't end all be all, but I think shorter people took for granted how protected you felt in the arms of someone bigger than you. Which was why short women didn't know how selfish it looked to take all the tall partners. *Umm, can you save some for the girls who don't want to wear flats every time they go on a date?*

Luz. *Chill. You not supposed to be talking about how protected you feel in someone's arms and shit; you supposed to making this about sex!* And even then, you should be able to focus on more than just the outstanding ability that was Evan's pelvis. Despite my co-workers asking and texting their concerns about me coming back forty-five minutes late from an already long lunch break, when I'd come back to the office, I wasn't fooling anyone. They all knew it had to do with the green-eyed stallion that they saw whisking me away the other day.

Adult Evan? I actually liked this version of him. He was passionate in a way that went beyond just centering all that energy into one hobby like he did when I first met him. He was confident with the perfect balance of alpha and gentleman, and I couldn't forget funny *and* fine as hell.

I can't help wondering that if we had met up before this event, even after our ill-explained break-up that maybe I could have avoided a handful of relationships that soured my outlook on love.

This wasn't the first time I'd felt this level of happiness. I could get it from having a piece of mine go viral, and sometimes, happiness was just as simple as freshly baked mantecaditos with a cup of cafecito. But this was the first time in a long time that a mutual attraction felt deeper than just my body parts jumping.

I actually wanted to see Evan, smell him, kiss his cheek and *more* than just our planned get-togethers. When it came to cisgender straight men, when they were interested, I made them work for it. Since there wasn't often that instant connection like when I dated other gender identities, like shared worldviews, I created labyrinths around myself because in my experience, cis guys made the least effort to be decent partners.

Imagine my surprise to find out with Evan, I didn't even have to do any of that. He put 100% into everything when it came to me. He went out his way to plan things, a first for me when it came to boys. The only reason we ever did anything spontaneous was because I couldn't resist him long enough to wait an entire weekend to hang out him.

A last-minute lunchtime romp was not enough for us to change our plans for Saturday, but I was bold and didn't think I could wait until then. I took out my phone, surprised that he had texted before I got a chance to spring one up on him.

Evan: Hey beautiful. Today was fun, but I can't wait to see you Saturday.

Damn, I was going to have to dig up something to say that wouldn't sound thirsty.

Way to go. Now I just sound like I'm trying to set out a thirst trap. Whatever was on Evan's mind, I couldn't tell from the instant thought bubbles appearing on the screen.

Evan: Hanging out before Saturday means we'd be doing something last-minute. I thought you didn't do last-minute.

How rude. Using my own words against me.

Me: Well...I thought wrong.

Evan: I would love to hangout tonight, but my fear is anything we decide to do will only end up the same as lunch.

Me: And?

He took a little longer to write his reply, but before I could put my phone away, a message appeared.

Evan: I know you weren't always a fan but would you want to catch a basketball game?

While I was in the spirit of going out of my comfort zone, I figured it couldn't be any different than watching him play when we were kids.

Me: What did you have in mind?

Evan: I coach basketball at a youth center after school. That usually takes up a portion of my Tuesday-Thursday nights, but if you'd like to see each other, you're always welcome to sit in and watch. Basically, no funny business. I was serious about taking things slow.

Shit, I was too, but you couldn't ask a coyote to go against its nature.

Me: Sounds promising. What should I wear?

Evan: I'm not going to tell you this again. Just be yourself. Whatever you wear is fine. You'll look beautiful either way.

Me: Well...when you put it that way...

Evan: Cool. It's between Lexington and 101st. The doors open at five, but any time between seven and nine is fine. I'll be there tomorrow after work.

Me: I will be there.

Evan: Great! I can't wait to see you.

And I couldn't wait to see him.

CHAPTER TWENTY-ONE

Evan

We were down in the last quarter and somehow managed to pull things back. At the last minute, I'd put in Emmanuel, which helped J.C. from getting too fatigued. He was the strongest player, but even stars needed to rest. With only five minutes left, the harsh reality was this game would definitely be a loss.

They had worked together—no showboaters this time— showing up for one another and playing as a team. With how strong they had played, never giving up just because it wouldn't be an easy win, in my book, that was a win. No matter what the outcome was, we were still going to celebrate for playing with heart.

Rounding them up for a quick timeout didn't take long; within half a minute, they were all huddled up to hear my words of motivation. "You guys are doing good out there. Hustling hard, sharing the ball. When that last buzzer rings, it doesn't matter what that scoreboard says. Y'all were down twenty-five points, but you never let that discourage you. Get back out there, but don't overthink things. Make it quick but make it count," I encouraged, my signs flowing freely with my verbal speech.

"Remember what I taught you. Go out there, have fun, and afterward, we're all going out to celebrate whatever outcome." When the game started back up, I turned around just in time to find Luz looking for a proper seat a few rows away. Since she'd caught me peering in her direction, I waved, blowing a kiss for good measure.

Playing along, she pretended to catch the kiss and pressed it to her cheek with the cutest coquettish expression. We knew neither of us would be able to hear one another from this distance and the boisterous crowd, so I held up my phone, gesturing that she should expect an incoming text.

Me: Glad you could finally make it ❤

Luz: You know, when you invited me, I didn't know it was gonna be smack dead in the hood. You got me out here looking uptight and bougie; meanwhile, worst-case scenario is some of these kids prolly goin' home to an empty fridge. I wish you woulda told me to dress more approachable.

Me: It's cool. You look nice and there're only a few minutes left anyway, so you're dressed appropriate for dinner. Let's talk more after the game.

There were just a few seconds left in the final quarter, and with the boys finishing strong, they'd only fallen behind six points from the winning score.

"Alright, good game, guys," I clapped, anticipating their approach. "That's what I call hustle."

Many of them were clearing out of the gym and making their way toward the showers, but I wanted to prepare them for our unexpected guest. "Meet me out here when all of you are ready to go. I have a friend coming along, so don't make us wait too long." Knowing if I didn't say that, the final kid would lag and drag their feet.

Luz sashayed down the bleacher staircase, never missing a

beat in her four-inch pumps. Unlike most times we hung out, her hair was smoothed into a neat bun and upon closer examination, the stud usually adorned in her right nostril was replaced with a mini hoop.

"Hey, sexy."

"Hey, Number twenty-two," she flirted back as I bowed my head down to keep myself from grinning like a hyena. When I did return her gaze, from no control of my own, my mouth settled on grinning like the Cheshire cat instead.

"You remembered?" Twenty-two had been *my* number. All throughout middle school and high school, I'd managed to always secure that number on the basketball court. To know that she remembered gave me an enormous ego boost. It meant she'd still thought of me.

"Boy, of course I remembered," she teased. "You wore that letterman everywhere you went. For years, I couldn't even think about that number combination without having severe flashbacks. Not all of them good, might I add."

"C'mon, though. You dug it, right?"

Her lips pressed into a straight line, her earthy brown eyes drifting off to the side. "Yea, maybe a little bit but mostly when you let me wear it. I was stunting in the hallways, thinking I was fly."

In fact, she was fly. At least to me she was. With no words, every time she wore it, it was like she was telling the entire school she was mine. What a time to be a self-centered teenage boy.

"All this chitchat and not once have you offered me a hug," I said in jest. "Is it too much to ask for a hug?" She laughed, flicking her fingers in that signature way she did right before she paid you a compliment.

"Look at you, being all respectful and asking for consent. And they say chivalry is dead," she jeered, clasping her arms around my neck, pressing her torso into mine. The way her warmth felt in my arms more than made up for her late arrival as the sultry scent of jasmine blissfully calmed me.

"Again, thank you for coming. I can't wait for you to meet my boys. They're really good kids." Her smile beamed with genuine excitement as it wasn't long before all the boys began spilling back into the court. They hooted and hollered as if they were in the middle of a game when I pulled away from Luz, second-guessing my decision to introduce them the moment words started coming out.

"Okay, Coach. I didn't know you were down with the swirl," Yousef joked, relaying the message to Kyvon in ASL like he was so clever.

"And shorty thick. Okay, I see you," J.C. said, rubbing his hands together, wearing a cocksure grin that made me cringe. The discomfort in Luz's stance was hard to ignore, especially since a second before she'd been cheerful and friendly.

The sad thing was when I had been their age, I hadn't been any different. I knew better, but until Luz, no one I cared about had actually challenged me. Watching Luz's body language forced me to act, and if I didn't do it at that moment, none of my boys would learn and I'd probably lose my woman.

"All right guys, come here. I want to talk to you all for a minute," I signaled for all of them to surround us. From the looks on all their young faces, it was obvious they knew nothing of what they'd just displayed was problematic.

"Okay, fellas. I get that you're excited to be in the company of a beautiful woman such as my friend Luz, but what you all said when you walked in here? None of that shit was cool." Luz's lips pursed to the side, her arms hugging her middle as she dipped her head in shame. Only it was me who should be ashamed. I regretted not talking to them about the opposite sex first, but the truth was, I hadn't thought I'd have to. "Some of you guys are looking at me, confused. I want to explain something to you. Women exist in this space where they feel like they constantly have to protect themselves and it's mainly from us. As boys, we're not raised to think with that mindset. That the same rules that apply to some don't always have to apply to us. Most of you have likely been told your behavior was just *boys being boys*," I explained with a reflective roll to my eyes, ashamed of that free pass on shitty etiquette.

I brought it back up to fix my expression as it wasn't Deaf-friendly unless the face was made with the comment, as I tried to be just as consistent with my spoken words as with my ASL. "We need to start operating with logic that challenges our toxic tendencies. I know it's hard to believe it, but I was your age once, and I didn't have friends that called me out on things that made other people feel small. As a result, I behaved poorly."

When I was a teenager, we thought girls liked hearing that we found them attractive. We assumed that girls found it cute when we obnoxiously cat-called them, and from the looks of it, this generation hadn't been taught any differently.

"We grew up the same way, but all things can be unlearned. If you learned it, then you can also do the work of unlearning that girls like that kind of behavior when it couldn't be furthest from the truth. Newsflash, most girls don't give a shit what you think about them, not about their looks, not about their bodies, not even if you think you're complimenting them. You're just teaching them to feel unsafe around you, even if you think you're doing no harm. Stop being comfortable with making girls and women feel uncomfortable. Learn how to read their body language when you speak to them. If she's holding herself protectively when you talk to her or if she scrunches her face or looks away when you call her out of her name, then you need to check yourself, capiche?"

A brief silence followed that made the entire moment tense and awkward. Since Luz had been the only person who couldn't address many of them by name, there was no logical reason she would challenge a bunch of teenage kids she didn't get to know or humanize.

The boys and I discussed a lot of things, hard topics, particularly how society treated them as young Black boys, made even more challenging if you had a disability and were forced to adapt to a mainstream culture like Kyvon had to.

We talked about how things in the media made them feel, working on how to manifest frustration and anger into avenues they could control, like school, or the arts, or just about anything that brought joy and allowed them to think critically. The biggest lesson of all was going to be how they treated others, especially women.

That kindness and respect weren't and shouldn't be tied to just feminine energy and that they could feel emotions like remorse without being labeled as less masculine. All those contributed to toxic masculinity and the mistreatment of women and even if Luz hadn't been here, it would have been necessary to check them.

"You guys, I'm not telling you all this to be an asshole. I'm addressing it because I want you to stop and think before you say things. You are all *so* young. On the strength of that, I knew Luz wasn't going to say anything, which is why I spoke up. My hope is that when you're in your own spaces, when you see stuff like that happening, you care enough about people in your life to check them. It's not always going to be easy, but most of it starts with us. With that being said, I hope you all have something you'd like to say to her. And as a reminder, her name's not "shorty"; it's Luz."

With that, Luz managed to regain her confidence, mentally releasing the biggest sigh of relief.

"Make it quick but make it count."

The first one to approach her was J.C. He lowered his baseball cap from his head and brought it behind him, out of view. "Hi, Luz. Um...I'm sorry for making those comments about your body. That was really rude of me. I didn't mean to make you feel bad or uncomfortable."

Luz held out her hand for him to shake, choosing forgiveness over writing them off as degenerates. "Thank you for taking the time to apologize—"

"J.C.," he interrupted, filling in the blanks.

"It's really nice to meet you, J.C." Her eyes widened in preparation for Randall stepping in to perform the same act of humility.

"Sorry about that thing I said about the swirl. I think I was just trying to be a clown. Next time, I'll just shut up," Randall said with a nonchalant shrug that made Luz giggle.

Kyvon signed a joke about this being why he didn't talk; despite all finding the humor, Luz was the only one lost in translation. "This is Kyvon. Kyvon, this is Luz. Be patient with Luz. Her ASL is worse than Randall's," I signed and spoke, prompting a laugh from Kyvon as well while Randall did his best to fight his case about how he was trying.

"Evan speaks so highly of you all, so I'm honored to be joining you guys for dinner. He says you always go out for pizza, but would y'all be willing to switch it up a little? Maybe try sushi or this really cool Brazilian spot on 49thSt?"

Most of them got excited at the option of all-you-can-eat Churrascaria. Convincing the minority who would have rather tried sushi proved an obstacle, but none Luz or I couldn't handle. Being in the mood for both, I promised everyone who opted for sushi that we'd just try it next time, and that sent us on our path to the closest subway station.

Churrascaria Plataforma was our next destination.

———

"So, what was Coach like as a kid?" Yousef spoke and signed, despite hosting a mouth full of food across from the table. Shooting Luz a look, hoping she'd stay on code and talk me up, she ignored it based on her familiarity she gained with the boys. It was already their first instinct to poke fun at how un-cool and old I was to them, but she was going in.

"Ya boy was straight up full of himself. He thought he had it like that, but that obnoxious little charm he had didn't work on me." Underneath the table, Luz hooked her ankle around mine, the sting of all her teasing melting away with her light touch.

"I guess that explains why you're sitting here now. Clearly, my charm is on the fritz," I gently teased back. My boys typically found me to be the biggest cornball, but at the very least, that got a laugh out of it. Luz *had* to give me that one.

"Okay, but let me be straight with y'all. Evan was really sweet. Not to mention, smart and talented. He was too popular for me back then, considering I was the nerdy weird girl that read manga and watched anime."

"What's wrong with manga and anime? That shit is fire," Randall argued, confused that was even a thing.

"Y'all Black and brown Gen Zs have it easy. Y'all got groups like PLANETEJOBN: The Extraordinary Journey of a Black Nerd Group to express your blerd and Black geekiness. Y'all got whole ass communities and safe spaces. Wasn't no Black Twitter when I was sixteen. When I was y'alls age, we were on our own."

J.C. took a sip from his tropical smoothie, brows furrowing in confusion. "I have a hard time picturing you ever being nerdy. I think I'd have an easier time believing Evan was the dork. He never shows us how he got down. When we ask, he's always like, 'I had my time' or 'It's your time to shine'. 'I'm not your competitor, I'm your coach'."

Which was true. I was shy when it came to showing them my skill level because my time had already passed, but after spending months of them trying to teach me the Milly Rock, it didn't surprise me that many of the boys had a hard time picturing me as popular, a jock, or just anything that wasn't their stuffy coach.

"Y'all are all so precious. That means a lot." Luz over-exaggerated her facial expressions in a fake cry.

"But no, Evan was an amazing player. I wasn't into sports much, but people loved watching him play. Y'all are lucky to have him as your coach."

My phone vibrated in my back pocket, and while I wasn't a fan of answering phone calls and texts when I was with company, watching Luz task with her phone made me assume she was the culprit as to why my phone went off. A quick glance confirmed my suspicion.

Luz: *Just so you know, I'm having a good time but wanted to know if we could step out for a bit. It doesn't have to be now, but I'd love to talk before we leave.*

Acknowledging I had read the text, I looked up and nodded, politely excusing myself while I left J.C. in charge of watching the crew. "Hey guys, you don't mind if we step out for a minute, do you? Think you all can behave like gentlemen until we get back?"

A quick assurance from J.C. told me he had everything under control as Luz and I disappeared outside, making sure to leave our credit cards with our waitress as good faith that we weren't trying to walk out on the bill.

On occasions like this, I did usually front the bill, but Luz insisted on going half so that the experience to try new things came from both of us. Interesting thing was most of them were a sucker for pizza, but it had been nice seeing them enjoy something new for a change. I had to thank Luz later for suggesting trying something different.

We finally found a quiet spot on the outside of the restaurant, against the bright brick walls painted to match the colors of the Brazilian flag. "Your boys are really sweet."

That comment made me involuntarily wince. "When they want to be. They're still figuring themselves out, so thank you for being patient with them. I'm really trying to give them opportunities for growth, on the court and off."

"I'm sure it's not easy, though. Dedicating your free time to coaching kids when you have a time-consuming career? Doesn't it get hectic sometimes?"

I hadn't put a lot of thought into it until now. Coaching was actually one of the easiest aspects of my life. I loved basketball and kids, so being present for them and my love of the game came naturally to me. It was especially important since the basketball programs for areas they lived in sucked or were non-existent, and anything that could help their futures made it feel like it wasn't work.

"Hectic, *no*. Fun? Yes. Growing up, I never realized how privileged I was to have a decently funded sports program. I just want them to have the access that I had growing up. I know it's a little hard to understand since you were never into sports, but many of them were in tough places before I started working with them. I'm not ashamed to admit they're like family now."

"You know? I remember a certain someone mentioning all those years back about how they wanted to somehow make a difference. Imagine my surprise that you actually kept that promise. At seventeen, you hear that and all you're thinking is 'this kid's full of shit'. Being a decent human being looks good on you. I'm proud of you."

I wasn't sure I was actively trying to make an impact, though. At least, not the way she was painting me out to look. As important as it was for me to be a role model, all I wanted was for these kids to feel like someone outside of their families gave a fuck about them. Every kid deserved to have an outside system that wanted to see them succeed, but kids living below the poverty line didn't always have that.

Some of them were going to be amazing at basketball, but the others? I wanted them to know that with mentoring and resources they had options. Coaching basketball had never just been about basketball; it was about molding young leaders, building bonds, and having somewhere they could turn to when they felt like giving up.

"I'm not trying to get all mushy on you, but these kids are like my little brothers. I just want what's best for them."

"You know, I think my brain just had an orgasm. Don't mind me if I space out on you," she joked. "Does that count toward your article, or do we have to have our clothes off for it to matter? Just wondering." With a playful slap to my chest, she found no issues with telling me how I was so goofy, but I chose at that moment to remind her how beautiful she was.

"Oh my god, Evan. Stop!" she whined, stomping her heeled feet.

Confused, I shrugged. "Stop what?"

"Stop being so cute."

"There's no incentive to stop if it makes you laugh," I teased. Besides, I needed something to look forward to before our first date. We were taking it slow, weren't we?

"I think we have company." Luz pointed behind her that another person had taken up our space. It was one of the boys, Kyvon, humbly signing if it was okay if some of the boys ordered ice cream.

"Sure. Go nuts," I signed back, verbally informing Luz that I'd be more than happy to cover that part of the bill.

"Can I ask Kyvon something?" Luz turned to me as I confirmed whether she wanted me to sign it for her or let her have a go at learning basic ASL.

"It's okay if I let him read texts on my phone, isn't it?" She focused on me as I signed whether it was all right if Luz could ask him something. Kyvon nodded, closing the distance between him and Luz so he could be in better view of her screen. Whatever she had asked him made him laugh as he pulled her a few inches away so that their backs were to me. What was she asking him and why was it top-secret? I could tell that Kyvon was showing her something with his hands and wasn't planning on leaving until she got whatever he was teaching her right.

Once Kyvon was satisfied with her progress, they leaned into hug one another as Kyvon waved and made his way back inside.

"What was that all about?" I asked with quizzical apprehension.

"Nothing, I was just wondering if he could show me how to say something. Let's see with his instruction if I retained any of it." With a shaky yet understandable attempt, Luz signed the words 'I want kiss'. She was asking if she could kiss me. How could I not find that darling?

"*Cute*. No wonder you two were giggling over there. Now, he's probably in there telling everyone we're outside fucking," I quipped.

Relaxing my body language, I signed "Yes. Kiss me."

Luz closed the distance between us, but I couldn't wait. Leaning down to meet my mouth with hers, I tasted everything good about her (in addition to some amazingly seasoned lamb chops) as she leaned back, but not before gently taking my lower lip between her teeth and making me yearn for more to come.

Saturday could not come soon enough.

CHAPTER TWENTY-TWO

Evan

Between work and the team, which could be stressful at times, nothing made me more anxious than going out with Luz. Typically, taking a woman out rarely made me nervous, but this was Luz we were talking about. A woman I thought I'd never see again, let alone her wanting to be in the same room with me after our high school break-up. With all the pre-date meet-ups, I couldn't stop thinking about her—what her perfume smelled like, how her face would light up whenever I said something corny, which body part she'd choose to highlight when saw each other in person. Was this fucking normal to be thinking about someone from the moment you woke up to the second you went to sleep?

Considering how quickly our first afternoon together escalated in Midtown, my plan was to keep us out each other's beds and choosing a first date that would force us to give each other our undivided attention without involving sex. I wouldn't be able to halt any freaky shit should she be the one that initiated, but I intend to show her that sex wasn't the only thing I was interested in. After a shower and quick shapeup of my beard, it wasn't long before Ms. Mary Mack was helping me pick out clothes for my date. I wasn't a fashion expert, but I did spend enough time before dates being conscious of colors and moods I wanted to invoke. Small things about my personal appearance had changed since Luz and I dated in high school, but the one thing I knew to focus on was to wear colors that made my eyes stand out. Luz loved my eyes. What did I have in this closet that could help me accentuate that?

As if reading my mind, Ms. Mary Mack hopped around excitedly in the deep trenches of my walk-in closet, drawing my attention to a blue sweater I almost never wore. It was a cashmere blend and looked good on me, not to mention the calming effect the color blue had on most people. "Good girl." I rubbed Mary's head before rushing to my ringing cell phone on my bed. It was Luz.

"Hey, you're up early," I answered on the second ring, choosing not to miss her call should any change of plans on her end occurred.

"And ready early. Do you think it's too much of an issue if I meet you at your place instead of you picking me up at mine? I sometimes get my nails done on 23rd St and I just happen to be close by."

Looking at the clock on my nightstand, it was an hour earlier than my plan to pick her up, but if I remembered anything about Luz, she was stubborn and liked to do things her own way. Perhaps, this was even part of her testing me.

"Are you asking or telling me?" I teased.

"Neither. Just trying to save you some time. I can totally hop on a train back to Brooklyn and wait for you there."

If I let her go back home, chances were, she would have me waiting longer to change her outfit, hair, and would probably even take another shower. She was definitely testing me. I had to get Mary set up in her room before Luz got here because the last thing I needed was for an eighty-four pound cane corso battling for master's attention. First encounters weren't Mary's strong suit but as long as I got her calmed down and in her room before Luz got here, I didn't have a problem.

"You know what? Sure. Meet me at my place. I'll send you the location and give a ring to the doorman to let you up. You'll just have to show your license."

"Great, because I'm a few blocks away and should be there in less than ten minutes." Less than ten minutes?! Knowing how agitated Ms. Mary Mack got when she knew I was preparing to leave soon, I now had a problem.

———

One knock at the front door thwarted any progress I'd made getting Mary to her bedroom. Knowing her, she probably thought it was Bernice, a nice, older Jewish lady who lived a few floors down and looked after her when I was away on vacation or spent longer days at work. Each time, I could count on her to get Mary some fresh air, but I knew Bernice wasn't standing on the other side of that door and things only got tense when I opened it.

"Hey, I'm sorry; I'm still getting ready. I thought I'd have more time to get my dog settled before we left. Ms. Mary Mack isn't what I would call a fighting dog, but if you know anything about cane corsos, then you'd know that they're very protective of their owners. Once she knows you, though, you can't get her to *stop* being affectionate. If she had her way, I'd never leave the house. She just has this strong separation anxiety that's linked to her being a rescue. I just need a few minutes with her."

I was fighting endlessly to edge her toward her room but failing miserably. I hated leashing her inside because she reacted calmer when I wasn't forcing confinement, but her reckless fidgeting was tempting me to do it this one time, if only to get her to her room so I could finish getting ready.

"Well, aren't you the cutest little dog dad? All the more reason to end up back at your place after our date," she flirted, only putting the idea in my head that if we did end up back here later, I was going to see her naked again. Maybe that was optimistic of me, but I was doing my hardest to play by her rules, yet here she was changing them as she went along. Now, I'd never stop thinking about it.

"Look, Cattaneo. You don't even have your shoes on. Why don't you let me work out things with your dog; what's her name again?"

"Ms. Mary Mack," I reminded.

"*Right*! You finish getting ready, and I will make sure Ms. Mary Mack is all taken care of."

If she hadn't sounded so confident, I may had doubted her, but the moment she bent down to pet her, Mary calmed down with unrecognizable orderliness.

"You sure you don't mind?"

"Of course not! Us girls will be fine, okay? Finish getting ready."

In the short time that it took me to style my hair and slip on some socks and shoes, I returned to the living room, bewildered by the *lack* of noise I expected to hear.

"Everything alright in here? Things are eerily quiet," I admitted, my eyes widening in shock to see that Mary was not only obeying Luz's commands but also begging for her attention and admiration. She ignored me, a rare thing for her to do even when the company she liked walked in. She was always loyal, cuddling up next to me over the faces that came and went.

"I don't know what you were talking about when you said your dog was overly protective. We've been having a great time, haven't we, Mary?" Luz cooed, laying a long, comforting stroke along Mary's silky black coat.

Truthfully, Ms. Mary Mack was protective. She never let anyone new touch her in the way Luz was. Even women I had dated for years had taken months for my girl to warm up to. Obviously, we didn't last.

"You're probably just spoiling her. She always gives her attention to someone who acknowledges her," I lied. Mary was as good with people as that one ornery elementary school lunch lady, but even they wouldn't growl and bark in your face if they saw you as an instant threat. Which led me to my next conclusion; Ms. Mary Mack actually liked her. Ms. Mary Mack didn't like anyone she just met.

"Your dog makes me wish we could've afforded a dog when I was growing up. I might actually be good at this dog mom thing," she kidded.

Mary getting along with Luz was the sign I wasn't expecting. Maybe, Luz could be the one.

CHAPTER TWENTY-THREE

Evan

The first thing I noticed about Luz on the way to my garage was how fucking hot she looked. The way the dark wash jeans she wore hugged her hips and thighs made me contemplate a thousand and one reasons to walk behind her, just to get a continuous view. She kept it casual with a crisp white tee but trendy with sexy fitted leather jacket. Style wasn't something that always grabbed my attention, but Luz's unique style never failed to wow me.

"Did you get my message about wearing something comfortable?" I asked, my subtle acknowledgment that her high-heeled boots wouldn't be the best choice for where we were headed. As I played with the key fob, the doors opened with one click of a button. "You sure you're going to be comfortable in those things? We may be walking around a lot." And by those things, I meant the highest, pointiest, probably most uncomfortable, ankle boots a woman could own. She definitely looked sexy, but she looked more downtown than small town, which was our destination.

"It's not like you'd tell me where we were going. I wanted to look cute on our first date. Besides, I packed a pair of sneakers in my bag just in case. See?" She opened her shoulder bag, revealing a pair of dark blue tennis shoes that looked barely worn, as I surprised her by pulling her in for a kiss before I opened her door. Her lips were so hard to break away from when she reached in again for another one as I tried to pull away; I couldn't resist her.

"I'm sorry. I haven't had breakfast yet. I'm not myself when I haven't had *you*." A grin pooled across my face at the sound of her laughter that followed. I didn't know what I liked about Luz's laugh. It wasn't girly, cutesy, or even controlled, but it was such a turn-on. She didn't know how much I loved it. "All right, we've got a bit of a drive, so we should get going."

She climbed into the passenger seat as I closed the door behind her. Once in the driver's seat, I cranked the ignition, and it didn't take long until we were on the road and headed to the closest freeway.

"Thanks for making me coffee." After taking a sip, she put down the mug of black coffee with three sugars in one of the cup holders. She moaned as she swigged it down, a smile creeping up my face at the sight of her enjoying something as basic as coffee. She was damn cute when she enjoyed something.

"I have to say I'm really surprised you have a car, living in the city, Cattaneo. I only have one other friend who has one, and I've been living here for fourteen years."

"So, you're saying you don't drive when you go back home?" I didn't do much driving in the city, but the city wasn't the entire world, and driving made traveling simpler.

"I'm saying I don't have a license and have never learned how to drive at all. When I do visit home, that's what the train is for so that I don't have to drive," she stated matter-of-factly. I couldn't believe a word I was hearing. No woman in my life was going to be without the ability to drive. What if we took longer road trips or had an emergency? That burden had to be shared.

"Okay, then that's my next date idea—teaching you how to

drive so that you can get your license. I see us going on longer trips, and there's no way I'm driving all the way there." The moment the words left my lips, it dawned on me how optimistic I sounded at a future past the next few months but she just went with it.

"You might not want it to be in this car. This is really nice and I'd hate to get into an accident. I'm sure with those wall street checks, this is the latest model" she teased.

Trying to keep it a surprise until absolutely necessary, I set the destination in my navigation's GPS. "Apple Crisps Orchards? We're going to a farm?"

I nodded. "Not just any farm but a farm with adult activities. I was in the mood for apple and pumpkin picking, but this place also has a wine and hard cider distillery. Once we've had our fill with partaking in what every American should experience at least once in their lives, we can drink ourselves silly in adult beverages."

"Listen, I'm sure I'll have mad fun but pumpkin-picking? Watch me be the only Black person. This is about to be the whitest thing I've ever done." I rolled my eyes.

"Excuse me, I thought I was the whitest thing you've ever done? I mean, I know I'm suave and all—"

With a pointed manicured fingernail, she pressed my mouth closed. "Don't finish that sentence. You're lucky that last thing you said was kind of funny." She shrugged. "But maybe you're right. One for Evan." She held up one finger as if keeping imaginary score.

"So, I was wondering since we've got a two-hour drive ahead and assuming the weather stays good and we don't get caught up in any major traffic, are we allowed to have third and fourth date conversations? I asked, looking in her direction, her face morphing into an expression tinged with intrigue.

"We've already had sex before our first date and there's the familiarity that comes from knowing someone from your past, but there's so much time in between. I don't know as much as I'd like to know about present Luz, and I just want to know her as much as I did past Luz." Past Luz, I knew *everything* about.

"I don't see any issues with that. As long as you're as honest as I plan to be with you." I nodded in agreement. With her, the truth came out easily. Adjusting the satellite radio, I settled on a channel that was smooth and relaxing. The last thing I needed was a song like "Area Codes" by Ludacris blasting through the speakers when we were talking about fidelity and past relationships.

"Can I go first?" she asked as I shrugged, trying to hide that my heart was beating a mile a minute, fearing what she might start with. "What was life like for you after high school? I know you moved down to Philly to go to Temple, but I don't have the whole picture. Did you give up sports altogether? Did you have this epiphany that you had to get out of Rochester? What made you move to NYC?"

Life after high school? I hadn't thought about it in so long that I really had to rack my brain to remember. Details came back in bits and pieces. My collection of acceptance letters. The sting of my breakup with Luz. The chance at a fresh start. I hadn't entirely given up basketball, but I knew if I wanted to make a way for myself, it would have to be doing something I earned and wasn't just naturally good at. Basketball was something I played because I loved it, but I didn't want to be thirty-three asking myself what I could have done differently. In college, I liked being nobody. I never had to worry about if someone liked me for who I was and not just someone's fantasy of me. Leaving Rochester helped me see that more, but coming back to New York helped me to realize how hard it was finding a good pizza spot that came close to yours. After my explanation, she nodded in agreement.

"New York is home, ya know? Once you've lived other places, you realize how much you miss it. What brought me here was an internship for a Fortune 500 Company, and I was fortunate. The person I worked the closest with was also Italian, so I think he just saw himself in me. He helped me to get the job that led me to the firm I'm at now, so NYC, being the finance capital of the world, was just a good fit for me. My dad knew taking over our family restaurant wasn't my calling and my mom wanted me to make the most of my degrees. It was nice to just pick up and start someplace new."

Luz's version had been simpler. She dreamed of living in the city and, like me, had family in New Jersey and looked forward to family visits just to get a glimpse of the Big Apple. She was so excited applying for colleges, but I remember when she heard back from her top choice, she applied for every scholarship she qualified for and took out loans just so she could be in attendance come September. It didn't surprise me that she ended up working her dream job. Everything she had ever wished for had seemed to come true. So, why was she still single?

"You know, I always thought if I ever saw you again, you'd be married with kids by now. That you would have this super-hot wife who was some neurosurgeon from Gabon or Sierra Leone." In the past, she mentioned her Uncle Jidenna's ties to Nigeria. Her cousin Demeter bragged about spending summers in West Africa, so after lots of research, Luz made those two countries her top places to visit once she completed a semester after her first year of college. Her left eyebrow lifted in amused interest.

"Okay, tell me more about my made-up wife." Her warm smile beamed but I wasn't even done reassuring her how much her presence was needed in my life.

"I want to know why someone as amazing as you didn't catch someone else's eye. I know the offers have been plentiful."

She shrugged, taking her jacket off to lay on her lap. "Offers will always be there, but once someone betrays your trust, it's hard to open your heart to someone else. I promise I'm not talking about you, but after I had one bad relationship, it just felt better to be by myself. I was tired of giving more that I was receiving. It only resulted with me getting hurt in the end. Were you trying to turn this conversation into a confessional?" she asked with a fake smile, leading me to believe there were something she wasn't ready to talk about and for that, I was patient.

"What about you loverboy? You're thirty-three, make an incredible living, and you coach youth basketball. You know where we come from, no one like you would be single right now. What's the deal? Do you not make enough time to date or are you just unlucky in love?"

"Sadly, it's had been a little of both, but more or less with my last relationship, I was falling into a routine that I hadn't found fulfilling. I wasn't motivated. I didn't like myself and it only got worse when my ex and I moved into together. It was as if I was forcing it to work because of the years we put in together, but the sparks hadn't been there. Until now, I was never sure of what I wanted, but let's see how things work out for me." I just wanted a love that felt like my first. I couldn't call Luz the first girl I slept with, but she had been the first girl I fell in love with. Everything before that paled in comparison. Everyone else wasn't Luz.

After a long drive and deep conversation, I felt closer to believing that a relationship between Luz and me could work. After playing forty questions and counting, we couldn't be any more different. When it came to politics, I was a stark Libertarian while she was an issue-swaying Independent. I was all action, all the time, while she was still a lover of all themes magical. We couldn't even agree on the greatest musician of all time because in my eyes, Jimi Hendrix reigned supreme but she was not backing down on her argument that Beyoncé was the greatest *living* artist. The only thing we didn't disagree on was that despite all that, we enjoyed spending time with one another.

"Usually, long drives with someone had me ready to kill them, but all I want to do is kiss you, so that has to mean something."

Once we got there and drove into the parking lot, we both agreed to use this time to unplug and take the time to enjoy being out. That meant no pictures, no phones, and absolutely under no circumstances would we skip the distillery tour. Tours were cheesy for a reason and that reason was linked to creating cherished memories. Screw the coolness factor. As she was stashing her phone away, the smile on her face was so adorable that I had to know what it was about. I thought she only smiled like that at me.

"You know, you should tell your other man to stop texting you because I have you this weekend," I half-teased, prompting her to show me the thread of messages she was sending to her mom. The only messages I could make out were the ones easily translatable. Te extrano and my name surrounded by words in Spanish I didn't already know. "My mom doesn't believe I'm on a date with you," she admitted.

I was more shocked that her mom even remembered me. Fifteen years was a long time, and I'm sure to her, we were just kids in love. Luz's mom was the few of my exes' moms that I could've actually seen becoming my mother-in-law. Who *still* could end up being my mother-in-law.

"Before we do anything, why don't we do this?" I took her phone, flipping through a page's worth of apps, looking for the camera icon. Setting it in selfie mode, I pulled her close and we posed together in a picture that had screensaver potential. We looked pretty damn good together, so if that didn't convince her mom, I didn't know what would. "Now, send it and let's get started. We've got apples to eat and pumpkins to pick." She sent the photo, choosing to shut it off and throw it in the passenger seat as she joined me.

The starting point was a quaint, rural cottage-style gift shop permeated with the scent of homemade pine-scented candles, apple-infused incense, and cinnamon brooms that evoked all things autumn. Charlotte, our counter person, looked especially cheerful in her red gingham apron and matching framed glasses. If I had to guess, I would say she was in her forties, but even some of my boys' moms looked too young to have teenage sons, but I was positive most were my age or older. With hair of white and grey blended strands that contrasted her dark skin, to guess this Black woman's age would only frustrate me.

"How are you doing, Charlotte? My beautiful companion and I would like to buy some pumpkin-picking time, and while we're at it, let's throw in that farm and distillery tour? We're city folk, so we don't get out here too often," I flirted.

Quickly Luz left my side to explore the gift shop's wonders, only to return with a bottle opener in the shape of a man in flannel and overalls with a pumpkin-shaped head. "Isn't this cute? Can you get this for me?" she added with a kiss to my cheek.

Upon inspection, it was the silliest bottle opener I had even seen but when in Rome. "Why don't we throw this in there too? Anything else?" I asked, handing my credit card to Charlotte as she stared at us with a soft expression, her head tilting to the side.

"You two are adorable. You remind me of me and my husband when we first got together. Have you been seeing each other long?"

With raised brows and failure to fight back a smile, I took Luz in my arms. "You know, actually, this is our first date."

With widened eyes, Charlotte looked back and forth between us, sharing her blessing on our visible chemistry. I felt guilty for not disclosing that we had a history prior to today, but the joy she exuded from seeing the beginning of what she referred to as "our young love", I didn't have the heart to break it to her. Plus, it would be a nice little story to tell her husband when she got home. After a quick probe, I learned that he, too, was Italian. What can I say? We had good taste.

"Enjoy Apple Crisps Orchards" was her final greeting as we made our way to the line forming just outside the cottage. I hoped this wasn't some Hunger Games exercise because between Luz in her sky-high boots and the stiffness from a two-hour car ride, our odds weren't high to pick the brightest and freshest offerings. After what I assumed would be an afternoon of walking, by the end of the date, I would have to do some carrying.

"You heard what she said, right? Our friend Charlotte over there thinks we're in love. Don't you have a notebook in that big purse of yours? Shouldn't you be writing this down?"

CHAPTER TWENTY-FOUR

Luz

"Here. Why don't you open the door?" Evan handed me the keys to his apartment as he wrapped his arms around my waist. His feather-light kisses to my neck had caused me to drop them before I could angle them toward the keyhole. I had always been a fan of neck kisses, but what Evan's lips did to me; I could barely walk in a straight line, let alone open a door.

"See, the Luz I remember could handle two tasks at once. Is someone distracted?" With a playful shove, I warned him that we would be standing out here all night if I didn't get this door open and voila, with a quick flick of the wrist, the door swung open. His dog came rushing from the hallway with a smile on her face and a pep in her step to find her handsome owner had returned. To my surprise, the black-coated beauty pranced toward me, showing me the same love and affection. While I wasn't used to a dog's tongue licking my face, Ms. Mary Mack's taking to me wasn't a bad thing. I didn't mind sharing the title as Evan's favorite girl.

"Just a minute, girl. I'll take you out in minute." Evan met me with sympathetic eyes as Ms. Mary Mack headed for the door and began what I interpreted as her ritualistic bathroom routine. When nature called, you had to answer.

"Hey, is it okay if I take her out for a walk? I have a lady that comes when I need her to, but she could really use some time to run around and do her business."

Shocked that he was even asking me for my permission, I waved my hands dismissively and told him what he needed to hear. "Oh, of course. I wouldn't deny the girl getting herself settled for the night. As long as you don't mind me making myself comfortable with that sixty-inch TV in there just dying to be watched." Remote in hand, I plopped down on his plush sofa, praying that he had Disney+ so I could do a quick catch-up on The Mandalorian as he readied his four-legged friend for a relaxing run around town. After the door closed and minutes had passed, I paused my program to give myself a quick tour of his condo.

Not that I was suspicious, but a lot could be said about a person by the way they kept their house. My stopping by earlier than planned could have been a potential disaster if I had walked into a pigsty. Some men thought having a woman in their lives meant unpaid guaranteed maid services but that wasn't the case with Evan. His place was impeccably clean. Eerily clean. So clean that it put me to shame. I loved how his condo was so well-put together, like some high-scale ad for an interior design company. Entering what looked to be his bedroom, my mouth dropped at the view of a bed that was actually made. I hoped he wasn't the kind of person who got up at five a.m. on a Sunday just to make the bed up with you inside.

Either way, his place wasn't too pretentious or too plain and not that it was a bad thing, but as someone who wasn't an animal owner, it was nice that it didn't smell like other condos

I've been where it was obvious they owned a pet. With the view from his place, I could see myself spending the night a few nights a week.

Stepping out onto his bedroom terrace, the glimpse of the city this high was a sight few girls from around my way got to see. There was a sense of pride that I got in knowing the city like the back of my hand, but even after fourteen years, there were still viewscapes I hadn't seen, and knowing there were others only excited me.

It wasn't before long that the sound of man and creature broke my singularly focused train of thought. They'd either sniff me out or let me come to them; either way, they'd find me for sure, so I figured I should meet them halfway.

"Hey, I'm glad you're still here." Evan kissed me on the forehead, assuming I had left. "You don't mind if I take a quick shower while you're out here, do you?"

After a long day, I couldn't object to Evan getting all cleaned up. Plus, it'd give me time to spend with my ebony-furred homegirl. Ms. Mary Mack climbed onto the loveseat, eager to get a taste of the penthouse view herself. She didn't seem to mind my company, but it could've been because she was basking in the tummy rub I had reserved for her. Poor thing was getting attached to me. Let's see if I could get my new BFF to dish about her owner.

"So, now that we're alone, Ms. Mack, what do you think about me and Evan?" She perked up, as if she understood, and rested her chin on the top of my upper thigh. "Should I invest in more? Should I base everything on his bedroom skills? I'm asking you because I know you can keep a secret," I teased, causing her to bark as if she was giving me the 411.

"I really like him, but only if that's ok with you." Ms. Mary Mack was in tune with my emotions at the very least. She reached in and licked my face, cementing her approval, which could only mean a girl's night dedicated to mini makeovers and ridiculous rom-coms were in our future. She hopped off the couch the moment she heard the shower cut on.

She paced back and forth as if she was notifying me that all this time I was entertaining her, I could have been joining Evan in the shower. "Mary, I don't know. Evan seemed clear on his stance about going on dates that didn't lead to sex. If I hit up that shower, I can't promise what'll unfold."

Ms. Mary Mack barked as if her response was meant to convey *So?* Sex-positive *and* bougie? She was about to give Candice a run for her money as my official BFF. "All right, Imma take your advice. But if I end up staying over and taking away from your attention, it'll be all your fault."

Making my way into his room, I opened his bedroom door to let Ms. Mary Mack roam free. Not to say we were *going* to end up doing anything but I wasn't opposed to the idea that watching soap slide down Evan's body would end up in him throwing me on his king-sized bed and taking me.

Did it even count if it was all in the same week? Evan desperately wanted to space out our sexy times, but all I could think about was soap dripping down that sexy body and that the logistics of our bet had little meaning. Soon I stripped out of my clothes and was buck-ass naked in front of his full-length mirror.

I tiptoed into the bathroom, able to slip into the shower while his face was covered in soap. Once his face was free of suds, he turned around, wide eyes softening into a satisfying grin. "Mmmm...look who decided to keep me company," he said, biting his lip.

He ran his fingers down my now-wet hair, tracing them the slowly down my back until they reached the fleshiest part of my backside. "You saved me the trouble of finding you later." He leaned in for a soft, sensual kiss. Even underwater, his lips were spellbinding.

"Now I get the pleasure of getting you clean. As long as you don't mind me turning you on first," he flirted.

That was putting it lightly; by turning me on, he meant he'd set me on fire, watching his lathered hands caress me. His long fingers massaged my scalp after a mini-lesson on how to co-wash my hair. He handled my limbs with a level of tenderness that even I didn't always prioritize. By the time we were ready to hop out of the shower, the last thing on my mind was talking.

Evan adorned me in one of his plush-soft towels and with some expert scrounging found the perfect pillowcase to help dry my hair with. He disappeared into his bedroom, properly locking the door since Ms. Mary Mack had been known to crack a lock Da Vinci Code-style when it came to exploring her curiosity, but after our talk, I was sure she'd give us all the time we needed.

Evan swooped me off my feet as if I hadn't weighed an ounce. "Now that we're clean, I wonder how we should preoccupy our time," he flirted, pure lust in his gaze.

"I think I have an idea, but it involves your dick in my mouth and my kitty on your face," I suggested with a bite to my nails in an effort to look innocent. His thick brows rose in fascination, begging that I demonstrate by finding a comfortable resting spot inches away from his face.

"I love this view of you," he said, wrapping his strong arms around my waist. He playfully gripped me hard, my stomach pressing to his chiseled chest. "Normally you can get away easily when I make out with your pussy, but this ensures you're going absolutely nowhere," he laughed as he pressed a kiss to my embarrassingly swollen nub.

As much as I tried to move, he was right. I was trapped in his in embrace, but what he didn't realize was that his dick and my mouth would be a lethal combination. After I got finished with him, walking in a straight line would prove difficult to do. "You sure you can handle keeping up with me?" I teased, taking his already brick-hard length in my hand, letting my wet and willing mouth engulf the base of his cock.

He squirmed underneath as he let out a pathetic groan. "Fuck, I forgot how good you were at giving blowjobs," he confessed.

From the way he ate pussy, you would never know there was a time he didn't do it, but now I was paying for it with his out-of-this-world orgasms. "But I'm confident I can outdo you. After all, if I come, I'm out for a round, but you don't need that much recovery time," he challenged.

Talk was cheap when I had his dick in my hand, but once he got started, I couldn't help but feel that it would be me throwing in the towel. The way his mouth brought shivers to my spine with just one lick, I felt the urge to be selfish and take pleasure in riding his face. Part of the allure was that I couldn't see what he was doing. I just knew that it felt amazing and if I could, I would make him stay down there all day. The way he licked, sucked, and spread my pussy open was as if he owned it, as if he owned me. And I badly wanted to belong to him and only him.

Trying to keep up with him, I took his long iron-hard cock into my mouth, finding it difficult to concentrate with the havoc he was invoking on me. It was so much easier to sit back and come, but I had enough with him having all the fun. I wanted to give him something to brag about, even if it was just to his dog. The second my phone rang, I found an opening to put me ahead of the pleasure game, but it would only work if I could hold on long enough to put a dent in his performance.

"Oh my god, Evan, I have to answer it. It's my mother." He pulled back long enough to warn me not to, but with my phone at arm's length, I hit the answer button and greeted my mom.

"Hey, Ma," I answered, trembling at the change in speed Evan's magical tongue was working on me. Everything he did felt amazing, but the shift in his technique made the tickling sensation from his beard out of this world. With how wet I was, I was sure I'd be tasting myself on his face for days. "Yea, actually I'm still with Evan...we're in the middle of dinner," I half-lied. I mean, he was stuffing his face, but I left out what he was stuffing his face with. "You know what, Ma? He's actually right here; would you like to speak with him?"

The impact of Evan's hand stung hard as he slapped my left cheek. If he were upset, he was excellent at hiding it as I passed him the phone. Here was my in. He wouldn't outdo me with giving head. We could not have that.

"Hey, Mrs. De Los Santos, I mean Danyeli—" he said as his long toes curled at the hand/mouth combo I spent years perfecting. As much as he would try to fight it, the second his knees relaxed, I knew it was primetime to start unleashing some finishing moves. "Yea, it's been a really long time, Danyeli. No, no, no, we didn't go out to eat; we're having dinner at my place," he said into the phone as he drove his wild hips deeper into my mouth. Bearing witness to his ripped stomach clenching up in a moment of weakness was the kind of drive a girl needed to keep Evan's powerless cock at the back of my throat.

"Is your daughter taking care of me? Trust me when I say this; she's taking *real* good care of me. I'm not even sure I deserve the meal your daughter has so expertly put together. I'm sure she gets it from you," he laughed, his thrusting growing hungrier, more aggressive, and uncontrollably faster. He was going to come, and I was ready for it. It wasn't as if we didn't have all night.

"Yea, that's a good idea; why don't you call back when you're not busy? Plus, I don't want to waste a morsel of this beautiful meal Luz has in front of me. It was nice talking to you, Danyeli. Have a beautiful night, okay?" he blurted out with barely enough energy to mask his groans and frustration. When it was obvious that he had hung up the phone, he offered one last pump before flipping me over and holding me down.

"Okay, that was wrong...but strangely erotic." With my wrists still pinned to the bed, he leaned in and kissed me. "But I'm not wasting a perfectly good erection by coming in your mouth. If you want me to come, you have to do it the old-fashioned way." With that, he loosened his hold on me and rose to his knees. "Now, turn around. I want to see that sexy ass of yours."

CHAPTER TWENTY-FIVE

Before

Evan

"Are you sure your mom's not home?" That was always my main fear when it came to being alone with girls at their houses. Luz was a self-proclaimed free spirit, but my guess was she hated to be referred to as a good girl. She *sometimes* went to church and had a God-fearing mother just as any Catholic girl might, but even good girls had bad sides; I just didn't want to receive a lifetime ban from her house, so I was covering every base when it came to sharing alone time with Luz.

"The coast is clear. My mom works overnight on weekdays," Luz proclaimed before pulling me by the wrist to snake through the house. Things were quiet when Luz's mom wasn't home. None of the usual cooking smells lingered throughout. I was convinced Luz's kitchen had a permanent aroma of nutmeg and cinnamon for as much arroz con leche I ate whenever I was invited over for dinner, courtesy of Luz's mom.

Despite the confirmation that the house was empty, I found myself still tiptoeing down the hallway on the way to Luz's room. My anxiety didn't last long when I finally realized that I could kiss Luz openly and passionately and not just give the church hugs and pecks I was used to giving in her mother's presence.

"You smell really nice," I murmured, my face, lips and nose burying themselves further into the crook of her neck. There was a certain level of anticipation, not expectation, but the hope that our alone time would lead somewhere fun and explorative.

I never pressured girls to do things they didn't want to do, but I'd be lying if the promise of being in Luz's room unsupervised didn't make every nerve of mine stand on end. "Since we're alone, I wonder if you're open to a little more," Luz flirted, making my body react in typical, horny teen fashion. Calm down, body. She could just mean a lot of fabric-to-fabric dry humping, which I'd still be totally down for, by the way.

"Whatever you want to do," I replied as her lips pressed down onto mine. I'd always viewed Luz as shy and chaste, but it was clear she had a wild side. She was assertive in a way I wasn't used to, which worked in my favor because she couldn't keep her hands off me.

One minute we were making out; the next, she was unzipping my fly, her mouth too preoccupied to do much kissing. "Oh my god," I moaned, studying how hot Luz looked with her mouth was full of me. She hadn't even taken her glasses off; it was like I was getting off from a very sexy, very willing, sexpot librarian.

"I can't believe you've never done this before." I said throwing my head back in pleasure, unable to concentrate on anything more than how hot she looked on her knees. I could tell we weren't there yet when it came to sex, but I could definitely get used to nighttime blowjobs.

Her mouth was so warm; it only added to the texture of her

soft tongue. It had been a while, so I didn't have a strong last game when it came to head, and it wasn't long before I was reaching my point of no return.

"Luz, I think I'm about to come," I choked out in fair warning. I wasn't sure she was the type of person who would keep on going or preferred to catch the excess in her hand. Either way, no outcome would affect the way I felt right now. Luz was on a mission, and with my declaration, she apparently knew what to do. Instead of treating it delicately, her hand firmly gripped the base of my dick, followed by a jerking rhythm that accompanied her sucking. With her speed matching the intensity of her hand, inhuman sounds of satisfaction echoed from the back of my throat. All that tension built up to the final release, and it wasn't long before my body relaxed with the intensity of my spasms.

My gut reaction was to laugh, though it was more of a laugh of relief. "That was fucking amazing, Luz." And that was downplaying it. It was actually the first time I'd gotten a blowjob that felt just as good as sex.

She wiped her mouth off of all the excess saliva, prompting me to zip myself back up. "For a virgin, I don't know how you learned to do it so well," I added as I lifted my back to secure my belt back in the belt loops behind me.

"I already told you; I'm not a virgin." She was defensive but with good reason. She didn't consider herself a virgin because she had lost her virginity to her ex-girlfriend, but I'd never dated a bi girl, so my ignorance had always led to believe that it didn't count between two girls. Giving it some proper thought, sex was sex, no matter who or how you had it with.

"You know what I meant. For someone who's never been with a guy before," I clarified, hoping to get her to divulge where she's learned that from. She slipped her hand under her bed to retrieve a back issue of that magazine she liked. Modern magazine, I think. Rachel McAdams graced the cover, surrounded by all the topics the issue highlighted as its juicy selling points.

Tips to Perfect Your BJ Skills (even if it's your first time) was written in bold letters. I guess these magazines really did have useful information in them. It was a good thing Luz was such a dedicated reader; otherwise, that could have gone an entirely different way.

Luz excused herself to brush her teeth when I picked up the periodical and skimmed through its pages. Thumbing through its content this time, I surprised myself at how little I flipped past the photo layouts and pretty faces. There were real-life issues written in these stories, with subjects as heavy as insurance coverage for birth control to women's lack of leadership in corporate America.

Coming from a long line of conservatives, I never challenged conversations revolving around reproductive health and women's access to it, but some of the stories I read were downright eye-opening. It made me ashamed that I'd never considered that an alternative view on a women's right to her body, I'd just always been taught things like birth control went against God's way.

While I wasn't walking away with a complete understanding of the topic, I was much more perceptive to a view that may not have been my own. When Luz finally returned, she didn't seem to mind when I asked if I could borrow it so I could read through it on my own time.

Swiveling around in Luz's computer chair, I couldn't help but notice she started slipping out of her pajama shorts and wrestled with her long sleeve pajama top.

Luz had the most perfect brown skin, made more apparent once her toned legs were free of the confining material. If I didn't stop her now, there was no telling what my dick might do at the reveal. "What are you doing?" I laughed the moment she started tugging at her panties.

"I figured we would finish what we started," she suggested.

"I don't have any condoms." Imagine *me* not having condoms. I'd only assumed Luz wasn't the hit and quit type, so I chose never to bring any since I assumed she'd never gone past second base.

"We don't really need condoms. I just figured I'd freshen up before you ate me out."

I laughed but it became clear she wasn't joking. "Why are you laughing?" she asked, confused.

"So, you weren't joking about me eating you out?"

"Why would I be? Especially since not more than two minutes ago I was slobbing down *your* knob."

"Yea, but that was just head. It's not really as personal."

Luz's eyes narrowed to slits that were a cross between irritation and confusion. "But you're dating me. It's not like I expect a tit for tat, but I'm questioning why I'm dating a guy who doesn't want to go down on me when he claims to like me."

This conversation had me choking up. I didn't want to confuse her or make her more upset than she appeared, but I'd never had this conversation before and I was ill-prepared for the possible outcome.

"It's not that. I do really like you, but there's a lot going on down there when it comes to giving a girl head. There're completely different smells, tastes, and textures. If I'd known you wanted to have sex, I would've just brought condoms—"

"Let me get this straight," she cut me off, her tone going bolder as it was evident she'd been holding back to spare my feelings. "You're telling me that my body is good enough to stick your dick inside of but not good enough to put your mouth on? Oral sex and intercourse aren't interchangeable. Most girls can't even climax from penetration alone, so you're asking me to lay here like it's going to be as fun for me as it is for you."

My foot was officially in my mouth. All I'd done was make the situation worse, and I didn't even know how to fix it. Maybe if I just shared why I'd never done it before, she'd understand where I'm coming from.

"I've just heard so many horror stories. I'm afraid if I don't like doing it, I'll be totally grossed out by it forever—"

"Just stop talking," she interrupted, not even being able to look me in the eye but still able to convey her frustration through her body language. "I just want you to go. I can't even look at you."

"Is this just because—"

"Evan, you just admitted you're disgusted by my body or that I'm not useful unless I'm of use to *you*. Like I live and function for your pleasure." Luz slipped back into the shorts and long-sleeve pajama top that she'd shed right before this dispute went down.

"Fuck that. I have my own agency. Never mind that my body likes to feel good too. But it's only good enough if your body can get something out of it, too, and that's fucked up."

My mind was in a state of panic; I really liked Luz, and while I wasn't nurtured to be an empath, I tried to ask myself how I would feel if this situation was on the other foot. Would I be so accepting with a level of discomfort when it came to my body? I don't think I ever asked myself if girls really did like giving head or if they just liked the idea that I let them touch me.

No girl had ever argued about the lack of reciprocation, but I also never offered either.

"Could I finger you? Or—"

"You can leave. That's what you *can* do. I wouldn't want to subject your hands to such a messy task. I might even like it, and I know guys hate for girls to enjoy anything."

"Luz, I'm sorry. Tell me how I can fix this?"

Luz marched toward her closed bedroom door, slung it open, and pointed toward the exit to make herself clearer. She didn't even think I was worth a response after that.

"Fuck," I mumbled under my breath. I wish she had never given me head. From the way she eyed me leaving her room, my guess was she wished she hadn't either.

CHAPTER TWENTY-SIX

Evan

Luz refusing to answer any of my texts or phone calls had confirmed I really fucked up this time. The look on her face. Her tone of voice. The change in her attitude when she asked me to leave. Six months ago, none of this would have been a big deal to me, but for the first time in my life, I was embarrassed with how I conducted myself. Here she was, this sweet, sexy, and willing girl who took pleasure in satisfying me, and what did I do to thank her? *Nothing but refuse to return the favor*.

It wasn't about what I did, more of what I wouldn't do, and judging by her strategic avoidance of me, my actions spoke louder than words. Honestly, I never had a girl ask me to eat her pussy. Come to think of it, I never even considered what pleasure girls got from me because I never thought to ask.

I would never eat something that bled for seven days and didn't die.

I would never eat a girl out because I'm afraid of STDs, and it's not like they have condoms for mouths.

I just can't get past the smell.

Those were the things you heard floating around in the male locker room. I heard it from my teammates and worst of all, most of my friends thought that way. Everything I'd heard about oral sex with a woman had terrified me from even trying, especially since I didn't know one guy who openly loved doing it, as a result, I assumed I wouldn't like doing it either, but the shame I felt when I refused my own girlfriend made me feel like an *entire* piece of shit.

"Hey, Cattaneo, there goes your girl," Cotton pointed out, marking the first time I'd seen her all day on school grounds.

Instead of stopping to explain why she wasn't speaking to me, she walked in the opposite direction, making me the laughing stock of all my friends. "Uh-oh. Looks like there's trouble in paradise." My friends chuckled at my expense.

"Listen, I'll catch up with you two later," I said as I ran after Luz to catch her before her next class. She didn't stop after the first time I called her name, and the only reason she stopped this time was because I stood in front of her, blocking her path with my hulking frame. Whenever she was annoyed with me, she rolled her eyes with disdain.

"Ugh! Can we not do this now? I'm not in the mood to talk and in no spirit of getting used either."

Her words hit me hard, cementing me in place. Never in my life had I ever been accused of using a girl. I may not have been perfect, but I didn't need to use girls. That was how jerks treated girls, and I wasn't a jerk; at least I'd never questioned being one before today. The hallway cleared as I pulled her into a vacant hall. Though the late bell rang, signaling the start of next period, I needed to know *something*; otherwise, I couldn't fix it. "Look, I get that you don't want to talk to me right now, but can you at least explain how I used you? It's not like I asked you to give me head. I thought you did it because you wanted to."

Adjusting the arm strap of her book bag, she failed to meet my eyes as she returned my gaze with an unreadable, bemused expression. "The star basketball player wants to know *how* he used me. The fact that you don't already know is the problem. I know I'm just a girl who got lucky. I realize you can be with whoever feels privileged at sexually servicing a guy with your social status, but I found out over the weekend that I'm not that." Her shoulders slumped, her confidence wavering with every word that left her mouth. "I did it because I wanted to. Because I liked you. You gave me the impression that you liked me, too, until the thought of putting your mouth on my vulva disgusted you. Contrary to what most boys believe, dicks don't exactly taste like a lollipop, but it didn't matter because I wanted to make you feel good. The one thing I refuse to do is be in a relationship with someone who expects things from me that he would never do to me in return. Pleasure isn't one-sided, and if you don't see that, then you're not the guy I'd be proud to call my boyfriend."

Glancing at the clock hanging up above a nearby classroom, we were officially late for our next class with zero time to resolve this issue before we went our separate ways. My suspicions were right; she was mad at me for not reciprocating oral sex.

"Are we done with this conversation? If so, I'd really like to get to class," she said, attempting to walk away, but with this six four frame, she wasn't getting past me.

"Can I at least give you a ride home? It's hard to have a serious talk like this when we're not alone. I can explain myself better when we're alone. If you're open to listening, that is." I busted out the most pathetic puppy dog eyes and pouted lip I could conjure up.

"Evan, would you just get out of my way and let me go to class?" Her eyes furrowed in frustration.

"Only if you agree to let me give you a ride home," I countered.

"Fine. I'll meet you on the north side. But if I don't see you at five minutes after three, I'm just going to walk to my bus stop and go home."

"Cool," I agreed as she brushed past me with conviction in her step. The second she turned the corner, I was left with two things to think about, one being that from the time that we started dating, today marked the first day she hadn't kissed me. The second? It had been the first time she used the word boyfriend, but it was only to tell me that I was being a shitty one.

———

For the first few minutes, we hadn't said anything to each other. In fact, I didn't even fight over the music she decided to play. While an avid lover of anything that came out of Japan, she also had this guilty pleasure she didn't admit to just anyone. Over-the-top boy bands were her one flaw, and her favorite was one I couldn't stand due to all the girls at our school going nuts over the lead singer. It was bad enough I heard their songs all day when I went over her house. Being stuck in a confined space didn't make hearing their songs any easier, but I had to remind myself that if I even attempted to change the station, she would have another reason to be mad at me, so patiently I waited until the song was over. Now, she had to hear me out.

At a stoplight, I reached for her hand, relief flooding my insides when she didn't push me away. "I forgot to tell you how nice you looked today." Her thick, coily hair looked different today. Curlier, I guess? She was wearing this dark, long-sleeved red dress that was soft like velvet. Her legs looked incredible, and her tits looked round, full, and *wow*. If I didn't get this off my chest, I'd blow any chance of ever seeing them.

"Evan, don't waste my time. What did you want to talk about?" Straight to the point. I thought I'd have more time to work up an apology, but here went nothing.

"Luz, I've never gone down on a girl before. You're the only girl who's ever asked me to do it, so a part of me was scared to admit I'm not good at something people think you're just supposed to be a natural at. I wouldn't even know where to start." That, along with a whole list of reasons guys stupidly joked about. I wished I weren't that guy that bought into it, but it did influence why I had never brought it up.

"Have you ever offered to go down on a girl?" she asked.

"No," I shamefully admitted, which prompted her to bring up the one thing I had been insecure about, the topic of her ex-girlfriend.

"You know, the first person I've ever been with made me feel so good about myself and comfortable in my own skin. Kissing me and pleasing me were things that came naturally to her. She did stuff because she liked me. But you..." she hesitated. "Even with people growing up, telling me that I shouldn't be proud of my body, I've managed to build this self-love relationship when others have taught me to suppress. When you didn't want to go down on me, it made me feel like you were grossed out by me, and I don't see how anyone who claims to like me could be repulsed at the mere suggestion of pleasure that doesn't involve his own penis."

For the record, Luz and I hadn't even had sex. We hadn't even brought up the possibility of sex. I was trying to take things slow because I wanted her to mention it first. But so far, I was making her feel like I didn't love every inch of her body, which was not the case at all.

The way she talked about her ex-girlfriend, I wanted her to talk about me like that. Not because I was a guy but because she was the only girl I ever thought about. Her bringing up how her ex made her feel made me feel like I wasn't giving her enough reasons to think about *me* all the time, and that needed to change. "I've heard all these horror stories that have given me pause about performing oral on girls, but I would never want to contribute to how you feel about your own body unless it's positive. I need you to know that," I confessed.

I turned onto her street, parking a few houses down from her apartment building. She didn't rush out of the car like I thought she would. She sat there and let me explain how I was going to be the boyfriend she wanted, the boyfriend she deserved.

"I want to try new things with you. Not because I think I'll get something in return, but because I want to know you better as a person, as my girlfriend. I think I only got nervous because with my past girlfriends, I've always been the more experienced one, but I'm almost positive you're better at eating pussy than I am." She shoved my arm, her eyes reducing to slits as she pursed her lips tightly. Later, she set her book bag in her lap, making a comment about her having to go inside soon. Her mom was a bit of a worrywart and liked to see her safe inside before she left for work even though tonight was her one evening off. I'm sure she wasn't going to invite me up unless it was to say hi. They spent that one night doing mother/daughter things, and I didn't want to intrude just because I didn't want to say goodbye.

After offering to walk her to her door, I was met with a hug and a smoldering kiss that would keep me at bay for days until the next time we were able to be alone together. "Can I call you later?"

"Yea but only after nine if it's on my cell because you know that's when the minutes are free," she reminded me. "So, I guess you're my boyfriend now?"

I laughed. "Only if you want me to be."

She *so* wanted me to be.

CHAPTER TWENTY-SEVEN

Evan

How to eat your girlfriend's pussy

The Google search seemed pretty straightforward and brought up dozens of pages of search results on my quest to master the thing I've yet to conquer. The first thing I learned was the difference between a vulva and a vagina. We use the words interchangeably, but most guys didn't know shit about female anatomy. If I planned to be good at it, I needed to familiarize myself with its appearance. Did you know the clitoris had eight *thousand* nerve endings alone? Mind fucking blown. Besides the usual health sites, porn looked like the best way to broaden my findings.

Only it wasn't. The amount of time guys spent on the average cunnilingus scene (Yes, there was an official name for eating pussy) was only two minutes versus the average fellatio scene clocking in at eight minutes. When it came to oral sex, there was a clear winner on whose pleasure was centered on, so it was no wonder guys never felt the pressure do it.

The next words I typed into the porn's search engine led to a montage of lesbian porn that I never thought I could learn anything from, but boy, was I wrong. Who better to teach me how to properly go down on a girl than another girl who knew what girls liked? They didn't just stick to the clitoral area like guys did in MF porn. They went at it like pleasing a girl was a damn Olympic event. Swirling, licking, nibbling, and kissing in ways that made it look like just as much fun for the giver as the receiver. I made sure to bookmark those pages to go back to for future reference. Dating a bi-girl definitely had its perks.

In my quest in looking up advice from various online publications, I became plagued with shame at discovering how many girls had found themselves in Luz's shoes. Happily giving in to their boyfriend's requests for round-the-clock blowjobs but too afraid to ask for the same in return in fears of coming off as selfish. The number of women who were insecure about the look, taste, and smell of their private parts made me realize how guys played a huge contribution to that. The more I learned about what vaginas did besides providing sexual pleasure for a man, the more I found myself realizing a girl's vulva wasn't ugly or intimidating as I was led to believe. They were actually unique. Like hair texture or bone structure, no two vulvas looked exactly alike. If I were lucky enough, I'd get a chance to show Luz my findings tonight when her mom left for work. Until then, I had to accept that through my research, most girls who had oral sex reported higher chances of climaxing than through actual intercourse. I wonder how many girls had faked it with me to spare my fragile feelings.

"Evan, honey? You think if you step out you can grab me a carton of milk?" My mom barged in without knocking as I struggled to rid my screen of the dozens of tabs I had open relating to eating pussy, including the lesbian scenes I bookmarked for advanced techniques.

"Oh my god, Ma. This isn't what it looks like." I panicked to exit out of the screen until finally I fell clumsily at her feet, trying to unplug the computer. My mom fit the stereotype of your typical Italian-American mom: opinionated, street-smart, and at every given opportunity, a failure at the mere suggestion of whispering.

"Well, it looks to me like you're watching dirty movies. You think I don't know you watch porn on that thing? You forget who does your laundry." She leaned on the opening of my bedroom door, pointing to my computer.

Note to self: Start masturbating in the shower. It's the only way to get rid of the evidence.

"What I want to know is why you're looking up two girls. I mean, I guess I know but as long as you're staying out of trouble and staying good for God, I don't care what you watch. Just don't go out and act on it."

My mom wasn't naïve. She knew how many girls threw themselves at me; she just couldn't pinpoint when and who I'd broken that vow for. While my dad didn't encourage me to lose my virginity, he didn't discourage it either, but in my mom's mind, I was still her sweet little boy. I stopped being her sweet little boy two years and nine inches ago. I was practically a man now.

"Why do you want to know how to eat pussy for? Do you have a girlfriend we don't know about?"

Turning at an angle, I shielded myself with my hand over my face, but the reality was my mom didn't back down from anything. "Ma, can we not talk about this right now?"

At that, she laughed. "If you're this embarrassed to talk about it, imagine what it's going to be like doing it?" she chastised in her New Jersey accent. "Despite what you choose to believe, I've had my share of what it took to keep my innocence. Third base kept everyone happy."

"Ma," I said through gritted teeth.

"Fine. You don't want to hear your mother talk about sex, just remember; you didn't get here from me just hugging your father. Just do me a favor. Whenever you find yourself implementing this knowledge, no girl likes a thrusting tongue in her who-ha. If all fails, pretend you're kissing her lips up here," she advised, pointing a manicured fingernail to her lips. "It's generally the same concept."

I couldn't take it anymore. I had to get out of this house and fast. Slipping on the closest sneakers I could find, I zoomed past her without even telling her where I was going.

"Ma, I'll be back before dinner. Just need some fresh air," I said as I flew down the staircase to prevent my mom offering up any more sex tips. Some things you just didn't want to talk about with your mom, and for me, eating pussy ranked number one.

———

"Hey," Luz greeted me at her door as she closed it behind me. Her usually thick hair was wet and hanging looser than when it was dry. She was wearing an oversized hoodie that *clearly* looked like one of mine and shorts so tiny that at first glance looked like she wasn't wearing any bottoms. Very different than what she wore to school today, but with her legs on full display, I wasn't complaining.

I toed off my sneakers by her front door's welcome mat, and my nerves got the best of me when I thought about what I had really came over here to do. Sure, spending time with her was a definite plus, but I just really wanted to show her I had no fears when it came to pleasuring her body. We had all night, so when she asked if I wanted to watch a movie, I caved, knowing how easily I could make my move when we were both lying down and comfortable. As she sat on her bed, I curled up on the pillows behind her, giving them a quick fluff as I made myself at home.

"Hey, so do you want to watch Revenge of the Sith or Friday Night Lights?" What was a nicer way of saying neither? I had never even seen any of the Star Wars films to understand them, and the second choice I'd already seen three times. I shrugged.

"I'll watch Star Wars if you want. I know you like all that fantasy stuff." That's what being a good boyfriend was all about. Compromise.

"Cool," she said, scooting back to the head of the bed with me and finding a convenient spot in my embrace. This was going to easier than I thought.

———

Not even an hour into the movie and Luz found herself *too* comfortable. When I leaned in to kiss her neck, the hum of her gentle snoring informed me that my affection was being wasted on a girl who couldn't even stay up during one of her favorite movie franchises. What if my performance was so boring that she fell asleep on me? I'd never recover. Instead of letting her spend the whole night sleeping like the precious angel she was, I did the next best thing that never failed to wake me when I was having the best sleep of my life. I hit her with a pillow and not just once or twice; it took a good six strikes to coax her out of her slumber. Unfortunately, she wasn't a happy camper when she ripped the pillow out of my hands and struck back with a blow of retaliation.

"Evan, what the hell? I know I fell asleep on you. but you could've just shaken me. You didn't have to go full-on attack mode with a pillow." Another strike at my head forced me to dodge her next hit, but what I really wanted to get to was how nothing about my day was going as planned. I blamed the movie, but really, it was my fear at being terrible at something so vital to our relationship. What if I sucked at it and she decided that making out was all we were ever going to do? I wasn't exactly in a rush to have penetrative sex, but that didn't mean I wanted it to be completely off the table.

"Look, I'm sorry, okay? And I know I've had lots of reasons to be sorry a lot lately, but today was the day I was going to surprise you by going down on you and twenty-five minutes into my being here, you're already fast asleep."

"Well, I am in my bed, genius. *Wait*, did you just say you wanted to go down on me?" Her eyes widened with sudden intrigue, accompanied by a mischievous smile.

Here I was, hoping to make things all steamy and organic but doing the exact opposite by blurting out every detail of my plans. Normally, I was a fuckin' pro at hooking up and making out, but my feelings for Luz were making me an anxious, nervous wreck.

"So, is that the only reason you stopped by today?"

Letting out a deep breath, I shrugged. "No, it wasn't the only reason but I mean, it's probably, like, the *main* reason," I admitted, knowing I'd be in big trouble for being late for dinner but also realizing this was the only day out of the school week where Luz and I could be completely alone.

"Why didn't you just tell me? Watching a movie is fun, but I'd choose your face between my legs any day of the week," she said in all seriousness before climbing into my lap and leaning into kiss me.

"Your lips taste like berries," I said at the traces of her lip balm transferring onto my eager lips. I loved her full lips, and I loved the way she asked me to kiss her. Most guys would have thought of her as bossy but being told by a girl what she liked took out all the guesswork of wondering if she enjoyed what I was doing.

"Do you want me to take my shirt off?" she asked, pulling away, leaving my lips feeling desperate and lonely.

"Do you like having your shirt off when you're getting eaten out?"

She laughed, sensing my nervousness and had given me the honor of watching her strip down to just her bra and shorts. Through her bra, her nipples hardened, her breasts looking bigger without the usual three layers of concealment her clothes offered. When she unbuckled her bra, I had to remind myself to pick my jaw off the ground and stop staring. Man, she had amazing tits. "Wow." Shaking my head, I attempted to knock myself out of the daze that seeing Luz's naked breasts put me in. Clearly, I wasn't doing a great job.

"I know I'm supposed to say this sort of thing, but you're so fuckin' hot." As I flipped her on her back, I was finding every excuse for my lips not to leave her body, but it was her whimpering in between that made me hard as a rock. Kissing, and teasing, and kneading her naked breasts, it wasn't long before my mouth had traced kisses all the way down to her torso, her pussy only a thin layer of mesh shorts away.

"A quick reminder that I've never done this before. I don't want you to hate me if the first time isn't to your satisfaction." She rose up on her elbows, her breasts taking on a different shape of fullness. Fuck, she was hot!

"Evan, I'm not going to be mad at you. You know I'm about patience. I'll be right here, guiding you on what feels good and what doesn't. I won't sit back and let you fail at it," she said, as I helped her out of her shorts and panties with a gentle tug. Her pussy was nothing I expected yet everything I expected. It wasn't scary, confusing, or even bad-smelling. On the contrary, it was beautiful. Everything about her was beautiful.

"Are you ready for me?" I asked with a kiss to her inner thighs that caused her to wiggle and laugh.

"I actually like the teasing. Getting me worked up feels a lot better than diving straight in. You know, just as a suggestion."

"Guess you're in luck because kissing and teasing are two things I'm amazing at." Caressing the soft, delicate skin on her inner thighs, my lips and fingers took turns exploring the wetness of her pretty pussy, her scent making me want to devour her whole. If her taste was half as addicting as her smell, I was never going to want to come up. Before long, I was nose-deep between her legs, licking and sucking, adjusting my technique with whatever she asked of me. Pulling hard on my hair, she moaned my name, announcing her inescapable arrival.

"Whatever you're doing right now, don't stop." Her legs clamped down around my neck as her desperate pleas begged me to make her come, making me more determined. With a final cry, I was met with a side of Luz I didn't get to often see, her vulnerable side, as her body went limp and the power behind her legs loosened around my neck. As if embarrassed, she covered her face with her hands, making it a time of many firsts. I'd never seen her act shy before. It was actually kind of cute.

As I attempted to lick and kiss the delicate softness I spent the last half hour acquainting myself with, she pulled away, begging me to stop. A minute ago, she was telling me *not* to stop. I swear, girls instructions were mystifying. "Things get sensitive down there, okay?"

I climbed on top of her, pulling her hands away from her face as I leaned into kiss her. Where my mouth had just been, maybe I should've asked first, but her taste was nothing to be ashamed of, and I didn't want to waste a second of this moment not proving that to her.

"Mmm...that was so nice," she said with a bite to her lips as she reached for the painfully hard erection eating her pussy had given me. Who knew focusing on someone else's pleasure could make me as stiff as a board.

"Evan, I know this is kind of sudden, but do you have any condoms?"

My eyes widened to saucers at the boldness of her question. It wasn't like I didn't think about having sex with her. I thought about it all the time, but things were moving faster than intended, and I'd only *just* mastered how to bring her to orgasm with oral sex. Penetrative sex felt like a huge deal.

"Um yea, I do." It came out in a stutter. "Have you ever had sex with a guy?"

She shook her head, confirming my suspicions. "Are you sure

you want to go that far with me? I'm fine with not rushing. I'm going to have to learn to start breathing through my mouth, though. You don't make breathing easy when your legs are cutting off my air supply," I joked, leading her to kiss me as her hands pulled down on my sweats and took a firm grip on the length of my cock. All right, so this was happening.

Practicing patience, I took my time exploring her body, taking mental notes of how she liked to be touched and where on her naked body she liked to be kissed. Anticipation pulsed through me that today marked the day I'd finally be inside of her, losing myself to the inner depths of her warmth. Not in a rush to finish, I just needed her body under mine. "I want to feel you."

She cried out to me as I took her breast in my hand with a firm yet gentle grip, assaulting her neck and throat with hungry, carnal kisses. "I want to feel you too. I just don't want to hurt you." I leaned in for a tender kiss as she wrapped her arms around my bare back, my anxiety decreasing at the presence of her touch.

"You won't hurt me if you take your time," she cooed and with that, I slid in slowly, her welcoming entrance embracing me without any resistance.

Being inside of her was the best feeling in the world. Better than any home game. Better than any test drive of a car I couldn't afford. Better than any free throw that landed in the basket with less than seconds to spare. The only thing even close was the sound of her voice moaning my name and her lips pressing against me. I was desperate to pick up my tempo, but for her sake, I took my time. When she rotated her hips in slow, deliberate circles around my cock, I pulled her body closer, feeling as deep as humanly possible, and with possessive kisses, she took hold of my mouth, letting me know who my lips belonged to. As I spread her thighs further open, the sharp gasp that left her mouth almost forced me to slow down. She took my face in her hands, assuring me that she was enjoying it when she begged me not to stop.

"It feels so good, baby. I promise. Just take your time, okay? I don't want this feeling to end," she whispered as she reached down to her clit, her moans growing louder at the combination of touching herself and the thrusts of my uncomfortable hardness. Rising up to watch her play with herself caused my pace to quicken as I filled her with blunt promise. Instead of telling me to slow down, she lifted her hips to meet my strokes, and just that quickly, I didn't stand a chance.

Driving my hips into hers with speed and purpose, the walls were closing in on me as my orgasm approached. No girl had made me feel so good. So perfect. So whole. Having sex and fucking both had their purposes, but making love was an act I had yet to experience. Until Luz. I loved making love to her because deep down, I knew that I loved her. When she announced her arrival, too, I held back, wanting to experience the chance of a mutual surrender. Grasping and groaning, we gave into the joined pleasure our bodies had to offer and with sweat dripping down my forehead, I leaned in for one long, messy kiss.

"I think I'm falling in love with you," I panted, trying to catch my breath. It hadn't mattered that she didn't say the words back. I just wanted to tell her how *I* felt. In time, I hoped she could trust me enough to tell me the same.

"You think?" she asked, surprising me with what she said next. "Because I know I'm falling in love with you. I'm just not good at saying it all the time," she gushed. I didn't care if I heard it every day or once a week as long as I knew that she loved me. I'd say it enough for the both of us.

CHAPTER TWENTY-EIGHT

Now

Luz

Seriously, there was nothing like the overpowering sense of euphoria after some good, old-fashioned sexual healing. Yea, the feeling was temporary, but it was my favorite calm after the storm.

"Mmm...that was amazing," I cooed as Evan rolled into the open space at my side. My head had hit the pillow, but every limb of mine had liquefied to Jell-O. From the looks of things, Evan hadn't been affected. I didn't doubt that he was strong enough to go another round.

The only sight of him I was lucid enough to pay attention to was his chest, as there was just enough hair to give it a gentle tug but still appear visibly toned. It was making me want to mount him *one* last time before I fell asleep.

"One can only be as good as his teacher," Evan mocked before reminding me how much of this love bet we'd actually gotten through. I didn't realize we were even keeping track at this point. My piece would be inspired by the experience, but I couldn't see myself limiting our bedroom fun to *just* three times. The pitch was merely clickbait.

"I wonder what will happen after the third time." His expression sunk from warm to serious in that moment.

"Evan, just enjoy the moment. You don't think we're actually going to get rid of each other automatically after three sessions, do you?" My statement appeared to soften him despite his stare being laser focused on me.

Damn, did I have crust in my eyes or something? Please let it not be a dry booger hanging at the front of my nostril. To snap him out of it, I gently kicked his leg underneath the covers. "What?"

Evan smiled. "Nothing. You're just beautiful."

Gosh, he was so corny. I almost couldn't stop the forced laugh that escaped my lips. "Don't tell me you're catching major feelings already," I taunted. Apparently, Evan didn't catch that.

"Luz, I can't catch what I already had."

I sat up for the first time since my body had melted into the mattress. "Evan, stop playing."

"How am I playing?"

He was really going to make me say it. "You don't have to gas me up for my sake."

"Luz, do I make you that insecure as a partner? Because every time I have a good feeling about us, it seems that you're okay with us failing, and I'm not okay with that."

My face dropped as his comment put me in defense mode, and I wasn't sure where this conversation was about to go.

"Evan, I'm not intentionally trying to sabotage us. I just want to be realistic when it comes to what we're doing right now. Falsified or not, I don't think you understood how it felt when I thought you betrayed me," I defended softly, hoping I didn't sound as upset as he did.

"I know," he fell back. "I just can't help thinking no matter how much I show you've I've changed, you'll keep using our past against us, and I just want us to move forward and the outcome of this won't be determined by your pride over an article."

Ugh, I hated when his tell-it-like-it-is persona forced me to reexamine myself.

"Evan, half of the social experiments that I write about have to be interesting enough to get readers to click. I have to make things compelling enough for millennials to care while making sure I also capture the eyes of Gen-Zs. I'm probably going to leave out half the stuff you and I went through, just because I want something for myself. I'm not going to sabotage what we're doing to make it more interesting because that's what it always sounds like you're suggesting." Hoping that set the record straight, I hid half of my face into my pillow.

"Luz. I know what you're doing," he accused. "You're trying to manipulate me into not being mad at you because it works." His reappearing smile convinced me he wasn't as upset as he wanted me to think he was, but it did seem like he was holding onto this conversation for a while.

"I think I'm secure about us but I'm also insecure about you. That we're going to blow this second chance, and I'm going to go another decade and a half wondering what I did wrong." He had definitely been holding on to that when I was too comfortable and sexed-up to move. We said we'd have an open dialogue about when things changed between us, and it was clear I wasn't holding up my end of the bargain.

"Confession time. A few years ago, I had a really bad breakup. It was so bad that I didn't even know if I can handle more than sex half the time." Very few of my past relationships affected my self-esteem, but this one relationship I was in affected me more than the rest.

For something that lasted so little time, this individual had been an emotional strain on me, and in turn, I became an emotional strain on my family, that as far as they were concerned, was my fault I couldn't make it work. Admitting as much as I felt comfortable made me feel better but also made me feel weak. I hated everything that relationship did to me.

"Okay."

"Just okay?" I ask, now on the defensive. He wanted me to admit it, but now he didn't want to hear it?

"I think I get your reservation. There's still some pause when it comes to me based on what we were, but I'm trying to be understanding that other people hurt you too. I don't want to hurt you anymore. I just don't know how to show you that because you continue to hold a part of yourself back."

Evan had been going above and beyond. That fact that he needed me to reassure him had showed just how a nonchalant comment or two in jest affected him, even if he didn't admit it at that moment.

"You do show it to me. Every day. Maybe I don't tell you enough, but that's something I can work on. I just need you to work on your patience. I know you're trying to be understanding, so thank you." As I leaned in for a peck on the lips, Evan melted into the space between us until we were almost the same breath, drowning into each other. This communication shit was kinda nice.

"Maybe you think I'm moving too fast, but I'm not going to hide how much I love you. At least not anymore."

"That's a bold statement to make."

"Well, I don't have anything to hide from you."

It was as if once he said that, all the guilt I had from hiding things rose to the end of my throat like bile, trying to force its way through. I had my own confessions to make, maybe not as intense as love, but certainly something I could no longer hold onto if I were going to put myself in the position to admit I loved him too.

"I want to say it back...but I have something to confess that might make you hate me," I blurted out as I hid under the outer sheet, revealing nothing but my eyes from underneath.

"Nothing you say could ever make me hate you."

I don't think he knew what he was saying. Let's hope that he lived up to that statement once the truth came out. "So, remember long ago, when we were oh-so-young-and-foolish? Since we're not judging each other for shit that's in the past?"

"Okay?" Hints of confusion laced his tone.

"And we're *understanding* of things that happened that are beyond our control?" I tried to emphasize the word understanding so he'd be forced to remember things he had recently said about not being mad at me.

"So, I might have, kinda sort of...been the person who slashed your tires and keyed your car—"

"I knew it!" he growled through gritted teeth and a hard-to-read expression.

"But we said we weren't judging each other for past mistakes, right? Unless you want to go ham on them backsies."

"Luz Marisol De Los Santos, I'm not mad at you," he continued to lie through clenched teeth and a fake smile. Plus, he was saying my entire name too? "I'm just disappointed by your choice, but we were young. So, I forgive you, but I think it's only fair of me to ask for an apology."

"For what?" I asked surprised.

"Baby, you just admitted you destroyed the car that I spent four years saving up for."

"And it was because I thought you cheated on me. A low act of revenge, I admit, but I was justified."

"Luz, I apologized for something I didn't do. The least you could do is apologize for something you actually did."

He did have a point, but I thought we weren't judging for past shit, so he was already going back on that promise.

"I'm sorry I destroyed your car. I wanted to hurt you the same way I thought you had hurt me, and while I still feel I was justified at that time, it was wrong of me to do." Phew, that took so much energy to admit I was wrong. How does anybody manage that?

"Do you forgive me?" I asked impatiently, wondering why he hadn't had much to say after the fact.

"That depends," he smiled back.

"Depends on what?"

"How long you can take my face between your legs?"

CHAPTER TWENTY-NINE

Luz

"Ain't no way I'm missing my touch-up for you. From the looks of your hands, you could use a manicure too."

It had been a few weeks since Candice and I had a self-care pamper session, and after a beginning like 2020, Candice vowed never to take getting her hair, nails, and feet done for granted. Despite being so good at doing her own curly hair, she was a jack-of-all-trades yet master of none when it came to everything else about her upkeep.

When I started dating someone new, I always felt obligated to maintain most of my beauty rituals. But seeing how I'd been so comfortable with Evan, I didn't always bother with keeping up unnecessary appearances. When I suggested that Candice and I go to a movie instead of a nail salon, if you could witness a friendship deteriorate with one off comment, that was what I was facing if I didn't apologize immediately and succumb to the original plan.

"Bitch, this better be Black-owned," I said, trailing behind her into the establishment. A combination of musky incense and acetone assaulted my olfactory senses as Candice pranced over to the reception area to inquire about the wait time.

"They said fifteen minutes." She took the open seat next to me, reaching for the mini-brochure of nail color options to choose the colors for her mani/pedi.

"What color are you going with? I'm thinking white for my toes but robin's egg blue for my nails. It won't go with everything, but I love that light blue brings out my skin tone."

It went without saying that Candice's dark brown hue brought out the undertones of anything that contrasted it, but with so much on my mind, I couldn't process what might stand out on me other than the fire engine red I normally went with.

"I'm not picky."

"You're not picky, but you're probably about to go with the same red you always go with," she said pettily.

"I'm just sayin'. If it's good enough for Annalise Keating, then it's good enough for me," I shadily defended. Even when we threw shade each other's way, it was always in good fun. The fact that it's taken this long for us to hang out showed I need to make a little more effort when it came to the other important relationships in my life.

One of the receptionists offered tea, coffee, or mimosas as the shared look between us could only mean one thing. We were going with the mimosas.

"So, how is everything going with that Valentine's Day piece? Haven't seen you in a while so you must be dating—fucking—something," Candice said from the boldness of the champagne in her system.

I was hesitant to be completely transparent because I didn't want to sound like I was bragging, but I wanted her to know why our weekly hangouts missed a session or two. "It's been a couple of weeks since our first real date," I emphasized with air quotes. "But Imma be real, girl. We barely made it to the first one before we were...girl, you know?" I said in an arrogant huff, trying not to go into my usual familiar outburst.

"Wow," Her tone was accusatory and judgmental. "So, you out here getting your nasty on, and you didn't think to let me in on it."

"Look, when you're about to get broke off, tell me if you'd call me right after," I said, and from the looks of the other patrons, we were getting a little rowdier than the salon's etiquette required. If we wanted to keep our wait time, we felt it best to keep it down.

"So, is he the guy?"

"Girl, we ain't had sex but two times." Three if you counted the oral. "He's got some major pluses, but we are taking it *slow*."

Candice shooed me away as if she didn't believe a word I said. "You out here crooked smiling and bragging like you don't got sense. If you're happy, what are you waiting for?"

Was it really that easy? Candice certainly made it sound so. I won't pretend as though Evan isn't special. With all the qualities that complemented him, the ones I loved the most had only gotten better with age, and physically, I was ready for him in my life, but emotionally? I wasn't sure I had the emotional stability to take it there yet.

"Evan actually likes the pace in which things are going. I like the way things are going. I'm probably not going to go into as much detail as other situations, but I want to make it at least look like I'm trying to make an interesting piece." Plus, we had reached two-thirds of our bedroom fun in less than four weeks. What kind of person realistically fell for someone in a month?

"You better than me. If I felt half of what you're feeling now, I wouldn't be out here kissing frogs and dodging busters," she said as if she were exhausted with her dating pool. If nothing had changed from last time, she was practically celibate and that was where she differed from me.

"So, I'm happy. Was that what you wanted me to say?" I defended, hoping the admittance would silence her comments about the whole thing once and for all. I didn't want to jinx what me and Evan had until I knew what it wasn't. And even then, we respected each other's boundaries not to share the pillow talk between potentially serious partners.

"What is up with you, anyway? How are all those nieces and nephews?" I wanted so bad to put the attention on her, but there was so little I could bring up that wouldn't put her in a negative mental space. Her family life outside of her sisters wasn't ideal; she wasn't in love with her career path, and I couldn't bring up things she had chosen not to share. However, she loved talking about her niece and nephew.

"I don't have either of them for the weekend. Marcia took her son to Universal Studios with her husband. Which who the hell goes to Universal Studios in 2020? Joujou's daughter is staying with her father's family since my sister wanted her home for Thanksgiving." I wondered if she'd ever not have to be split between two sisters given that they didn't have a good relationship.

"So, I'll probably just be doing another self-care weekend. No big deal."

One of the nail technicians approached the couch where we found refuge and asked us to choose which one of us would go first. Since this was more for Candice than for me, I volunteered her and assured her that I would take the next one. "You go ahead. I'm only getting a manicure anyway."

Candice sat up and before she was led to the pedicure area, a scream left my mouth the moment I looked at my phone.

"Girl, are you crazy?"

"I'm sorry. I'm just surprised." I looked back down at my phone to confirm I wasn't dreaming.

Evan: Tickets to the Millennium Tour w/ a B2K as the headliners. Second chance to get it right. What do you say?

Anxious to text a reply, another message came from Candice as she hadn't enough time to ask me what happened.

Candice: Girl, what are you screaming for? You know they're already looking at us from earlier.

Not knowing who to text first, I replied in a rushed headspace and nearly replied to the wrong person.

Me: You know how I said I don't want to brag, but Evan got me tickets to a reunion concert this weekend. This thug about to cry *water-works emoji*

Candice: Good for you. I'm not sure what else a woman could ask for outside of a ring.

Me: You know I'm not worried about marriage

Evan: It's okay if that's too last minute. Just wanted to make up for old times.

Ugh, I hated when two people were texting you at once. I went into Evan's thread to ensure I wrote the right person.

Me: I would love to. Would you believe I still listen to them?

Evan: Phew. Was worried you would think it's corny but already bought the tickets, so that's a relief.

We went back and forth for a bit before I noticed I hadn't replied Candice back when another technician approached me. I wouldn't have both my hands free, so I opted to text Candice back after letting Evan know I couldn't talk.

Me: Candice, getting called up. I'll try to save you a seat when you're done with your toes. If you wanted me to admit I liked Evan, you're in for an earful.

CHAPTER THIRTY

Before

Evan

Time flew when you were naked and having sex with your girl-friend. Sweaty and sticky in all the right places, I knew I would need to shower soon but none of that mattered minutes after you busted a nut. "God, I could live between your legs all day. Tell my folks I'm not going to Temple. I'm enrolling in the Universidad de Luz."

She laughed, laying a playful slap to my shoulder and throwing a shot at how corny I was, knowing deep inside she loved it. "You came, right?" Bunching a sheet over her body, she reached for the closest shirt on the floor she could find, followed by the boy shorts I'd slipped off earlier.

"If you have to ask, then you'll never know." With Luz's body, her pleasures were still a learning curve for me. She was great at telling me what she did and didn't like and understood that just because I was more experienced in some areas didn't mean I knew what I was doing everywhere else. She could have totally been a writer for those magazines she obsessed over, but I was going to have to get better at telling if a girl was faking. Slipping on my boxers, I followed her to the living room and put my arms around her as she checked her answering machine.

"Can I get a hint? It sounded like you came, but you're the one always telling me not to assume things." She shushed me as her mom's voice poured through the speakers, wanting to know why her mother called twenty minutes ago while we were, *ahem*, fooling around.

"Ay negra. It's Mom. They're cutting back hours, so I'm coming home early. I wanted to get a head start on your cake—"

The message cut off. With an hour commute and a message that was left twenty minutes ago, we didn't have much time to mask the scent of sex.

"Holy shit!" I panicked as I hauled ass to get my clothes on Luz's bedroom floor. Pulling my jeans over my legs, I nearly tripped trying to put on my sneakers. "I wish I could've stayed longer." I threw on my jacket and freaked when I didn't readily see my book bag. "Especially since you won't tell me if I made you come or not. I would've happily gone down on you again—"

"Twice, okay?" she grumbled. "I wasn't even going to say anything because of that big goofy grin on your face right now."

Gosh, had I been smiling? I was really getting good at this sex shit. She hit me over the shoulder, pushing me toward the hallway as she managed to slip her bra back on without ever taking off her shirt. "I'm sorry, I just got distracted. *Twice, you said?*" I held up two fingers to gloat.

"Evan, instead of focusing on that, you need to focus on remembering it's my birthday tomorrow and that my mom is probably going to want you to stop by for food and cake," she scolded as she directed me to her front door.

Whether or not her mom suspected, it wasn't a good look to have her find me here while we were alone. "How could you think I'd forget about something that important?" I said as her features softened.

"I guess I'm used to just being around only family for my birthdays. Since it's my eighteenth, she asked me what I wanted and I told her I nothing big. So, it'll just be my mom, you, and me."

As I leaned over to kiss her adorable forehead, I assured her I wouldn't miss it for the world. "I promise I'll be here bright and early, so tell your mom to bake whatever she needs to. I will fuck up my whole diet just to make room for whatever Dominican dessert she has planned." Luz laughed, edging me toward the door again, and I pulled her close to me and left her with one last kiss. "I love you, silly." This time when she pushed me through the door, she did so with finality but opened the door to whisper a quick I love you back.

———

Not to insult my mom's cooking, but if there was anyone that cooked better than Ma, it was Luz's mom Danyeli. I'm not sure I ever tasted a cake this fluffy before; hell, I was even tempted to get the recipe before I left. I didn't think anything could top her deditos de novia or girlfriend fingers in English, but like most things, I was proven wrong. Her bizcocho was so airy and moist like no other cake I had ever had; it practically melted in my mouth. The pineapple filing added this tart surprise I wasn't expecting and the icing was so sweet, I wasn't ashamed to have licked my fingers clean.

"Have some more cake, papi." Her mom added another plate in front of me before I could object as Luz explained to me not everything she cooked was traditionally Dominican. They were more like things she tried and liked and then added Dominican touches to it. The plantain cups she prepared had this amazing tasting avocado mash with a catering-style arrangement of shrimp. With her culinary talents, she could have owned her own restaurant, and I would've gladly been her first regular customer. Bachata played in the background, and by the fifteenth attempt of asking, I let her mom teach me how to dance to it. Dancing had never been my strong point, having tree trunks for arms and javelin polls for legs. I felt like it was destiny to be that awkward white boy who needed liquid courage just to do a simple two-step.

Danyeli was definitely a better teacher, but she was so small in stature, it proved difficult not to step on her tiny feet. Luz was definitely a better fit and more talented than she let on. The way her hips moved made bachata look so simple, and I was in love with how sexy she looked dancing. "Papi, you dance so good!" her mom said, laying it on thick. When the next track was a slow song, I asked if we could sit down, prompting Luz to mouth the words thank you for the third time tonight.

"Evan, mira! Come see the pictures we took at her quince," her mom said as a photo album materialized out of nowhere ready to humiliate Luz in her fifteen-year-old awkwardness. She opened up to a page of Luz wearing a poufy blue dress fit for prom and a tiara adorning her once shorter fro. Luz's mom loved showing how proud she was of Luz as documented throughout photo albums; there was a new one every time I came over.

"Wow, Luz. Is that you?" I fought back laughs as she met my gaze with furrowed brows.

"She didn't want to have one, but it's tradition and the one birthday when a girl becomes a woman." Flipping through the pages of more memories, I concluded that Dominican get-togethers mirrored Italian ones with the wall-to-wall guests at every party. She was so cute as a kid; if I had been lucky enough to see her at the playground, I would have totally begged her to be my girlfriend at five. She probably would've been one of those girls that let you have it in the sandbox, but what could I say; I would've proudly been her victim.

"Time to open your presents!" her mother exclaimed, the guilt building up inside me knowing I had been fearing this moment. Danyeli handed her a collection of moderately sized gifts, along with a few gift bags she claimed were from her aunts and uncles. Luz tore open the first gift, her face scrunching in confusion at the CD in her hands. "Thanks, Mom," Luz said with forced enthusiasm. Before I knew it, the spotlight was on me.

"Papi, what did you buy for Luz? Por favor, don't keep us in suspense."

"Ma, he doesn't have to give it to me now," Luz whined, which only made me feel worse about the bad news I'd be delivering on my girlfriend's birthday.

"Luz, you don't have to speak for him. He can talk," she said in her thick accented English that made me feel like I was on trial.

"Umm, so, the thing is I did get you something, but it didn't arrive yet." I was relieved when the house phone rang, and her mom excused herself to answer it. "You don't look that happy with what your mom got you." I attempted to throw the attention off me. Sooner or later, I'd have to explain what happened and it was better with just her there than her and her mom.

"So, the thing is I know my mom did her best, but I don't even listen to Hikaru Utada. She's more like J-pop and I like J-rock. She doesn't know the difference because they both sound the same to her. I didn't want to sound ungrateful for pointing it out, but I'll try to give it a chance." She tossed it with a bag of hair supplies she received as a gift from her aunt in Jersey. It was now or never.

"Luz, I feel terrible for not bringing your present on time; it's just I wanted to surprise you because even though you play it off like your musical taste is so edgy, when I took a glance at your most-played songs, seven out of ten were from B2K. That's when

I found out they were playing at Kodak and saw their tickets were sold out, so I found some tickets on eBay."

Her eyes lit up, taking a nearby pillow on the couch to conceal her cries as she screamed into it. She fanned her face anxiously, and I almost didn't have the heart to tell her the whole truth. "Oh my god, Evan. Please don't tell me you got me tickets to see them?" She only calmed down when she sensed my grim mood.

"Well, that's just it. I thought that was what I was getting, but it turns out when I got them in the mail and tried to redeem the tickets in person, the venue told me that I got scammed. I can definitely get my money back, but it's going to take seven to ten days, leaving me broke until then. I didn't have the time or the cash to get you something else in time," I shamefully admitted. I felt like an idiot for getting scammed but an all-out loser for ruining her first birthday with me as her boyfriend.

"Gosh, I'm so sorry that happened. When was the concert supposed to be?" she asked with a long face.

"Tonight, at the Kodak Center. In my head, it lined up perfectly with your birthday. But I guess it was too good to be true."

Without explanation, she grabbed her jacket and pulled me toward her room. As I stood outside her bedroom door, I watched as she grabbed a pile of CDs and zoomed past me to tell her distracted mother we would be back before curfew. Rushing me to put my shoes back on, I had no clue where we were going, let alone what we were doing. By the time we made it out to my car, I paused, knowing I didn't have the gas to be driving around with no set destination.

"Luz, can we stop for a second? Where are we going?"

With a straight face and a calm tone, she informed me we were going to that concert. "There's nothing the venue can do about getting my money back. Besides it's like eight bucks to park in their parking lot, and I don't even have *that*. That's how broke I am."

She took my hand and led me to my car, promising she would fit the bill for the parking but only if we left *now*. When we got there, as expected, the parking lot was packed with a mob of teenyboppers dressed head to toe in the groups' memorabilia, entering the venue in packs of three of more. "Okay, we're here. Now what?"

As I put my car in park, she gave me this look as if it was obvious. From her bag, she popped in one of the CDs she brought with her, turning the volume to the max. As the music played, her dance moves became obnoxiously adorable, her off-key singing only a mother could love. She was pretending that she was inside the venue having the time of her life and making the best out of a bad situation.

"Just so you know; I like you despite of your boy band obsession. I literally have to be in love with you because if I were by myself, by now, I would've taken this thing out and backed over it with my car." I teased as I turned the volume down a few notches.

"Baby, I'm so sorry for not coming through for you on your birthday. When I get the chance to make it up to you, it'll be a big thing."

"You know, if you really want to make it up to me, you'll stop pretending you don't know the lyrics and sing along with me."

Why did that have to be one hundred percent true? It wasn't as if I knew the songs by choice. Pep rallies, dances, and house parties proved that everyone listened to them at our school.

"You know what? Fuck it." I turned the volume up and joined her in her off-key singing. You only turn eighteen once, and I wanted this to go down as her best birthday ever. When years went by and we were still together and in love, possibly even married with kids, we would remember all the times we shared, when it was just us against the world.

CHAPTER THIRTY-ONE

Now

Luz

The night air was cool but warm for an early November evening and because I was on such a high from the concert, instead of taking a cab back to Evan's, we opted to let our feet take us home. It wasn't until he reached for my hand that I realized I was shaking, not yet down that this had all happened—and in front row seats, no less.

"You know, Evan, I think I can finally call my existence complete now. I finally got to see Omarion in concert and with all the other members of B2K. It's like I know it happened and we literally just left there, but it really feels like it was a dream."

With a raise of his unique eyebrow, he shot me this look of confusion. "You do realize after that R.Kelly scandal, your so-called *man* made a promise to retire all the songs you happened to be singing the loudest to right? Because you know he wrote those, right?"

He had no problem reminding me. Even when we were kids, he had found my obsession with them obnoxious, especially since I had my whole J-Rock stage, and let's just say none of that sounded like the hip-hop and rock he and his friends listened to. While I was aware that Omarion had vowed that this tour would be the last time they ever performed those songs live, they could've retired their entire set list for all I cared. I'd not only seen it but also danced my ass off until my legs were sore, and after that horrid special airing of all the details of how many lives that man destroyed, I understood that this would be my last time indulging in those songs.

"Correct," I replied snarkily. "But that still doesn't take away from tonight. I had the time of my life." Dressed as if I belonged in another decade, I looked ridiculous and out-of-date in my throwback basketball mini dress. I had to score this thing on eBay because after sorting through my old clothes, everything I owned looked like a Japanese rock star wore it first.

Evan had chosen *not* to take it all the way back to 2005 with his clothing choice, but he was dressed more reminiscent of how he looked as a teenager, choosing a pair of sporty sweatpants, an oversized hoodie, and a pair of classic three-striped white Adidas. He'd nearly pushed it with his baseball cap to the back, but we'd reached a stage in this whole experiment where I'd found him attractive no matter what he said or did. I had to admit that he was cute with his hair out of his face.

"You know, I wasn't sure you'd enjoy yourself half as much as you did," he smiled warmly. "I'm thrilled you had such a good time. Remember when I wanted to take you to the concert for your eighteenth birthday and it didn't turn out the way I'd planned?"

I did remember and how devastated he'd been breaking the news to me that he had been scammed. As great as it would have been to experience it then, it meant more to me to experience it now as an adult because I rarely did anything that I wasn't embarrassed to admit that I'd enjoy. Plus, if I was being real, at eighteen, I wasn't even trying to be critical. At least now, I recognized some songs weren't sending out the right messages or weren't as genius as I thought back then.

I was just happy to have this memory. Few things made me feel like a kid again, and being there reminded me of a time when I thought I could conquer the world. I wish I could say it was the concert alone but no. Evan's presence made it feel more complete.

"Evan, trust me when I say this. I have not had this much fun in a long while. I can't thank you enough for giving me this experience. How will I ever repay you?" I feigned, knowing damn well tonight would be when I got a head start on repaying his kindness with his cock in my mouth and suffering through all his beloved sports programs without a single complaint.

"It's funny you should mention repaying me." He brought our locked hands up to his mouth, planting a soft kiss on the back of mine. "I already know how you can. It's actually something I've been dying to ask you, but I always talked myself out of it, thinking it was too soon or not the right time or some other insecure reason I stopped myself from popping the question."

Popping the question?! I know he hadn't planned on asking me to marry him. Don't get me wrong; things were going well, but they weren't going *that* well. This had only been our second date on paper, but I was almost positive that tonight was going to be our third time being intimate. Would he really ruin things by throwing something as foolish as a marriage proposal out there? It had been some time since I last prayed, but if that was where this conversation was going, I prayed he would survive the big fat no I was prepared to tell him.

"Um...as long as it's appropriate at this stage of our relationship," I threw out, hoping it would deter something that felt too soon. Given the ambitious look on his face, whatever he was going to ask of me, he was sure I'd say yes.

"I think it is, but you're welcome to disagree." He shrugged and carried on with his lengthy explanation. "I was going back to Rochester for the holidays in the next few weeks."

That's right; Thanksgiving was upon us. As much as I missed my mother's pastelón, I didn't go back home as often as I liked and for good reason. My family was easier to deal with all split up, but the second we were all gathered in one area, it was a recipe for disaster. Instead of focusing on the good in my life, everyone always seemed to zero in on the bad. It was mainly my aunts, or rather one aunt, but she was an expert at making everyone see how much of a failure she thought I was. It didn't matter that I had this great job, or living independently in the city, or checking off all my goals. She was always quick to remind me that even if I was a success in work, I was shit at keeping a relationship. No matter how many times she said it, it always hurt like the first time.

"I was wondering if you'd planned to go back home too, would you have any time to break away for a while? I know you most likely have plans with your own family, but it would really mean a lot to me if I could steal you away for a bit to meet mine."

My mouth dropped in surprise. That was definitely *not* the proposal I was expecting, but I suppose I should have been relieved. It was *a* proposal but only an invitation to meet his folks. We were having fun, but neither one of us had put a clear label on it. Meeting parents felt like we were in the headed for serious category. Were we already getting serious?

"It's just that Thanksgiving is the only holiday everyone makes time to get together, so you wouldn't just be meeting my mom for the first time or meeting my father again. It'd be my entire family."

"So, would I be meeting everyone as your girlfriend or just

some girl you know because I need to prepare before I walk into that ring of fire."

We were soon in front of his apartment building, but instead of heading straight inside, he took my other hand as he turned to face me.

"That depends. Are you comfortable with the title of girl-friend? Because if not, I'm fine with telling everyone you're just a stowaway," he snorted as his face softly transformed as he awaited my answer.

Truthfully, I wasn't sure how serious an invitation made us, but what I did know was that I liked Evan—a lot. So much that the thought of him pairing the words *my* and *girlfriend* in reference to me had sent a jolt through my body and a chill up my spine. I'd met his dad on several occasions when we met at their family restaurant where Evan worked after school sometimes, but it always felt like his mom was off-limits and only a viable option once we got serious enough.

It worried me, though. If I accepted the invite, would I be the only Black person there because what I knew about Italian Americans was they ran deep and mostly stuck to their own kind. Lots of Italians I knew were pleasant and helpful, but there was always that percentage who were ignorant and didn't want their blood-lines tainted by anyone that looked even ten percent Black. I'd been there already, dating white or indigenous Latinos, and I just didn't want to be put through that sort of abuse again. What if they didn't like me? What if I wasn't a fan of their food? What if; what if; *what if*?

All these questions were making my mind spin in circles, espe-cially considering I had only a few weeks to turn in my article. Giving it more thought, I could make the holidays the cherry on top to my nearly finished piece. Whether good or bad, I'd been prepared to turn in more than one version, depending on the outcome, and the holidays could be a make or break addition to it. Reminding myself how many times my mom asked me whether

I was making Thanksgiving this year, I had more than one reason to return to my old stomping grounds. Plus, as much as I hated getting all mushy about this sort of thing, I was excited that he actually wanted me to meet his family.

"I'm comfortable with you introducing me as your girlfriend." The tense lines around his eyes eased when I gave him my answer.

"So, that means you'll come?"

He smiled wide as I bit my lip and nodded my head enthusiastically.

"How can I say no?"

He leaned in and kissed me as he wrapped his snake-like grip around me. As cheesy as it sounded, I loved seeing him this cheerful. The fact that he was excited about it convinced me his family didn't have the toxicity that my family usually brought with them. But then again, I didn't really know, so I had no choice but to wait and see.

"As long as you don't mind me splitting the time between our families. It would look sort of bad if I spent the entire time at yours and my mom found out I was back home." Because trust me, my mom was a regular Inspector Gadget when it came to finding things.

"That would be actually great. We can drive up together, and I'll drop you off at your mom's. Then you just call me when you're ready." As we walked through the lobby and into the elevator, I turned to him, asking the one question that would stay on my mind and riddle me with anxiety if I didn't.

"So...Evan. Am I going to be the only Black person there?"

He smiled widely, scratching the tip of his nose before turning to me.

"Listen, I don't want to lie to you. *Maybe*. But I wouldn't even invite you if I didn't know you would be one-hundred-percent comfortable. I would never put you in a situation where I couldn't protect you, even if it meant I had to check my own family. Besides, you're not the only Black girl I've ever introduced to my family; you're just the only one who wasn't African American. But that's not going to matter because no one's going to be anything less than welcoming. Is that cool?"

Letting his words sink in, I couldn't remember the last time a person I dated made me feel safe and didn't require me to act stronger than I was.

I could just be soft. I could just be girly. I could just be...me.

CHAPTER THIRTY-TWO

Evan

"Mary, you good back there?" I asked from the front seat, resulting in a loud bark from my girl in the backseat. Luz turned around and scratched underneath her chin, calming her enough to lie out on the seat. With both my girls in my ride, we were on our way back to our hometown of Rochester.

The holidays were upon us, and I couldn't be more nervous yet excited at the same time that my entire family was about to meet the girl I was serious about.

"Looking forward to any particular dish your mom is known for during the holidays," I asked, trying to keep myself entertained during the long drive. I was wired on caffeine and sugar, so a quiet car wasn't going to keep my mood and energy high.

"I'm not sure. My family didn't celebrate Thanksgiving before they moved to United States because it's not a Dominican holiday. The meal plan isn't always the same, but we try to keep things as traditional as possible. There's obviously some crossover with dishes served normally at Christmas."

That made sense. Most of my family back in Italy had never heard of Thanksgiving, let alone celebrate it. Since both my parents were American and their parents before them, most of our traditions had been set in stone before I was even born.

Luz mentioned that while they sometimes have turkey, they typically had a few other meat dishes to choose from that were more in line with Dominican culture. Sides like rice and beans along with festive casseroles and desserts made the menu. While I loved our traditional antipasti platters and hard-to-replicate pasta dishes, remembering her mother's cooking made my mouth water.

"So, is this your first time back since March?" I asked, prompting me to think about my last visit. It had meant she hadn't been back to Rochester in nine months. My schedule made it challenging to come back for every holiday, but I did my best to juggle attending weddings, birthdays, God forbid, funerals, and any Catholic holiday or major family event. Thanksgiving and Christmas were non-negotiables.

I would be too scared to come back if I came for anything less than that, but having met and developed a relationship with Luz's mom, I couldn't imagine not coming to see her only once a year. If she were still as warm as I remember, it wouldn't have been a challenge for me to pop in if I had known my company wouldn't be unwelcome.

"My family is a bit—overwhelming at times. It used to be that I would come back for every major holiday. Maybe celebrate birthdays. But now, they're lucky if I make it for Easter, Christmas, or Thanksgiving." She admitted that it wasn't uncommon for her to get into highly sensitive arguments with an old-fashioned uncle or nosy aunt on occasion. We all had that one family member. The one that complained that women weren't what they used to be. That men used to be "real men" back in their day. It was easy to ignore in my own family, but I wasn't sure how she navigated it in hers.

"Well, at least you'll get to spend time with your mom. I can't help but feel that she didn't even believe it was me, even when I talk to her over the phone," I admitted.

To set the ambiance for the ride, we both detailed how a typical family holiday went down. For the most part, my family was harmless, but they did mistake shyness for weakness, which I didn't think would be a problem for Luz.

Telling my parents I was bringing a girl home was like telling my entire family. Everybody knew, and I had to silence the family group text to prevent all the interruptions along the way. It has been years since my breakup with my ex, Amanda, and despite how well she could've fit in my family, they had never embraced her into the hive. She was never shy around me, but the louder and brasher the crowd got, the more introverted she became. Not exactly a selling point in an Italian-American family.

"Are you looking forward to anything in particular?" Luz asked, desperate to shift the conversation away from herself.

"Just you meeting my family, but only because they're so anxious to meet you."

She pretended to *aw* after gagging at the cheesiness of it. Her mom's place came first on the GPS, so the moment we started seeing Rochester city line signs; it wouldn't be long before I'd be dropping her off.

Her mother had moved to a new area, one that seemed safer and decimals quieter. I had never been intimidated by the neighborhood they used to live in, but for someone her age and size, I'd be worried about traveling alone at night. "Alright, Mary, I'm going to help Luz up. Stay here, ok?"

Ms. Mary Mack rested her chin on her paws as if she had planned to do that anyway. Luz exited out the car before I could open the door for her, so I met her in the middle by beating her to her suitcase in the trunk.

We barely made it past the sidewalk before a high shriek came from the front door of Luz's mom's house. Danyeli, with hair that was bigger and curlier than I remembered, greeted us with open arms. Her face hadn't changed much; hell, her looks hadn't changed at all. They always said don't judge a woman's beauty by how she looked in her youth since beauty fades, but that wasn't true about her mom. If that were true, Luz would probably never age because her mom looked like she just stepped out of a time machine. An excited squeal of recognition sounded between me and a hug.

I never forgot how tiny she was, barely reaching my chest. I picked her up and swung her in place. She gave me a kiss on the cheek and I put her down, as she made every excuse to touch me —in an appropriate way, of course— claiming she couldn't believe it was actually me.

"Evan, you stayed so handsome over the years. How did you manage?" she flirted.

"When you tell me your secret, I'll tell you mine." I winked back, which seemed to get a quick blink-you-missed-it eye roll from Luz.

"Did you get taller since the last time I saw you?" She pulled me into the apartment, and I was immediately assaulted with the calming aromas of seasoned meats and sweet pastries. I didn't even get to bring in Luz's suitcase.

"Come, come. I made some empanadas just like you used to eat when we invited you for dinner."

Good times indeed. I could guarantee I'd never leave hungry after having dinner with Luz and Danyeli. Since it was the holidays, I didn't want to ruin my appetite, but I was sure I could find room for a pastry or two.

"I guess I'll just grab my own bag!" Luz yelled from the threshold of the apartment.

I immediately stopped what I was doing so I could help her drop it off to the desired room.

"Luz is so fussy. One minute she wants to independent; the next, she doesn't know what she wants," Danyeli deadpanned.

I promised I would help her to get settled, so it wasn't taking any time of my way to bring it upstairs.

Danyeli followed us both upstairs, too impatient to let me get further than the highest step. "You should meet mi mamá, Luz's abuela—"

"¿Como? Come on, Ma, her English isn't as good. I don't want her to feel insecure."

Danyeli waved her hand to dismiss Luz. "She just doesn't want you meeting my mother. Once she knows, everybody will know who you are," Danyeli explained. After pulling me in the direction of a room that looked spacious from the outside, Danyeli disappeared, confirming something in Spanish before she invited both of us in.

When I thought of a grandmother, my mind defaulted to a certain aesthetic that wasn't the women sitting before me on the bed. Luz's mother was a vision to behold; I don't think I'd ever met someone with a complexion that deep and with eyes that light, but the grey in her eyes made her appear fey-like, almost as if she wasn't real.

If I did the numbers, she had to have been at least in her seventies or eighties, but since her skin was so smooth, even darker than Danyeli's, her face was free of the lines I associated with a woman her age.

"This is Lourdes, Luz's grandmother and my mother."

Lourdes tapped the space beside her, an offer for me to take a seat. This close up, she was striking, so I can only imagine what she looked like when she had been Danyeli or Luz's age.

My ASL was ten times better than my Spanish, but considering Luz was concerned that her English wasn't strong, I wanted to try my best to use the Spanish that I knew. "Estoy encantado."

She shooed me away like she couldn't believe I would flirt with her considering Luz was just a few feet away. "You speak

Spanish?" she asked me in English with an accent not like her daughter's.

"Un poquito." As I held up my thumb and index finger to indicate how small the amount was.

She smiled and pointed to Luz. "¿Eres su novio?"

I was relieved to have been able to answer with a simple, "Si."

Lourdes laughed and spoke in the rapid-fire Spanish that made it hard to sound it out—something about babies, maybe? Luz rolled her eyes and then dragged me out the room.

"Gosh, what did she say? You got worked up all of a sudden," I observed.

"Boy, just take your empanadas and go before my mom and grandma decide they don't want you to leave," she said, forcing a cynical smile.

"Are you going to think about me while I'm gone?" I whispered, followed by something dirty about the after-hours we could spend getting frisky in my old room when it was time to switch places.

"Boy, you better stop." She pushed me away but only because she knew if I kept reminding her, she'd have a lot to answer for if her mom happened to walk in on us. Reaching in for one last kiss —in our case, a few last kisses—she wrapped up my pastries to go and walked me to my car and to see Ms. Mary Mack off until she joined us at my parents' house.

Danyeli watched from the second-floor window, waving assertively to make sure I saw her before I took off. Waving back, I secured my seatbelt, hoping it'd be as smooth integrating Luz into my family as much as it'd been meeting her grandmother.

———

"Alright, Mary. It's curtains up," I announced, pulling into the one free space on the street across from my parents' place. Different family members normally took turns hosting, but I always loved it best when Thanksgiving or any other holiday was held at my parents' home. The sense of familiarity was what made the holiday more inviting for me. I checked my phone to find two messages from Luz. My nosiness got the best of me as I gave her one more opportunity to share what her mom and grandmother had said that had gotten her so annoyed.

I also wondered if it wasn't rude of me to know why her mom and grandmother's accents we're not the same. To my surprise she answered both.

Luz: my Abuela said "They would make beautiful babies" and my mom agreed with her 🤦

It hadn't been as bad as I thought. I was hot; Luz was hot. But I know Luz was sensitive to certain topics when it related to colorism and how it was expected of some Black people to date and marry someone White. There was no way Luz was only with me for that reason but she feared that sometimes it would look that way to people who didn't know her personally.

There was one more message.

Luz: my abuela is Haitian. She moved to the Dominican Republic as a teen but lived most of her life there. It contributes to her accent, but she speaks Spanish more than Kreyol now.

Before I could reply, I felt an overwhelming sense of déjà vu as another wailing woman opened the door, screaming my name, arms wide spread.

"Evan, my baby!" My mother screamed, alerting just about every member in the house to exit stage right just to greet me. I was met by my uncles Luca, Vinny, Richie, and all the wives, cousins, and in-laws they brought along.

That wasn't even half of the family projected to be there either. In an Italian family, it would be a shocker *not* to shut down an entire street with all the family we invited.

"Where's your girlfriend? Don't tell me you got rid of her before you got here." A series of random thick New Jersey accents spoke all at once on top of each other.

"She's coming later tonight. She'll let me know if I have to pick her up or if she's taking an Uber, but she does have her own family, you know." That seemed to disappoint the crowd.

Once I convinced everyone to head back inside, a handful of my younger cousins took turns helping Ms. Mary Mack out the car and keeping her company while I got situated. Her temperament was neutral around family. As long as they kept her exercised, I couldn't see why she wasn't in good hands.

It was a full house, adorned with festive decorations and delectable smells coming from the kitchen. Every time I came here, I could never comprehend how the house that I'd grown up in never changed. All the photos on the wall detailing different stages in my life, the piano in the hallway, and not to mention all the furniture that remained in tip-top shape with the help of my mother's obsession with keeping most the company off the "good" sofa.

"So, should we be expecting wedding bells?" my father imposed, rustling his fingers through my hair as if I was still four foot three child and not a six foot four grown man.

"I like her," I underemphasized, knowing he found it weak to wear my heart on my sleeve. "Let's just keep it at that, okay?"

At the topic of marriage, it was as if my mother emerged from the shadows. "Well, I just want to make sure she's not a floozy. You know you're getting up there in age, so you don't know how to pick them as well as when you had better sense."

What was deemed appropriate and inappropriate had changed over the years, and with Luz's presence expected in a few hours, I had a to put a halt to all that well-intended tone of "telling it like it is" when company that didn't think like you was in attendance.

"Ma, I'm gonna need you to take it down a notch when it comes to comments like that."

"Like what?" she asked, feigning ignorance.

"My girlfriend isn't as old-fashioned as you guys. If I find *half* the things you say offensive, she's going to find 100% of the stuff you say offensive."

"Don't tell me you found one of those tree-hugging hipsters hell-bent on gentrifying the neighborhood."

"No, and she's also not Italian, so—"

"Well, what is she?"

I was tempted to answer that she was human, but I knew that level of sarcasm only encouraged my mom to hit me. "She's Dominican-American, Ma."

"Oh, so she's Spanish?"

"No, she's Dominican, and she will correct you if you call her Spanish. She's also Black, so please don't just go saying anything you feel like. Especially comments that are going to make you sound anti-Black."

"Anti-what?" Ma couldn't help sounding confused. If I had said racist, she would have given me a long list of how she could never be such a thing; the term anti-Black made it easier for me to challenge her without her ticking off every time she went out her way to be nice to a Black person.

"I know you're not trying to say we'll come off as not liking Black people. Your father's 100% Sicilian. Why, I'm sure if he hadn't married me, you'd be half Black yourself—"

"See, stuff like that. *Resist* the urge to say stuff like that. She's going to be the only Black person here, but we don't have to make her feel like it, okay?" My parents didn't fully understand my request but promised to be on their best behavior when it came to Luz spending time here.

She could be with her own family, but she was choosing to spend time with my family and me. I wanted this to be a good memory for her, not a bad one. After checking my parents for the final time, I took out my phone to shoot Luz one more miss you text before challenging my uncle to a game of Briscola, an Italian card game, and accepting the plate of food my mother made for me.

CHAPTER THIRTY-THREE

Luz

"Ma, would you get that dopey grin off your face?" I demanded of my mother. "You knew for a few weeks now that I reconnected with Evan." The second she saw him, she wouldn't stop smiling. You would think she was dating him and not me.

"I know, it's just I hadn't remembered how tall he was. The photos that you sent me don't do him justice in person. I hope you're doing what you need to keep him."

Sometimes, my mom gave the most antiquated, impractical advice. This was but one of the many reasons I hated telling my mom about any man I was dating. Comments like that just worked my nerves. *Keep him?* What about what he needed to do to keep me? When my mom said shit like that, it was as if she was living back in the DR, worshipping men that just gave you crumbs. In her head, there was a checklist on how to keep a man happy.

Praise him for anything and *everything* he did, practically be his sex slave, and always keep yourself looking like a model. I, for one, praised no man, unless he was an amazing person, and as far as sexual servitude went, that was a slippery slope for me. Evan never had to beg me to be intimate mainly because I was the one hitting him up for it. In the short time we'd rekindled our romance, we both respected each other's sexual boundaries. As for the last one, I looked cute only for myself, and if someone benefitted from my appearance, then so be it. When the time came to giving a partner what they needed, I didn't take advice from others. I just asked the person I was dating, flat-out, what they wanted from me. Most times, I could fulfill those needs, but if they were asking for the impossible, then it just meant that we weren't compatible. "Ma, I wish you wouldn't say things like that. It's misogynistic and old-fashioned."

"Misogino? I swear you're always trying to make me feel silly with all these words I don't know."

Turning away from her, I rolled my eyes but was sure to fix my face before I went into further detail. "It's a word that means saying or believing things that are harmful to women," I peacefully explained, only to have her shush me since my Abuelita had retired to a bedroom upstairs. Tito Gadiel and his wife usually took care of her most the year, and while my mom lived alone and could have, she preferred the peace and quiet. My mom liked having her around, though, and I noticed she called me less when Abuelita was staying with her. Her company made her feel less lonely.

"I'm only curious to whether it's serious, negrita. When you told me you had spent time with him, I thought maybe you only ran into him. But if he drove you here, does that mean he's your boyfriend?"

With a come-hither motion, she insisted I follow her to the kitchen to help out before the guests arrived. This was always my least favorite part of Thanksgiving. Being with Evan was spoiling me because every time I slept over his house, he took the wheel and always cooked for me, and when I did cook at home, it was usually just enough for one except for when Candice would drop by. Helping to cook for ten plus people was a thankless job only my mother took pride in. My ass just wanted to eat and pack several doggy bags, but I also didn't want to leave it up to my mom to do alone. Ugh, this trying to be a good daughter was exhausting around the holidays.

Most years, she volunteered to host at her place, but sometimes, family preferred not to drive as far as Rochester, so, my aunts have also hosted in NJ. I had a list of my family members that I dreaded seeing this holiday but also a handful I loved catching up with. My mom checked on her famous Pastelón, a Dominican-style Lasagna that was made with ripe plantains instead of pasta in the mini oven, and the robust smell coming from the oven let me know that the turkey was nearly done.

"Ma, can we just talk about something else for now?" I asked, not trying to hide that I wanted to keep some things to myself regarding my former high school sweetheart. Don't get me wrong, I actually loved talking to my mom about what was going on in my life, and dating should've topped that list, but sometimes, I would've been more open if she showed the same interest and respect for the women I dated. This selected interest made me not even want to discuss it, so it was either all or none.

Lifting the lid of the many pots she had simmering on the stove, it became apparent that my mom had already done most of the work and all she really needed help with was washing the mountain load of dishes that came from an entire days' worth of cooking. I wasn't mad because cooking with my mom had its challenges. I was all about measuring, and she was all about throwing what *looked* right in there. Story short, we clashed, but I will say everything with her on-sight measurements made everything taste like heaven on an island.

Her new place was quite spacious. Ever since I got the job working at the magazine, I was able to help her in ways I was never able to when I was in school. She was working full-time, renting a chair in a salon, and soon, her plan was to switch gears and open a bakery. Doing hair was something my mom loved but cooking? That was my mom's passion, and I fully supported her in her journey and planned to help with the down payment once she found a space to lease. In the meantime, I was just happy my mom found a safer place to live, but with a safer, bigger place meant more people could fit into her home. As much as I loved my family, certain people's presence was going to test my patience.

"So, Ma, how many places am I setting? Is it going to be just Tito, his wife and kids, and Abuelita?" I asked hopefully. Of course, she confirmed my worst fear by letting it slip that my aunts Zahira, Noelia and whoever came with them would also be in attendance.

After the last family get-together that ended badly, I'd forgiven all the people involved who made me unreachable for two-and-a-half years. I hoped, no *prayed,* that another disagreement didn't ensue; otherwise, this was going to be my last family holiday. "Ugh. I don't see why Noelia and company have to come. You know she only likes to brag about how Mikayla got into Yale. We get it; you're proud, but it's been two years since she graduated. Can we just move onto another topic?" I said, wrestling with the collection of trash bags I prepared to take out into the blistering cold.

With a final grind of salt in my favorite habichuelas, my mother gathered her thick, curly hair into a small, multicolored scrunchie and gave me that look when she was about to ask me to do something I didn't want to do.

"Luz, mi amor. Can you just be nice for me this one time? I know you don't think family is as important as I do, but for one day, I just want my daughter and my sisters to get along. I don't ask much of you, negrita."

There she went on that guilt trip again. If I let her tell it, I was the problem and not my aunt who had the superpower of tapping into your wildest insecurities. In truth, I really loved all my family, so what my mom assumed about me wasn't true, but my aunts often weren't the sweet, nurturing, supportive aunts to me like my mom was to their kids. If they had been, it wouldn't have even been an issue. But like my mom said, she hardly ever asked me for anything, and as much as it pained me to potentially endanger my mental health, I decided I would just keep to myself and not play into my Titi's games.

As long as I didn't engage with her nonsense, in a few short hours, I'd be at Evan's cozying up with *his* family and then we'd be on our way home back to the city.

"Fine, Ma. I won't cause any trouble," I said before stepping outside to take out the trash. My cell phone screen lit up, revealing a text message from Evan.

Evan: Hey, Ms. Mary Mack is settled in. Call me when you're good to go. Things are already picking up here. My family is wild. They're going to love you.

The thought of fitting in with his family lifted my mood and made me smile, but now, for this trash had to be taken out. A reply would have to wait.

CHAPTER THIRTY-FOUR

Luz

By now, some of our colossal-sized family had flooded in, more than I was expecting but less than my mother had planned. Tito Gadiel and his three sons were already posted up in the living room, not offering to lift a finger while his wife was helping my mom in the kitchen. One of my cousins had brought his girlfriend and surprise, surprise; she was in the kitchen asking how she could help trying to impress my knucklehead primo. I'm not sure why it was expected of just the women to do all this while the boys got to relax and play video games. All them were capable, and I knew damn sure they were all going to eat.

When my cousins and I were in charge of organizing holidays, we had to have a talk about getting these entitled boys to pull their own weight. Peeking my head in and out the living room, I felt like spoiling all their fun and just unplugging the TV, but then I remembered what I promised my mother earlier: be on my best behavior and try not to start any trouble. For now, it seemed simple enough to do, but my Aunts Zahira and

Noelia and their families hadn't arrived yet, so only time would tell.

Before I knew it, my cousin Mikayla and her younger brother Jassiel were putting down trays on the counter and greeting my mom and uncle's wife with proclamations of how long it'd been since they saw each other last and how tall my bigheaded cousin had gotten.

"Hey, fea," Jassiel greeted me as I was losing the fighting battle to hit him upside the head.

"Stupid. That's why you need a haircut. Titi and Kayla came out looking red carpet ready and you out here looking like a scrub."

"Negra, be nice to your cousin," my mom whined, and the second she turned her back, he stuck out his tongue and raised his middle finger.

"Kayla, you better go get your brother before he goes back to Newark in a casket." Damn, they were already working my nerves. Mikayla, being the voice of reason she always was, sent him to join the other boys in the living room to chill. "You look nice," I complimented her on the bright pink halter dress and latest designer heels. A part of me wishes I would've at least attempted to dress up, but I didn't want to come off as high maintenance in front of Evan's parents. Instead, I went for the whole jeans and tee-shirt vibe. Now, seeing what my mom had changed into and what all my female family members were wearing, I felt like I had set myself up to be picked on by looking plain.

"So do you," she said before she cut the conversation short as her mom walked in looking especially grandiose in her upscale blouse and pencil skirt accentuating her lean but prominent curves. She didn't have the height of a typical beauty queen but always made up for it with her sky-high stilettos.

"Everything smells delicioso, Danyeli. Let's hope you didn't overcook some things trying to take the big load of the cooking this year."

That was my good, old auntie, dishing out backhanded compliments. Once everyone started eating, however, she couldn't say much else. My mom was the best cook out of all my aunts, whether they wanted to admit it or not. She was also the sister that liked to keep the peace by not defending herself when my aunts fired shots. Everyone was lucky Abuelita was around today and wanted to see all of her grandkids or else I would've been at Evan's.

"Que lo que, mi gente? Dime lo que hay?" My aunt Zahira announced loudly as she entered the room with her eldest daughter, Demeter, and one of her twin toddlers Ngozi. Her husband Jidenna wasn't far behind with the other twin, Nairobi, in his arms as Zahira added four more trays to the many trays of food on the counter.

"Demeter, what do you have on? I can see your breasts and everything. Leave something to the imagination." Noelia went straight for the easy target, and for the first time in my life, I was glad I wasn't it.

Zahira jumped in with a quickness I hardly ever saw from my own mom, defending her daughter's right to wear whatever she wanted. "Leave my daughter alone; she is grown. Not everyone wants to wear turtlenecks and church pants just to leave the house. Like you weren't walking across stages in bikinis and high heels on for the whole damn world to see when you were her age. Let these girls be young, coño!" Zahira gave her middle sister a hug and kiss, looking taller than normal in stacked heels and short-for-her skirt. Her usually tamed hair flowed free and wild into a head-turning afro.

"I know y'all are not going to just stand there; give your Titi a hug," she addressed Mikayla and me after complimenting how pretty Mikayla's hair looked after months of doing her own hair. "We can't all be blessed with that good hair Demeter has, but we all learn to get by."

It was comments like that that made me glad I had my hair

pulled back and out of everyone's line of vision. Unfortunately, it was normal to use terms like good and bad hair; half the time no one realized they were doing it. My family wasn't intentionally colorist or featurist; how could they be? We were all phenotypically Black, and unless we were speaking Spanish, our lineage was always questioned. However, the things that left my aunts mouths sometimes, hell, even my mom, just made me want to crawl into a hole and die until they all unlearned their casual anti-Blackness.

"Look, whatever good my daughter has, she got it from me. So, what if some of us don't have hair falling down our backs. We're not all meant to." She picked at her fro that made me shed a tear at how proud I was of her at that moment. Ecstatic that my aunt Noelia had completely ignored my appearance or anything else about me that she usually liked to pick on, my mom unlocked my number-one fear, trying to add some positive vibes to the room by talking about me.

"Luz, why don't you tell everyone about your boyfriend, Evan? The boy is so sweet; he used to date Luz in high school." My mom's warm smile lit up the room as Noelia's eyes widened.

"Luz has a boyfriend?"

I wished she wouldn't act so surprised. It's not like I live to let them in on my entire love life. For all they knew, I could've been dating him secretly for months. Popping some caramels from her purse into her mouth, my aunt Zahira and my cousins fixed their gazes in my direction. Now, everyone was waiting for me to bring up my lovely boyfriend, including my Abuelita, who had just entered the room from her long nap. If there was anyone's attention my mom and aunts fought the hardest for, it was the love and admiration from their over-critical and over-demanding mom, hence the generational put-downs.

Abuelita was old-school, so none of that feminist, women-who-could-do-it-all impressed her. For the longest, she admired her youngest daughter for elevating herself off her beauty, but my mom had outdone all of that when she gave birth to me, her first grandchild. I wasn't Abuelita's favorite; no one was, but as Titi Noelia grew older and had a few miscarriages it was clear Abuelita had deemed her as underachieving when she wasn't popping out kids fast enough to her liking.

Like most boy-worshipping families, Noelia wanted a boy so she could stand out, like she was so used to doing, but instead, she had Mikayla and my Tito Gadiel beat her by having the first son in our family. I loved them, but if there was a definition for Momma's boy, my cousin's Jassiel and Augusto's pictures would replace the words. And it didn't matter how accomplished the women in our family were, nothing came close to the praise and admiration my male cousins got.

Which was why I missed the relationship Mikayla and I used to have. Sure, she used to follow me around like I was the cool older cousin and I could do no wrong, but she was smart like me, and at the time, our five-year age difference didn't matter. But like most families that didn't heal their generational traumas, rivalry was also inherited.

"And he's so handsome," my mother kindly boasted. "So tall. Like a basketball player. Negra, didn't he play basketball in high school?"

I shrugged, uncomfortable that the conversation had shifted to me and my business. "Used to, Ma. He only coaches it now."

"So, he's a basketball coach?" Noelia's amused smile formed on her face, trying to find a chink in Evan's armor. I would've been perfectly fine not bragging about his occupation, but I just wanted to get that smug look off her face, so, I went into petty mode.

"Actually, he just does that in his spare time, working with at-risk youth. He's actually an investment advisor in the financial district. He's one of the best in his field," I ended with a grimace.

"And he has these beautiful, pale green eyes," my mother gushed, causing me to roll my eyes at praising his Euro-centric features. "And he's so respectful."

In a perfect world, I would've been glad to brag about how amazing Evan was, but right now, it just didn't feel right. Not when I was doing so just to one-up my aunt. I got why my mom was pressing so hard. In my families' heads, my being in a relationship made it appear as though my life was together. Maybe to some people, romantic relationships could potentially cure unhappiness, but it didn't necessarily make you complete. Why was it so hard for my family to understand that?

Noelia faked one of her pageant queen smiles, masking her malice with a benevolent tone. "Will your boyfriend be joining us then?"

Matching her energy, I informed her that he was spending Thanksgiving with his own family, but that he would be picking me up later so I could meet them, but that didn't satisfy her; she just had to keep adding fuel to the fire.

"I guess we should just be grateful that it's not another Antonio. You know, you haven't always had the best taste in men."

And that's when I snapped. It was one thing to think toxic shit like that; it was another thing to say it. My aunt had never learned the concept that if you didn't have anything nice to say then don't say anything at all, and I could not be silenced any longer.

"God, could you just be quiet for one minute of your life? We all get it. You see your husband and kids as perfect. That doesn't mean you have to shit on me and everyone else in this family."

Like always, my mom jumped to her sister's defense, demanding that I apologize, but I was tired of my aunt holding the fact that she brought this entire family to the states and that everyone should be indebted to her and kiss her ass. That didn't excuse her abuse and didn't mean we all had to walk on eggshells just for her to feel superior.

"Ma, I'm not apologizing. Tell your sister to get over herself and mind her own business before she comments on my life."

From the corner of the room, my aunt Zahira clapped in full

agreement and made a slick comment about how everyone should try her ensalada rusa since it was so bomb this year. With a pinched expression, my aunt Noelia approached me, my mom not far behind to calm both of us down.

"You think you know everything about everything. You're practically an abuela chasing stories about love and putting your entire private life online like it's cute to fail at relationships. You may know how to catch a man, but you sure don't know how to keep one—"

Before she could finish her comment, my mom's hand met her pale cheek in a hard, silencing slap. Shock was evident on everyone's faces as my mom, the most passive of her sisters, had been the first to shut Noelia up all night.

"Like I was saying, my Jollof rice, a la Dominicana, is about to be the best thing y'all ever had," Aunt Zahira added, trying to pivot from the situation at hand, but the room was just too tense. As happy as I was that my mother defended me, I couldn't keep from tearing up from my aunt's harsh words. Was that how everyone really saw my last relationship? My aunt Noelia adjusted her blouse and went back to prepping the food she brought, but I knew one thing. I couldn't be here crying in front of my entire family, so without looking back, I ran to the only place that felt safe in this house. My mom's bedroom.

CHAPTER THIRTY-FIVE

Luz

See, this was why sometimes family was best dealt with in small doses. Once all those opposing personalities were in a room together, it was only a matter of time. Sometimes, it'd be quick. Sometimes, you wouldn't have time to run for cover, but in the end, it always resulted in a ticking time bomb.

There was never a time where Aunt Noelia's tell-it-like-it-is personality didn't affect my self-esteem. Her attitude was loosely translated as "I can say what I want, but you better not saying anything back. Not after the sacrifices I had to make." She was constantly up my ass about any little thing, and I wasn't sure why she was so comfortable using me as her main target. I was done with consistently getting ridiculed for nothing and everything, but Aunt Noelia?

Often, she just took it too far.

I hadn't even realized I was still crying until my sleeve got damp and wiping my face with it no longer helped. Should I have just gone to Evan's? I didn't want to disappoint my mother and despite some of the choices I had to defend, I was having a good time until my Aunt Noelia had to go and ruin it.

Sometimes, I was convinced she resented me or any woman in my age group because of the choices we had. The choices that were available to me, that she somehow managed to remind us all the time, were because of her singular opportunity that brought my mother, aunt, uncle, and grandmother here.

Maybe I wasn't the luckiest in my personal life, but I had options. I could heal and move on from things I'm sure women of her day couldn't. Considering that almost made me understand her better, like her even, until she had another opportunity to deal a death blow to my self-esteem. I should've been stuffing my face, listening and dancing to merengue, and preparing myself to meet up at Evan's later.

Yet, here I was, wiping away the crust from dried tears, curled up on my mom's bed and wishing I could climb out the window before anyone saw me. Not that I wanted this to happen, but about the only good thing that came out of it was learning my mom did have it in her to defend me.

I had spent nearly all my thirty-two years of life watching my aunt belittle my mom with her snide comments. Along with that, my mother spent even more time advising me not to talk back to her. My mom had always been the quietest and most timid of all her sisters. As far as I'd witnessed, no act or show of words from Aunt Noelia would provoke my mom to come to my aid.

While I didn't condone anyone putting their hands on another person to solve a problem, one could only be pushed so far before the trauma you put them through made them snap. I just didn't know that tipping point would be me.

A singular knock came at the door, but I didn't want to answer it. It could only be two of three people, and I didn't think my aunt would be coming up to apologize anytime soon. If it were my mother, I could see it now. She'd either be disappointed in herself for me disrespecting her sister or disappointed that I spoke up to defend myself. I wasn't sure there was a world where this ended in my mother having a certain level of pride defending me, even when it came to her sister.

I didn't have long to consider it before the door opened and someone sat in the empty space on the mattress, opposite of me. I knew it wasn't my mom by the weighted impression on the mattress.

"You alright?" a silky voice surprised me in the distance.

The last person I expected to check on my well-being was sitting inches away. We never fed into the rivalry or mirrored the relationship of our mothers, but it had been more than a decade since we participated in more than small talk when in one another's company.

I don't even think I had her new number, and I'm sure as hell certain that I'd never asked for her social media handles. We were a long time away from her being my little cousin who used to follow me around all the time, but she was here, and I wasn't sure I was strong enough to turn down any wise words or comfort.

"I'll be okay. But just know," my voice lowering in the chance someone was listening, "your mom is exactly one of the reasons why y'all don't see me more than twice a year."

Usually, I either hid and ate or shut up and took the abuse. "What's your mother's problem anyway? Seems like she has a personal vendetta against me or something." My head hit the pillow, but I wasn't stressing it. With so little makeup on, I wasn't likely to ruin it.

Mikayla tucked her knees underneath her chin, bringing her naked feet onto the mattress. "I sometimes wonder the same thing. Trust me, it's harder when you live with it than just to hear it around holidays."

Urgh. Here I was complaining about the two or three times a year I showed up for these events when I didn't even think about what Mikayla had to endure her entire life.

"I always wondered what it would have been like if I had been the daughter she wanted." Admitting that through all that arrogance and self-assurance Aunt Noelia exuded, *no one* was excluded from her opinions. To be honest, I was caught off-guard most by what Mikayla admitted next.

"Mami always had to make it known that she was always the pretty one or the gregarious one. The sister everyone instantly liked. She's never really said it in words, but I can tell she means because she was thinner," she took the deep breath necessary to admit what she did next, "and considerably lighter. So, imagine her surprise when of all her sisters, of all the daughters born from the three of them, I'm the only one who looks like me."

She didn't have to say anything else. Demeter, Mikayla, and I all had similar features. We were cousins, but it would have been intellectually dishonest to ignore the obvious. Demeter was light-skinned, maybe even bi-racial presenting, despite having parents who were considerably darker than her. I was brown-skinned, the shade of the typical Hollywood Black actress invited to the table could look like to make it seem like they were being *diverse*, but Mikayla?

She was a shade between chocolate and coffee and the most feminine presenting out of all of us, but it wouldn't have mattered unless our entire family was willing to challenge their own internalized colorism.

Colorism affected everyone in the Diaspora but proved especially difficult in a culture that both celebrated and struggled with its relationship to Blackness. I had cousins in Santo Domingo who would tell you in a heartbeat, "*Orgullo negro*", Black Pride, while being forced to deal with American-bred family members who would solely identify as Dominican. We had little problem calling out other people's anti-Blackness, especially when we were the victims of it, but to address our own often proved to be a hypocritical challenge.

I didn't subscribe to this notion that Dominicans were inherently more anti-Black than other cultures in the Caribbean because that shit simply wasn't true. However, things got especially tricky when any Black person was forced to exist in a space that wasn't intended for them. From the time that we were born, we were constantly reminded of our proximity—or lack thereof— to whiteness.

Mikayla didn't have to tell me that despite the front Aunt Noelia put on about how beautiful she found her daughter and that it probably wasn't uncommon for Mikayla to hear things like "She'd be so much prettier if she stayed out of the sun".

My own mom criticized me for going natural once I went to college as the thought of dealing with my own 3C/4A curls had been too troublesome for her to manage as a kid. That was tame compared to what I can only imagine Mikayla heard behind closed doors.

"I try to be understanding of the sacrifices my mom made, you know? I tried to mirror her in all the ways that mattered to her, but mostly, things didn't change. I think it was why I clung so much to you growing up. You were like the big sister I wanted but never had."

From my standpoint, I had never seen myself as much of a role model. I saw her struggle when she was old enough to wear makeup and gave advice on how to select the perfect shade. Even though she came from a two-parent home, they never spoiled her the way they did her brother, so I taught her how to dress nice for cheap because if she were anything like me, she'd need it. And all that powder room talk about how to flirt, even though I wasn't very good at it, had showed she'd been paying attention. With her dating coach business, it was clear she had surpassed the teacher.

But with the tense relationship between my mom and aunts, I assumed her choices in life had been ones to be in direct competition with me. Only now did I see that she wasn't copying me; she was likely just following a path that wasn't her mother's. Damn. I was starting to understand why her mother projected so much negativity toward me.

"No lie, our mother's sibling rivalry made us miss out on *a lot* of invaluable hoe stories we could've shared," I joked.

"Hey, there's still time!" Mikayla challenged, even though I knew it'd likely be mainly me sharing and her listening. Casual sex went against her "rules" of dating.

My phone chimed, indicating I had a text message, prompting Mikayla to ask if that was the *man* my mother had been bragging about.

"Oh, pictures, pictures!" she demanded as I slid her my phone, suggesting that if she didn't want to see smut, then she'd better keep swiping right.

"He's *cute*," she giggled as I managed to mention that he was just the right height for taller girls like us. Her eyes glistened as she mouthed "A real one" under her breath.

"So, I have to ask—" she started before I interrupted her.

"Yes, I set boundaries."

"And you make sure he plans and pays for dates?" she added, watching my body language to see if I'd slip.

"Yes, mom!" I said, annoyed as she asked me one last question to confirm I let him text first before I replied to old texts.

"Mikayla, I know the checklist required to weed a dude out; you remind me every time I see you. But real talk, a lot of times I don't need to. He shows he cares a lot about me, but we often go off-script. I'm not as hard on him as other guys I've dated, so it makes me feel that I like him more than I lead on."

Mikayla handed my phone back to me, probing me for details on how we met and what it's been like to have a high school sweetheart. My mood was still in shambles, but at least talking about Evan didn't put me in a worse mood.

"Why don't you get out of here and head to his place?"

I sat up from the most comfortable spot I'd been in a long time, most likely because I remembered at this house, I didn't have to pay bills. "I don't know. I didn't want to leave you guys doing all the work while I'm out having fun at someone else's house—"

"Trust me, if it were me, I wouldn't even be thinking about you," she interrupted.

As much as I wanted to, I considered my Abuela's health. My mother probably wasn't any better, but this could be the last Thanksgiving my Abuela was around for, so I decided to tough it out.

It'd exhaust my emotional labor quota for the year, but I couldn't abandon anyone until the time felt right. Evan's family would have to wait a little while longer.

Right now, I had another dilemma to face, and I wouldn't be going anywhere until I faced the women downstairs.

CHAPTER THIRTY-SIX

Evan

Listening to my Uncle Dom's impossible stories had been a rite of passage for as long as I could remember. Not only were they unbelievable, but also the man spoke so fast that half the time you could only understand the last few words of his anticlimactic conclusions. As a kid, I used to think this guy was a superhero. But now, as an adult, I had to question the validity of his famous fables. Either way, no one made walking to a corner store quite an epic tale like my mother's brother.

With all the laughter and excitement floating throughout the room, I couldn't help thinking about how Luz was missing all this. I just hoped she was having as good of a time with her family because being back home for even a day made me miss these good ole times, especially my mom's lasagna, a staple at Italian-American Thanksgiving tables. It didn't matter how much effort I put in to recreating it myself, it didn't replace the love and extra something my mom put into hers.

The startling vibration weighed heavy in my pocket as a

collection of texts came in. Anxious, I pulled my phone out during story time only to have my heart sink into my stomach. The texts were from Luz, and they weren't what I expected to read, especially when I didn't have a clue as to what was going on.

Luz: Hey bae. Looks like I won't be making Thanksgiving.

Luz: I hope you have fun spending with your family.

She wouldn't be making it? What the hell did that even mean? I needed to get to the bottom of this, so I excused myself from my spot on the couch between my cousin Nancy and my Uncle Carmine, promising to return to the living room with more beers when I got back. Spirits were the last thing on my mind as Luz wouldn't just cancel on me. There had to be something up since she knew how invested I was with her meeting my family.

Me: Is everything okay? What happened?

After minutes went by with no reply, I ran out of patience and called her. If something terrible happened, that would've been reason enough to dip out on my family. Instead, I got railroaded with her voicemail. Feeling frustrated, I had no choice but to leave a message.

"Hey, Luz. I got your text about not being able to come, and I'm worried now. I just want to know you're all right. Can you give me a call and let me know what's going on? I love you. Call me back, okay?"

Not long after I hung up, two texts from Luz came in, indicating that her phone had been nearby and that she had made a conscious decision not to answer any of my phone calls. That wasn't like her at all. She always answered, even when she was at work.

Luz: I'm actually on my way back to the city. In a bad place and I didn't want to ruin your holiday.

Luz: Sorry for not telling you sooner. Just have a lot going on right now.

I read the texts back no less than ten times. *On her way back to the city? Didn't want to ruin my holiday?* I told my entire family that she was coming, and now I had to go back to the living room after I spent the whole night insisting that everyone was going to love her and tell them she wasn't going to be meeting them. If she hadn't wanted to ruin my holiday, it was too late for that.

I dialed her number again, wanting to throw my phone across the room when it went straight to voicemail. The worst part wasn't even about facing my family. It was going in there and pretending that her cancellation didn't affect me because truthfully, her meeting my family would've meant a lot to me.

This really meant a lot to me.

CHAPTER THIRTY-SEVEN

Before

Luz

Ugh, why was it so hard to be satisfied with the clothes you owned? Had I really tried on everything twice? My wardrobe was centered on the fall, so all my sweaters and tights felt a little too overdressed and heavy for spring.

There was this sense of relief that my mom bought clothes for me every season—even if I had no intentions of wearing them. She'd probably be jumping for joy knowing the only options I considered consisted of the assortment of lightweight, girly clothes she bought on impulse.

Ma had overdone it with the pastels; while I lived in dark colors, she was hopeful that I'd grow out of that. Most of the time, the extra clothes burned holes in my closet. I kept thinking they were best suited for the Easter bunny than a girl like me.

Seeing, though, how Evan marveled at anything I wore besides the standard black, all the robin's egg blues, powder purples, and bubblegum pinks stood out to me in ways they never had before.

I didn't want to be the only basketball girlfriend to show their support looking average. One of the reasons I'd never worn bright colors was because sometimes, I didn't want to be noticed. I was already one of three girls in my grade over five three. Bringing attention to yourself when you were already a tall girl was like a permission slip to the taunting of these immature boys posing as men.

Evan made it easier not to notice how tall I was, thanks to his stature, so I wanted to feel as pretty as all the other girls supporting their boyfriends did. Some choices I nixed since I'd be riding the bus, but a loose but tucked in sweater toned down the somewhat short skirt I choose so old creeps wouldn't think I was fair game to hit on.

Passing the mirror everyday wasn't ritualistic for me. I didn't actively avoid it, but I didn't take much pride in being in front of it either. Getting a load of myself, I looked—no *felt*—like a completely different person.

After today, I'd have to consider a wardrobe haul. I'd never be into fashion, but I still liked to look nice. It was hard admitting this, but softness suited me and for the first time in my life, I hoped people would take pictures. Tonight, I'm sure I'd be giving all the other girlfriends a run for their money. Not trying to sound conceited but I looked too cute to be modest.

Tonight was special. Since Evan had gotten into Temple and Penn state and I got into NYU, we'd be spending our autumns separate from each other. This would be the last game I'd get to attend, and I regret it'd been the one of three I showed up to. I never did school parties or dances, but after today I was totally considering prom.

We had little opportunity to hangout, preparing for college, so I wanted to make the last ones count. Evan had been lucky enough to get two offers for an academic full ride, something he had worked hard for so that he didn't have to rely on a sports. Also, he had an awesome girlfriend, so he was pretty much pulling a hat trick.

My phone alerted me a few minutes before I was set to leave, but since it could only be Ma or Evan, I answered it.

Evan: *Nervous but psyched you're seeing me play today =)* ***This game's the last one of the season***

Evan: *Let me know if you need a ride. My buddy Ty* ***already told me he'd have no problem picking you up***

Me: *It's ok, I don't mind taking the bus. My mom won't* ***like me taking a ride from a boy she doesn't know, but you*** ***can drive me home =)***

Evan: *Wish I could have picked you up myself =/*

Me: *Just worry about you playing to impress me tonight* ***;p promise to be there soon***

Evan: *I love you*

Me: *I love you too*

Even though we were going to different schools, I hoped tonight solidified that we could make it past the summer. After his game, I had been planning to bring up how we could make long distance work, if he wanted to. All I knew was I was willing to wait for a guy like him, so I hoped he was willing to wait on a girl like me.

———

"You look really nice, Luz" was constantly thrown my way, and all I could reply with were confused thank-yous, playing myself down. It was interesting how people could ignore you all year then when you looked nice to them, they acknowledged you.

My mother taught me to always accept a compliment because you only received them when others found you exceptional. For once, I was convinced I was more than the daddy long legs, keep-your-head-down type of-introvert. I was the pretty girl and it wasn't half-bad.

I almost ignored Joe Cotton, that weird kid that never had anything nice to say to me since I started here. It toned down after Evan and I started dating, although I still believed he was adopted or brainwashed because he never said anything nice about girls who looked like him.

He'd joke about my big lips or coily hair—never too much in public to raise other people's suspicions but just enough that the person receiving the comment knew. Not to mention, he always wore this look of disgust whenever he was around me, like he was seconds from throwing up or something.

Please don't come up to me; please don't come up to me...

"Hey, Luz," he greeted as looked me up and down. Not a compliment but nothing negative either. So far, so good. Maybe, he was maturing.

"Evan sent me to give you this message. He didn't give me much to go on, but it sounded like he had a surprise for you in the gym."

This was uncomfortable admitting, but I didn't have a good feeling about this. My gut was telling me to head for the gym myself as everyone else had been doing. I knew my boyfriend; he wasn't the type to send his boy to relay any messages for him.

But I couldn't totally dismiss it. What if he left his phone in his locker? What if he needed to see me before the game? If he needed words of encouragement, I didn't want to *not* be there for him. We'd refrained from physical intimacy leading up to the game since he claimed he had superstitions about having sex before his games and didn't want to chance it. "Um, ok. But only if Abagail comes with us." Abagail was Ty's girlfriend and arguably the only girl I'd had a real conversation with in relation to the team. She happened to be walking by and because girls sensed a weird vibe around other girls, she silently agreed to accompany me to the gym.

There wasn't so much a fear for my safety as much as not trusting my host. I didn't put it past him that I'd be walking into a door of pig's blood and could use an eyewitness should some shady stuff goes down.

"So, I hear you're going to NYU," Joe attempted weakly at conversation. Maybe, if he wasn't such a douche, I'd prepare more than three-word responses for him. I wasn't used to him being civil toward me, so it proved difficult to pretend his past treatment toward me hadn't bothered me.

"Yea, I am. Studying journalism and minoring in gender and sexuality. Hopefully, to become a writer," I confessed, not sure why I shared that or if he cared. My guess was the latter as there was an uncomfortable silence from that moment until we made it right outside the gym.

Any other time would've felt normal; I wasn't clumsy in the slightest, but the image staring in front of me forced me to nearly trip. Now, it was as if I'd witnessed a long-winded scene in a movie, but I knew it couldn't have been more than two seconds. Would I have needed more than that, though? It was like my heartbeat was on standby, trying to make sense of what my eyes saw.

Evan was there...but he wasn't alone. He wouldn't. He couldn't. Evan was kissing her. How could he...

Evan

Before I had any time to figure out what the hell was going on, all I could process was Luz running in the opposite direction. It was just one second, but that's all it took for any observing eyes to pass judgment. I don't think I even knew this girl. My instinct caused me to pull away without hurting her, a goal I achieved. But that didn't make me feel any better about it. The only thing I could make out from the situation was that Luz had been right there, and if I didn't go after her now, she wouldn't believe a word I said.

Giving it thought, I'm not sure *I'd* believe a word I said. One minute, this random girl is wishing me good luck on my next game, and the next? She's all over me, asking if there's any way she could make this last year special. Was she even a senior?

None of that mattered right now. By the look on Abigail and Cotton's faces, I knew it hadn't looked good, and I still hadn't caught up to Luz to explain what had happened. She'd be understanding; she had to be. There was no way she'd believe I'd ever cheat on her. I all but begged her to come see me play.

"Luz, please. Slow down. If you just let me explain—" I did my best to keep up, surprised that she had no problem turning back to me once she knew I was gaining on her. She was inches away from the school's main entrance, and by the tears streaming down her face, it was clear she couldn't argue with what her eyes had saw.

"I don't even know who that was," I defended.

"It looked like you knew her well enough from my point of view. Evan, don't even waste your time trying to come up with a good lie. I'm so done with this, and I'm so done with you." She edged toward the door and I couldn't help but stop her. If she didn't want to be with me fine, but the least she could do is hear my explanation.

"I know what that looked like, but I'd never do that to you. Please, listen to me, Luz." By now, I'd grown desperate, hoping the warmth of my embrace was enough to convince her to hear me out. "I love you—"

"Evan, I can't ignore how I feel right now. My heart is telling me you would never do that to me, but the fact you're going to sit here and lie to me like I'm an idiot when I saw with my own eyes, I can't believe a word you've ever said."

She asked me to let her go, so I let her leave without making a scene. She even said that if I ever cared about her then that was the least I could do for making a fool of her.

All I could see was Luz disappearing in the distance; by the time she was out of sight, I was on my knees, wondering how I got here. When I finally did muster up the strength to stand, I took out my phone, hoping she might be more receptive hearing me out without having to see my face.

"Luz, please..."

Already exhausted after my sixth attempt, I sent a final text. *"I just wish you would listen to me."*

What the hell was happening right now?

I found my bearings not long after, rushing to the gym to find this mystery person hell-bent on making me look like a cheater. There had to be a reason. There had to.

Once I reached the gym, she hadn't been hard to find. Standing outside the gymnasium doors, she was twirling her hair and popping her bubblegum without a care in the world. She smiled as if expecting my appearance post-breakup.

"You need to start talking. Where did you go off just kissing me like that?"

She rolled her eyes, annoyed. I hadn't realized how much ownership I didn't have over myself in that moment. Most guys thought it would be cool for some random girl to start kissing them, but I felt violated and it had cost me way more than my personal space.

"Relax, I didn't know your girlfriend was going to walk in on us. It was *supposed* to be a joke," the witch giggled, but I didn't find it funny.

After a brief, intimidating stare, she finally admitted that she was a sophomore from the school we were playing tonight, which explained why I knew nothing about her. So, what could the person who ruined my life have to gain by all of this?

Before I knew it, the gym began to swell with school spirit on one side and tons of unfamiliar faces of the opposite. I was there in body, but my mind had all these plans for me I wasn't prepared for. My legs had a mind of their own; they guided me in their desired direction but I did not feel in control.

In no position to play, as I walked past my teammate Cotton, he called out for me to get my shit together, but I only had a few words for him. "Tell Coach I'm sitting this one out."

Something told me Luz wasn't going to be the only thing I lost that night. If we won tonight, I'd be surprised. We were up against an amazing defense and couldn't afford to lose a good player, but I couldn't find it in me to care.

A game loss wasn't going to make me wonder for months what I'd done wrong. How was a moment that was supposed to be one of our most defining of the school year turn into the biggest defeat of my life? The worst part was I never even got to tell my side of it. After today, I doubt I ever would.

CHAPTER THIRTY-EIGHT

Now

Luz

Just a few hours spent with my family and I couldn't wait to get back to the city. In a toxic sort of way, I knew we all loved each other, but breaking generational trauma wasn't for the weak. One positive, though? I had my cousin back, the one I'd always missed; the one who had always felt like a sister to me.

Knowing she was a mere train ride away, I planned on making the most of our mended relationship. Even when I couldn't count on all my family, I knew I could always count on her. She would definitely be meeting Candice and me for drinks one of these days.

Until then, I couldn't wait for my week to go back to its regular routine. Getting time off was necessary, but my safe haven was at Modern, even on a holiday, I missed that place like crazy.

Not to mention, I wanted to reconnect with my very sexy, heart-warming hunk of a boyfriend.

Me: Hey baby. No rush, but once you get settled in from the holidays, let's do something fun.

By now, Evan had to be in the city. The six-hour drive there had been taxing, probably harder without a riding buddy. Sure, Ms. Mary Mack was that bitch, but I'm positive my presence would've been fun on the way back too. Even if it was just to get on his nerves.

Evan: Like what?

It wasn't like him to text something so brief unless it was an *I love you* text. As someone who was a romantic at heart and with a million dates up his sleeve, I got the sense he was too tired to respond. Two-word replies weren't like him.

Me: Why don't you tell me?

Hopefully, that was playful enough to get a decent reply. The cold shoulder and distance his texts gave off were starting to scare me.

Evan: Not a mind reader. Don't know your definition of fun.

Given his recent snark, I knew what the *opposite* of fun was, and it was this conversation. Maybe I just needed to see his face. Sitting with Evan in person would help me to decide if he was being grumpy or if something else was affecting his mood.

Hitting the Facetime icon, I waited...and waited. And waited, letting my nerves get the best of me when he finally took my call by the sixth ring. His face streamed in, green eyes piercing the screen, but they didn't appear soft or kind. They were eerily calm but peered into me like deadlights.

"Hey, handsome." I was surprised he didn't follow up with his typical, *hey beautiful* or any other cheesy term of endearment he'd reply when I greeted him in such a way. My guess was his holiday had been as hectic as mine. If he didn't want to talk about it, we had that in common. We just needed to spend some quality time to forget all this holiday stuff. It was only a few days later, but I already missed him so much.

"Everything ok?"

Evan looked down at the screen to assumingly give Ms. Mary Mack some much-needed attention. When he shooed her away, something appeared off. He never let her run off without me saying hi to her first.

"Everything's cool."

That didn't give me much to follow up on, so I'd best get to the point of this call.

"I miss you. I'd love to see you in person. Do you want to get up tomorrow, or even tonight if you're not busy." Christmas wasn't far away, and a part of me could've gone for something festive and cheesy like ice-skating or even toy shopping.

Expecting a smile or just a break in his dismissive demeanor, Evan replied detached and collected. In the whole time I'd been with him, I'd never seen him this way. Like he was distracted or that my phone call had been an inconvenience to him. As much as I wanted to probe deeper, a Facetime call wasn't the way I would have wanted to do it.

"Well, I'll let you go. You seem tired. Should I reach out to you when I've figured something out? Or did you want to think of something"

"Just let me know what's up and I'll be there."

Now, I knew something wasn't right. I didn't downright hate making plans, but Evan was admittedly better at that type of thing. All Evan did was ask for a time and place, to which I suggested an intimate night in.

Tonight would've been good, but he argued that I hit him up when he needed to rest. Evan didn't seem *fine* as he horribly played it off. It looked like I was going to have to drag it out of him. Whatever he was feeling now felt like rejection to me. In my assessment, Evan and I were *not* ok.

Forty-seven—no—forty-eight minutes late. I wasn't an expert, but I knew Evan well enough that he and tardiness did not mix. That man set alarms for his alarms. I wasn't naïve; often, things came up beyond one's control. I just wish, to ease my spinning head, he'd let me know something so I didn't worry.

Me: Hey, Evan. Did something come up? I got your fave from that sushi place we always order from. Didn't want start without you. Hit me back.

It took a whole seven minutes of my anxiety flaring up for him to reply. When he did, it wasn't the response I was hoping for, but I felt a little better knowing he was all right.

Evan: Yea. I'm still coming. Give me time, running late. Just eat without me.

Me: Ok, see ya soon.

Evan: K

With that exchange, I devoured my miso soup and finished off my classic and sumo roll. Eating alone reminded me that one of my favorite reasons to eat sushi with Evan was because neither of us was great at using chopsticks, so it was always a contest at who was more sophisticated at finishing their plate. It sucked that he was missing this.

Evan: Actually, I might be a while. Do you still want me to drop by?

Me: How long is a while?

Evan: Not sure. Yes or no?

Me: I'll wait for you if you make it before I hit the hay. Either way, I'll leave my key on the top of the doorframe.

I was disappointed at how vague his replies were. I couldn't read him over the phone but hopefully whatever was wrong could be solved in a much-needed conversation once he got here.

Evan

When I finally made it to Luz's place, she had been asleep for some time. I'd considered not coming altogether, or only reaching out when I was ready to talk, but it was clear she'd been oblivious to why I was acting the way I did. She hadn't even asked how my holiday had been, so I couldn't imagine her understanding how her absence bothered me.

She wrestled in bed for a moment or two, and I was halfway prepared to leave, knowing she'd never know I had even been here. When she opened her eyes, I knew it was best not to hide and confront her like I'd originally planned. "Hey, were you just about to leave?" she asked in drowsy confusion, yawning as she came to.

She closed the distance between us, placing her arms around my neck, leaning her mouth to mine. "If you're hungry, your food is in the fridge. Wasn't sure when you were coming, but I assumed it must've been important if you were running—"

"You know what?" I said, cutting her off. I wasn't interested in much aside from her, and I didn't feel like arguing. "It's been a long day for me. Can we just have sex? I'm not in the mood for much else."

"Everything ok at work today?" she asked in a last-ditch effort to dig deeper into my psyche. She didn't seem to care days ago, so why should she care now?

"I don't want to talk. I just want to fuck you." I lifted her up, prompting her to wrap her legs around my waist. Despite her confusion, she was more than enthusiastic at my effort to make it to the bedroom as soon as possible. She practically ripped my shirt from my torso before I was pressing her back into the bed.

"I'm not sure what's gotten into you, but I like it," Luz spoke before I covered her mouth with mine. Unnecessary words at this point. While her demanding kisses left me at a crossroads between need and confusion, I wasn't too jaded to move forward with the only release that would give my mind something else to think about other than anger.

After ripping Luz's panties off of her, my mind and body didn't have it in them to be patient right now. My hips met hers, sliding into her before I could get her panties past her ankles, her soft moans turning into agonizing Oh-my-Gods as my length thrust into her warmth, no barrier between us.

Each stroke made Luz dig her fingers deeper into my behind as I stretched her, milking her for all she's worth. "Damn, baby. I'm about to fucking come," she moaned in my ear, making my thrusts more frenzied and wilder as I reached my own peak.

Both of her ankles were in my hand, spreading her as I watched my cock disappear into the warmth of her arousal. Reaching for her clit, her slender fingers did half the work for me. I literally had nothing but my own release to focus on as I reached that point of no return.

My body tensed as all the blood in my body rushed in one direction. At the sight of Luz spread underneath me, my need to let out my frustration crashed down on me all at once.

My climax shook me in a way I didn't prepare myself for as I grunted and thrusted through my final stroke. Not everything became clearer after I withdrew from her, but my body had the clarity it needed. There was no need to stay any longer.

"Damn, I don't think I've ever busted that quick," Luz spoke in a jovial manner, reminding me we'd just gone raw as she hobbled her way to the bathroom to clean up the mess. I hadn't taken off much, but I climbed back into what made it to the floor, readying myself for a clean exit.

"You're getting dressed?" Luz asked, confused, as I was inches away from reaching her front door.

"I hadn't planned on staying."

Luz held her arms out angrily, but I didn't care. "What the fuck, Evan? You barely text me and when you do, you give these half-ass answers. I almost thought you were going to stand me up tonight but—"

"You mean the way you stood me up for Thanksgiving? Because all I could remember thinking was that something traumatic must have happened. A family member in the hospital, food poisoning—anything—that would have made me feel better about you blowing me off."

Even sex wasn't enough to melt away all the bottled-up anger I released. I thought I'd be calm when it finally came to the surface, but the more I spoke, the louder my voice grew. Not surprisingly, Luz was in her own little bubble.

"Wait, are you mad at me?" she feigned innocent when I wasn't in the mood.

"Gee, Luz, why would I be? You only made me look like an idiot trying to tactically explain that after ignoring all my calls and texts, nothing had happened. You just bailed because you didn't want to go."

"That's not what happened. I was dealing with some personal things. I wasn't even in the headspace to consider being around other people. My mental health had already been in the trash. What did you want me to do? Consult with you for prioritizing my self-care?"

"Luz, I would never dismiss something you asked of me like that, and if I did, you would check me on it, so that's why I'm checking you. Maybe you didn't want to come, but you didn't have to ghost me to get out of it. Not after I show up for you, not after I've proven you how much I love you."

Luz softened at my declaration of love; she knew I wouldn't have brought it up if this that wasn't serious. "Evan, I'm sorry I disappointed you. I didn't mean to ghost you. I just wasn't considering the consequences of going back home. I love my family, but they drive me crazy."

"You don't think I have family members that drive me up the

wall? Like I don't have people in my life I disagree with? I would've dealt with this better if you hadn't ignored me and then expected everything to be all right again, like it never even happened. What hurt the most is that I was never important enough, for one second, for you to consider someone's feelings but your own. You don't get to ask me to show up for you then only give me twenty percent of you in return. I'm not just a think piece or something you can play with for content and disregard when I'm no longer useful. If you would have just called me, I would've been there for you. I would have come to you and explained to my parents that you needed more time. I would've dropped *everything* for you—"

"Could you stop yelling, so I can explain?" she interrupted. Funny how she'd never given me the chance to explain my side, yet I was to entertain her explanation. Her family had left her emotionally drained, and she hadn't wanted that to affect my holiday. All things that would've been forgivable if explained at that moment, but I found difficult to sympathize after the damage had been done.

"Look, Luz," I started calmly, "I've known about your family since I've known you. Your mother has always given you good memories of her, and I badly wanted you to have that with my family. Asking you home for the holidays wasn't easy, and I didn't do it lightly. This would've been a big deal to them; this would have been a big deal to me. A phone call, a text. That's all it would have taken, but every time I reach a breakthrough with you, you find a barrier, and I'm exhausted at always meeting you ninety percent of the way. It doesn't even have to be equal, it just has to be more than this."

"Evan, that's not fair. I agree that I could have handled things better, but I didn't meet your family because I don't care about you. It honestly wasn't even about you—"

"Well, it's always about you. You are the door that has no key that can open you. You pride yourself on honesty, transparency, and communication, but someone can prove to you every day that they've changed and you will still pull away."

Luz paced uncontrollably. Tears and fatigue washed over her features as she asked what she finally wanted to know. "So, what are you saying?"

"I'm saying I can't do this anymore. I love you but I don't think loving you is enough to get you to care about anyone other than yourself. I can't say whether this is a break or forever. All I know is right now, I just need some time—away from you."

CHAPTER THIRTY-NINE

Luz

Do I have a force field over my body that just repels anything close to happiness? It had only been a few days since Evan asked for space. Even I knew that space was just another word for "I'm breaking up with you".

With so much going on since the last family holiday, I hadn't even considered that what he and I worked because he was good at prioritizing my needs over his own. Maybe being around my family during the holidays hadn't meant as much to me, but his reaction proved the holidays meant more to him than he let on.

It was one little get-together. Well, that's how it felt at the time. I didn't feel healthy enough to be around another family I'd have to step on eggshells to be around, but who's to say it would've been that bad?

I'd never know because I prioritized me. I talked a good one on the subject of compromise. I could dish it but couldn't take it. Even though our fall-out had happened fifteen years ago, it hadn't even been my worst relationship. Mentally, I blocked every emotionally draining relationship I had ever had, but I couldn't block the way those relationships affected my outlook on life.

Put yourself first. Be selfish. Don't give more than you receive. I could have been receiving genuine love and affection, but I was so traumatized from it all that even real love looked like a trap. I was bleeding on a man who hadn't cut me, and no matter how thoughtful or generous he was, I had to challenge things about myself and the cynicism I had about long-term happiness.

I missed Evan *so* much. So, why couldn't I show him that I did?

Why was it so hard to be vulnerable again?

Me: Busy?

The only other person I felt comfortable talking about things was Candice, so imagine my relief when she replied no more than a minute after reaching her.

Candice: *What do you need?*

Me: *Not all cried out but don't want to be by myself.*

Candice: *Have the wine and snacks ready...*

———

Before

All I had control over was the fact I didn't have control. I thought that it'd make me feel better to hurt him the same way he'd hurt me, but nothing helped when it came to feeling so easily replaced by someone who claimed to love you.

Am I proud of myself for defacing his car? Not really. In fact, I felt worse. It turned me into this person that I don't want to be. Jealous. Spiteful. Maybe even a little paranoid. Looking back at all the times he used to say he loved me, were they all lies? Was it all manipulation to have access to my body and then discard me when my services were no longer needed?

If love was so special, why did it make me feel so sad?

"Mija ¿Dime a ver? Tell me what's going on," my mother pleaded when I couldn't stop crying when I got home. My goal wasn't to come off as some lovesick teenager, but I was hurting and I needed a shoulder to cry on right now.

My only wish was that she had wanted to hear about my break up with Sol as much as my heartbreak with Evan. She was coming around to me identifying as bi, but I remember crying so much that I couldn't even wear eyeliner for a week because I kept messing up my makeup. I remember needing someone to help me get through the heartache, so to see her be more than willing to now, I felt some kind of way. Regardless, I really needed my mom right now, so I'd have to save the resentment for another time.

"I dumped Evan, Ma. I caught him doing something stupid and a part of me thinks if I had forgiven him, that I'd be happy but it would also give him an opportunity to do it again. He really hurt me." My nose was runny and I was surprised I could even talk with how bad my lips were trembling.

When my mother didn't say anything at first, I mentally prepared myself for a speech I heard my whole life when it came to problematic male behavior. That it was just what men did or some equally dismissive answer. It surprised me when Ma leaned in and comforted me in her open arms. Her next words weren't meant to be taken in a vicious way, but they stung in that way where she was right. I just didn't have the life experience to know that yet.

"People come and go, baby, but love keeps going on. It hurts now, and you're still going to get a lot of bad before a good one comes along. Now you know how to protect yourself. Don't let your first love affect your last love."

Now

Good thing my fridge was stocked for emergency breakups. It was tempting to take a scoop here, pour a glass of wine there whenever there was a special occasion in my life. But post-breakups were serious stuff; I was relieved there was something to binge on when I needed emotional relief. Even better when I had someone to share that relief with.

Since it was the holidays, my seasonal Trader Joe's treat overshadowed my typical Half-Baked from Ben & Jerrys. Jingle Jangle ice cream only came around once a year and because chocolate dipped in anything made every situation better, it was my post-breakup snack of choice.

"I don't think I meant to be as selfish as I'd come off, but at that moment, I was an emotional wreck. Sometimes, I get my family mixed up with other people's families. After all that drama, I guess I just didn't have it in me to fake the holiday spirit. But I know the holidays were important to him, so I messed up."

Candice's devoured the melting morsels of Candy Cane Joe's Joe's ice cream, making me envious that I didn't share the love for peppermint-flavored ice cream as she did, so she had it all to herself. With all that had been going on, with the piece, all my free time being split between work and Evan, it didn't dawn on me that I hadn't heard anything about her love life in weeks.

"Hey, remember that time you told me you dated some kid in high school?" I asked, kicking my ankle toward her side of the couch to gain her attention.

"What about it?"

"I don't think I ever probed you enough about it? I know he was some rich boy and that your mom worked for his family, but what exactly went down? He wasn't one of those privileged white boys that just saw you as a conquest, was he?"

Perhaps high school romances were supposed to stay where they'd been—in high school—but maybe if I heard her story, it would be easier to come to terms with that faster and gather my bearings and move on.

"It's kind of a long story."

The Christmas decorated tin fell to my lap as I held out my arms, hands full of chocolate-flavored goodies to stress we had nothing but time. Candice took a deep breath. This was probably going to be a doozy.

"I met him when we were both thirteen. My mother worked for his parents; in other words, we were the help." Candice played with her two-week-old manicure, a tell that she was embarrassed at the admittance.

"He was an artist and believe it or not, he didn't act spoiled or privileged at all. He was so sweet and soft-spoken, made a million times cuter by his English accent. By the time we had both hit puberty, he was my best friend and it was hard to control our attraction to each other."

Gosh, I was beginning to think that every girl I knew had this high school dreamboat that haunted their memories and spoiled their perception of reality. This shit mirrored my story with Evan, minus the wealth and English accent.

"He was my first kiss, my first boyfriend, my first everything, but we didn't think we could be open about it. For years, we smiled in our parents' faces like we were just friends, but by seventeen, we were madly in love." She rolled her eyes like even she thought it was cliché. "What's bananas is that before my mom found out, she loved him, but when she caught us together, something in her just snapped."

Candice confirmed the first thought that popped into my mind that her mom had jumped to the conclusion that her high school beau was just another rich boy who took what he wanted and would discard her once he got what he wanted.

"Looking back, I understand where she was coming from, but

he had always been so sweet and caring. Without even picking up her last check, she pulled me out of what she considered a toxic environment, so I didn't even get a chance to say goodbye. After that, we moved back to Newark and because my mom controlled every aspect of my life, I never saw him again. She doesn't know it, but I never forgave her for that. Like you, I just hang around family less. I keep in contact with my sisters, but my parents? They see me when they see me."

I know on the outside Candice came from a stable two-parent home, but there were other factors at play that made her living situation so much different than mine, and setting rules based on religion was one of them. I knew very little about her older sister, but I did know she was thrown out the house for not being Candice's mom's perfect little virgin. That made her parents even stricter when it came to her.

"Do you think if you would have done things differently if you could have?"

"Probably not," Candice huffed defeated. "It would have been naïve of me to fight for a relationship when I was dependent on my parents for food, shelter, and support, especially when there was no guarantee this guy would've supported me without them. I could have been smarter at not getting caught, but either way, I had no choice in how any of it went down. I hadn't even given it much thought until this thing between you and Evan happened. Now, I'm like, what if, tu sabe?"

Candice pointed out that despite all that had happened between us, Evan and I had a unique opportunity for a second chance. By some twisted piece of fate, Evan had never been married, had no kids, was single, and still into me. Not to mention, my mom *loved* him.

In trying to convince me to see her point, there was some slight judgment there. I wasn't so naïve that I couldn't see I was in the wrong. Unseen forces had been keeping us apart so long ago, but my inability to listen did the rest. Now that the present was upon us, my need to feel right all the time got in the way, and I had to get over myself.

Every time I made a choice, I chose myself. My pride was too important to consider another side. Watching Candice sulk in silent agony, pretending as though her past didn't bother her was heartbreaking. She had no choice in how her story ended. At that time, her mother had felt she was too young to make her own choices.

Sitting here, paying close attention to the antagonist in my own story, I didn't have to go far. My antagonist was me.

Every time there had been a pathway to Evan, I blocked my way through. I loved Evan; I wanted to be with Evan, and if we were destined to be together for the long run, being the road-block to all my blessings had to change...*now*.

CHAPTER FORTY

Evan

What the hell was I thinking ending things with Luz? Maybe I never used the words final but the fact that we hadn't spoken in weeks felt exactly that. Final. I hadn't even had the dreadful it's not you, it's me conversation, but in 2020, we both knew what uttering the words "I need time" meant. Having a chance to reflect on our last conversation, I didn't mean to be so harsh, though I was angry. I just wanted her to know how badly she hurt me. With how it all ended, it made it hard to see where we went wrong. Her pride was standing in the way of her apologizing and given the time we spent apart, maybe she was even relieved that I needed time. Was I wrong for asking for space?

I blew the whistle to signal the boys' attention as they stopped midway through their afternoon drills. It wasn't like me to end a practice short, but tonight, I just wanted to be by myself, sulking at home. Every minute away from home was a minute I risked taking it out on these poor kids.

"I was thinking we could end practice early today. Our next

game isn't until after the New Year, so consider it my gift to you to get a head start on your school break." Trying to keep my shitty mood at bay, I reminded them how important it was to spend time with the people they loved around the holidays, which was hypocritical of me since I wasn't even taking my own advice.

"Wait, so you mean no two-mile jogs around the court as a last-minute torture session?" Yousef spoke as he signed so his brother was in the loop.

"Boys, you know I can be nice sometimes. Missing a few drills a couple of weeks before Christmas won't throw off your performances. It's not like it's going to stop you from stuffing your faces with the Christmas feasts your parents will be cooking," I laughed, but some of them weren't buying it.

"*Nice*. I'm going home with use of my legs. That never happens. You know I was watching this movie on body snatchers and how people you've known forever start acting different. *You acting different*."

I rolled my eyes. Apparently, someone wanted to be a wise guy today, but seeing their smiling faces had instantly put me in a better mood. Kids were great at that; the way they took joy in the smallest thing was why I had dreamed of becoming a father someday. When the moment was right, it would happen. Until then, I had to count my blessings and be grateful for what I had now. I had family; I had friends and lots of fulfillment. A relationship that satisfied me was going to take longer. Luz couldn't have been the only person that could make me feel this way.

Who was I kidding? Luz was the *only* person who made me feel this way.

When I noticed the boys' attention wavering to something behind me, I turned around to see Luz walking in my direction, bundled up in a grey puffy coat and winter boots that seemed untimely, considering it hadn't even started snowing yet. Around her shoulder was a duffle bag, her expression full of sympathy and regret. A small part of me was happy to see her, but fearful of making a scene, I wished she had waited until after the boys were gone. I excused myself from the boys and directed Luz to walk over to the bleachers with me so at least *part* of our conversation could remain private.

"Luz, you shouldn't be here right now. I told you I'd reach out to you when I was ready to talk," I lied. I'd been ready a few days ago, but the downside to getting hurt was that it messed with your ego, which made you shut down.

"I know; I just knew you would continue to screen my texts and phone calls. Hell, I thought about stopping by your firm, but I thought about how that might make you look and decided against it."

"*Incredible*. Now, she cares about how I look to people," I mumbled under my breath and watched shame transform her once gleeful expression.

"I'm sorry about bailing on you over Thanksgiving. Please let me make it up to you."

"There is no way to make it up to me. What's done is done."

She dropped her duffle bag by the floor where she stood and held out her arms. "Evan, I'm not asking you. I want you to give me a chance, and I knew you wouldn't listen to me if I didn't make it worth your while. That's why I'm challenging you to a game of basketball. A bet was how we started, and a bet was how we found our way back to each other, but you have to promise me that if I win, you have to hear me out."

Tossing the ball between my hands, I gave thought to her suggestion. There was a chance she could give me a run for my money. I wasn't exactly the player I was at seventeen, and as much as I hated to admit it, I missed her. Entertaining the idea, I gave her my terms. If I won, she had to give me the space I asked for. No showing up uninvited. She had to wait until I was ready to talk. As she nodded with understanding, I blew my whistle, signaling for my boys to come over.

"You remember my friend Luz, right?" In a unanimous agreement, they all recalled the time we went out for Brazilian food. Kyvon being especially good with faces signed about her kindness and how appreciative he was that she was willing to learn a little sign, just to make him feel comfortable.

"Well, she wants to challenge me in a quick game. I know I said you could all go home, but for anyone that can stay and keep score, I'll arrange a Lyft for any of you should it get too late."

More than half of them had to leave, but the six that stayed were anticipating seeing me play because in the time that I spent coaching them, I had yet to challenge anyone to a game of one-on-one.

In the short time Luz slipped away to the bathroom to change, she had rid herself of her thick blue jeans and boots and into something more play appropriate—sneakers, a loose top, and annoyingly form-fitting leggings showing off the amazing legs and ass that no pants could ever hide. Letting the ball travel along my chest and arms in a grandstand arm roll, I finished off with a finger spin before tossing her the ball.

Luz had the minimum height to block me if needed, and while I never asked her if she liked to play, it didn't mean that she couldn't. I had the experience but fifteen years apart was more than enough time to develop new skills. She could very well beat me. I wanted her to beat me.

"Half court. First to seven wins."

———

Playing against this woman for eight minutes, two things became painfully obvious. First, it was that kids at any age were obnoxiously brutal when watching a game. Anything they could say to knock my opponent off her game, they shouted freely, something I'd learned to block out in my glory days. And second, it didn't matter what they yelled at Luz, the girl just...*sucked*. Keeping up wasn't even her problem. Speed-wise, she mirrored me on the court, but it was her shooting, her blocking, and even her dribbling that she had to be constantly reminded to do. I managed to get in five shots in before the poor woman landed one. Sure, there had still been time to turn the game around, but after my sixth shot, the next one meant game.

"Luz, at this point, it's hard to be upset anymore. You're fuckin' awful," I said, trying but failing to fight back laughter. "Even if you got one in, my next shot wins me the game. Why would you challenge me at something you knew you couldn't win?"

Her shoulders slumped as she admitted defeat but straightened when she finally spoke. "Because a while back, I made a bet with myself I didn't think I could win. I thought falling in love was impossible after three dates, and by my definition, I was proven right. I didn't fall in love with you by the third date."

The truth of her words stung. It was hard to face the fact that someone didn't love you the way you loved them. All I could do was accept it and move on. There was still hope for me; it just didn't include Luz.

"Listen, why don't we just call it? You just admitted that it wouldn't make a difference. Why did you even waste your time coming here?"

"When you're done not letting me finish, I'll tell you." She took a deep, heavy sigh, crossing her arms across her chest. "Because I didn't fall in love by session three. It only took the first time. It just took me longer to admit it to myself. Either way, I'm okay with calling it game and giving you the space that you asked for. I won't bother you again."

Her words left me light-headed and cemented me in place.

She loved me. She just told me she loved me.

Before I could react, six teenage boys surrounded me, telling me how dumb I was to let a girl like her walk out without going after her. "Look, Evan, I don't know how they do things in Rochester, but here in Harlem, dudes are going after that like the end of a cheesy Netflix rom-com. You feel me?" J.C. scolded. And Randall, who had barely spoken all day, made up for it by reminding me of how foolish I was.

"Yea, I mean homegirl just admitted she loved you and you're still standing here. Did your feet all of a sudden stop working?" Randall spoke and signed with a level of skill that left me impressed. With an engaged level of enthusiasm, Kyvon signed that even at thirty-three, I could still learn a thing or two about the opposite sex, which forced me to dribble the ball and toss it to Yousef.

"You know what? You guys are right. It's probably not too late to catch up to her."

CHAPTER FORTY-ONE

Luz

There was still time to catch the next train uptown, and given how ridiculously foolish I felt, I was ready to get home as soon as possible. I think Evan and I were really done this time. There wasn't anything I could do or say to fix this. I had to face the fact that I'd royally screwed up worse than I thought and just had to figure out a way to live life B.E. —Before Evan. Maybe I wasn't destined to be great at relationships. I mean, look at me. I'm thirty-two and as far as I know, single. I ruined what I had with Cattaneo just like I'd ruined every relationship I'd ever been in. Why did I think this time could be different?

Because the person was different. Evan was different. Evan was perfect, too perfect for insecure me and her million and one relationship hang-ups. When would I learn that letting negativity in was bound to cause me to do something irrational? Either way, I had to stop pretending like there was something I could do to change things around. I had to stop telling myself that I could hear his voice screaming my name. Was that what love did to you? You just started hearing shit that was, at one point, part of your everyday routine. Even something as small as the thought of never hearing him say my name again was sending me to the deep end. I couldn't wait to get to my apartment and just cry.

"LUZ!"

There it goes again. The sound of his voice was just engrained in my head now. How the hell was I supposed to get over him?

At the grab of my shoulder, I jumped back startled thinking for sure that I was being mugged. My bag fell to my feet, and the person that was behind me picked it up and offered to carry it for me. Evan.

"I've been running after you a few blocks now. Didn't you hear me calling you?"

Okay, so maybe I wasn't hearing things, but that still hadn't meant he was here to patch things up. Knowing him, he was only here to apologize for overwhelmingly kicking my ass at basketball. He had always made it look so easy. Who knew it actually took skill? "Maybe I did. I don't know. I guess I was in such a rush to get home that I thought my mind was playing tricks on me. Did I forget something at the center? You didn't have to come after me. I would've been fine with you mailing it to me," I lied. I would've been furious if he'd done that, but while I was balancing on a slippery slope, I thought it best to keep things civil. Easy.

At least until I got on that train.

"Actually, I did have to. I couldn't let you leave like that. I realize I never asked you about what happened that night. I was too busy being upset with you that I wasn't ready to hear it. But now I am."

I started with explaining the long history and rivalry between my mom and aunts because that's where it all began. I explained how everything is always a competition with my family and how everyone feels indebted to my Tia Noelia for using her opportunities to bring all her sisters, brother, and mother here and because of that, everyone felt like she had a get-out-of-jail free pass every time she wanted to diminish your spirit.

I told him how my aunt pushed me too hard this time, and for the first time in my life, my mom actually stood up to her. I expressed how it made me feel, only aided in me reliving it again, but it did feel good getting it off my chest. Having Evan there to just listen and understand felt like the first time I'd actually started seeing a therapist. Very therapeutic.

"Given the circumstances of that night, I knew that I was going to take my bad mood out on you and everyone in that house. I know you saw it as me blowing you off, but I really just didn't want the time you were so excited about me spending with your family to be compromised with how shitty I felt. I wish I could take it back, and I'm so genuinely sorry I couldn't be there with you. I really regret how that night ended."

With a nod of his head, his gaze shifted as his mind went into thought mode.

"Luz, if you had just explained that to me, I would've understood. It wasn't even that you cancelled on me last minute. What really hurt was you decided to go back home without even letting me be there for you. You only considered yourself at that moment, and yes, it would've sucked telling my family I was leaving early to bring you back home, but I would've done so in a heartbeat. Why didn't you feel like you could talk to me?" he asked as he pulled me closer and rested his chin on my head.

"I don't know. I guess it's been so long since I've had this kind of relationship with someone that I'm so used to dealing with problems on my own. I wasn't thinking." When I talked it over with my mom and best friend, I realized that a second chance like Evan wouldn't come around a third time. I didn't see just one season with him. I saw lots of seasons. Maybe even if I was lucky, forever. But if I didn't address this issue now, we were going to find ourselves where we were fifteen years ago, and I loved where we were now.

"But it's why I came to your basketball practice. I wanted to prove to you that I could make a fool of myself for love."

He loosened his grip a little to tilt my chin to meet his gaze. "Trust me, you did that *expertly*. Only next time, don't let it be basketball. I have a reputation to uphold. My kids are never going to let me live it down how *terrible* my girlfriend was," he laughed as I gave him a light slap on his chest. I didn't think I was that bad. Especially for someone who's rarely picked up a basketball.

"Let's say I accept your apology. You have to do me one favor before I make it official. Tell me you love me again."

With one look in his eyes, eyes I'd missed for so long, I found myself repeating the words like it had been the easiest thing in the world to do. "Evan, with all my heart and soul, I love you. And if you can find it in your heart to forgive me, I promise to never break a promise to you again."

Without warning, his mouth swooped in to steal a kiss, a kiss that had washed away all my fears and doubts and was everything I hoped for in a reunion kiss. The taste of him lingered long after his lips left mine, but if I was lucky, he'd be around for a lifetime of kisses.

"So, Ms. Modern Magazine, what do you make of your little love bet? Would you say that you lost?"

The fact that he had to ask was proof that he wanted me to get it all out there. After all, telling him that I loved him had just been the beginning.

"Look, I may have lost to you at basketball, but with my love bet, I won plenty."

EPILOGUE

January 23rd, 2021

Luz

"Hey, Ma, don't forget to tell your friends I'm going to be all over the magazine," Evan exaggerated, mere moments before he read the entire article to her. Both the dying print and digital decided three weeks before the Love issue released that they'd wanted to make this year's issue personal. Within reason, many of the guest editors, content creators, and writers came together and put faces to our work. The Galentine's Day piece was met with amusing pictures of a small gathering of the staff, and many of the photoshoots featured in this issue gave us a chance to glam up and put faces to the writers.

Modern dressed up my piece with an adorable mini photoshoot, featuring me with my test subject and even featured photos of us when we were in high school, courtesy of my mom.

As hard as it was looking at old pictures of us, the glow-up was an interesting turn of events, and it was safe to say our current energy had matched our past.

"Luz, Tesoro! You're going to have everyone wanting Italian boys after February," his mom's voice boomed over the ten-minute Zoom call. Relief set in when I realized Evan had skipped past all the NC-17 passages in the article, but it was nice getting feedback from someone who shared my enthusiasm. "Honey, you're practically famous. Do you think you could send me a few copies for my book club?"

I leaned over Evan's shoulder, low enough for his mom to see my face but not enough to see the bonnet on my head.

"Just let me know how many and I'll overnight them. Just tell this celebrity not to get too full of himself. He's already got a forehead the size of Newark." I said, poking a finger between his eyebrows before walking away to head to the kitchen. "See what I have to deal with, Ma?"

"Ask her if she used the homemade sauces I made for her? Tell her those are special ones. My great grandmother's recipes. I don't make them for just anyone so I want to know how she liked them." his mother spoke in the background, bringing me back to the Christmas I survived spending with his family. They were everything I thought they'd be, and like Evan promised, on their best behavior. The food, my God; the food was the best part about taking a break from my own family. I didn't even know I had a thing for Italian food until I tasted his mom's cooking. When she offered passing down a few of her famous recipes, I damn near fainted at the one sauce that had no less than thirty ingredients. As an act of good faith, she made me a jar of marinara, aglio, olio e pepperoncino, and carbonara sauces from scratch and dared me to go back to store-bought pasta sauce after trying hers. I'm proud to admit that I haven't, but since I was on my last jar, I may have to cave in and just learn to make them.

"She got them fine, Ma. She's been feeding me well." Translation: we took turns cooking, but so his traditional Italian mom wouldn't blow a casket, he let her think I did all the cooking. "Well, Ma, I have to get going. I just wanted you to know that all the superior genes and values you instilled in me finally made headlines in a magazine," he joked.

They wished each other good night as Evan ended the call and yelled loud enough for me to hear him from the kitchen, "Thanks for making me look good in the editorial, babe."

"Well, I did embellish an orgasm or two for dramatic effect."

Just in time, Ms. Mary Mack emerged as I bent down to pet her and picked her brain. "What do you think, girl? Do you think I overdid making Daddy look good?"

Ms. Mary Mack barked in full agreement. Looked like Cattaneo didn't have any friends out here, B.

Evan got up from the couch and picked me up, his thicker beard than usual rubbing against my cheek and chin. "How about I toss you in the bedroom and embellish *you* for dramatic effect?"

My pleas and faux cries for him to stop playing went nowhere as he whisked me off to the bedroom. After a few rough weeks, we reached our five-month mark, and I was certain we would make it to six. The love bet was out of the way, and the story was about to drop, so the stress of it all wouldn't plague me for another eight months. Now, that I was in love, who knew? Maybe my editor would look forward to an update next year if Evan and I made it that far.

I didn't want to jinx myself and plan that far into the future, but Valentine's Day had always been *our* day. Whether or not it was a cheesy greeting card holiday, it all started with a Valentine stuffed in my locker, and the rest? Well, you know the rest.

We had over a decade of V-days to make up for, and with the elaborate planner my Evan was, I couldn't wait to see what he had in store. Who would have guessed what started out as a social experiment would turn into my best second chance at love?

That was the thing about love. When it came down to what

the heart wanted, all bets were off. Evan Cattaneo had turned out to be my greatest prize.

The End

Thanks so much for making it all the way to the end of Luz and Evan's story! We so hope you devoured it! Before you go, we'd love if you could leave a few short words of what you thought of The Love Bet!

Follow this link to review and tell others what you thought. Again, thank you for your purchase and be sure to flip through the end pages to discover more addictive reads from G.L. Tomas.

Happy Reading!

ACKNOWLEDGMENTS

First we want to thank Patrice of Little Pear Editing. You're track change comments are hilarious and it's always so much red ink, but you help us weed out the inconsistencies that we often have being two separate people trying to write one manuscript. We know everything you do only helps make our books better, we just hope one day we'll create the perfect heroine for you XD

To Najla of Qamber Designs, you make the bombest covers and no one does it quite like you.

For all the Black women existing in Latinx spaces, we hear you. We are you. This might not be your story, but we always write with you in mind. Here's to the next book being about you!

ABOUT THE AUTHOR

G.L. Tomas is a twin writing duo and lover of all things blerdy, fearless and fun. When they're not spending their time crafting swoon-worthy heroes, they're battling alien forces in other worlds but occasionally take days off in search mom and pop spots that make amazing pasteles and tostones fried to perfection.

They host salsa lessons and book boyfriend auditions in their secret headquarters located in Connecticut.

Head over to our Official website @ GLTomaswrites.com There we have a list of our upcoming titles and you can purchase our paperbacks directly, along with other swag!

Jump on over to our official The Love Bet Pinterest board to see our fantasy casts and dream-ups of the characters!

Sign up for G.L. Tomas' newsletter.

You'll get exclusives, such as book release updates, chances to win or earn free swag, access to well thought-out book lists, and opportunities to save on books before anyone else!

Don't forget to connect with us on Bookbub and our exclusive Facebook Group! And be sure to send us an email to

talk books and about your fave characters! Drop us a line
at guinevere.libertad@gltomaswrites.com

If you liked reading The Love Bet as much as we did writing it,
please consider leaving a review! Reviews are a huge part of how
other readers discover and judge a book. It may seem like such a
small gesture but it's a small gesture that goes a long way and
makes the book you loved come up in more also bought searches
and has the chance to be featured in consumer newsletters.

Just a quick "I loved this book" is praise enough and encourages
your favorite writers to churn out that next favorite read. So don't
be shy, if you enjoyed reading, a review would mean the world for
a relatively new book! Follow this link to leave a review!

 twitter.com/Dos_Twinjas

 instagram.com/rebelliouscupid

bookbub.com/profile/g-l-tomas

patreon.com/GLTomas

pinterest.com/gltomas

Evan Cattaneo was used to getting what he wanted.

The successful career. **Check**.

The Penthouse apartment overlooking the city. **Check**.

Let's not forget the drop-dead gorgeous girlfriend. **Triple Check.**

Only now, being in the relationship of his dreams, he discovers one slight problem that puts a dent in his plans for the future. His girlfriend Luz doesn't see herself getting hitched.

Forcing Evan to confront their differences and understand their conflicting ideas.

The Engagement Plan.

A trip across the country, some much-needed therapy and their ability to work together as a couple fit into that neat little package. Only the closer he comes to uncovering the truth behind her reasons, he learns a devastating secret that will affect the state of their once happy union.

Pre-order now!

Leomie Coutard was looking to create a fresh start. New place, new job prospects, the task she's yet to conquer? Her non-existent love life. Considering her unique taste, sadly, not just any guy would do.

She met the man of her dreams presenting at a kink conference a year ago, but being oceans apart forced their two-week long connection to come to an end. Or did it?

Damien Karagiannis couldn't believe his luck. Settling into a different country and a new practice left him less time to meet people, let alone date. Through a wicked twist of fate, he not only gets the chance to reconnect to his budding Dominant stranger through matchmaker Mistress Alice she ends up being a part of his surgical team.

Leomie can't get the intimidatingly sexy surgeon out of her system. Damien craves that soft command he once explored. Their undeniable passion will have them breaking all their rules for each other.

Melt For You is a steamy May/December romance that features a gentle Domme with an appetite for masochism and an arrogant yet romantic male submissive who wants nothing but to make her wishes come true. It is BWWM with no cheating and a guaranteed HEA. If Dominance and submission aren't your style, sit this one out. If you like a little kink, let this Alpha submissive melt his way into your heart!

Pre-order now!

ALSO BY G.L. TOMAS

Love Unexpected Series:

Love finds even those not looking!

The Love Bet

The Engagement Plan(Pre-order now)

Kinky Matchmaker Series:

Kinksters find their perfect naughty match!

Meant For You

Melt For You (Available for Pre-order)

Friends That Have Sex Series:

A love pessimist and gentle bad boy can't get enough of each other...

F*THS (Also available in audio)

Friends That Still... (Also available in audio)

Friends That Collide (sign up to learn when it drops)

Bookish Friends To Lovers Series:

Book lovers find they have more than enough in common to take it there despite the circumstances.

Same Page (Also available in audio)

Next Chapter

Bookmark (sign up to learn when it drops)

Pagebreak (sign up to learn when it drops)